Black Rose

Black Rose

THOMAS A. CERRA

AuthorHouse™ LLC
1663 Liberty Drive
Bloomington, IN 47403
www.authorhouse.com
Phone: 1-800-839-8640

Published by AuthorHouse 03/10/2014

ISBN: 978-1-4918-5335-1 (sc)
ISBN: 978-1-4918-5334-4 (hc)
ISBN: 978-1-4918-5333-7 (e)

Library of Congress Control Number: 2014900921

Contents

In Loving Memory of my parents

Anthony & Joan Cerra

Also

Louise Cali

Stephen Dembral

Joe Morrison

&

Peter Calpin

4 lives taken from this world much too soon

Acknowledgement

My utmost thanks to those people who over the years have inspired me to want to be a writer and to the people who have aided me in completing this book. To my parents, Anthony and Joan Cerra, whom without knowing, filled me with stories. Funniest thing about this was that when I told them I wanted to be a writer they discouraged me, believing that it was much too hard a way to make a living; no argument there.

I want to acknowledge my cousin Meggie Calpin for helping with the editing. Without her tireless efforts, I could not have completed the manuscript. To the proofreaders, who were good enough to do me this favor and then had to endure my constant pestering, my thanks, and apologies. I would also like to mention two people whom I barely know. Amanda Collins and Valerie Koley who read each chapter as I wrote, enjoying and commenting on each scene and character. They lived and dying with them as I did.

The last two people I would like to mention, who influenced my sense of artistry in my life are William Teitsworth, a great artist whose love and dedication to his craft is unmatched. In addition, my former creative writing teacher Rory Giovannucci who once told me that I had a huge advantage over the rest of the students in his class; that I already knew how to write. This statement gave me the confidence to believe I could do this.

To my children whom I am so proud of: You inspire me every day with your boundless talent. Each thing you do amazes me.

Throughout the story, I have mentioned locations that have significant historic value. Each structure I am acknowledging is facing the wrecking ball due to neglect or misappropriation of funds. St. Joseph's Church in Belfast is the oldest and most historic of these sites. It deserves a better fate. The Hotel Sterling is already gone, soon to be followed by the Huber Colliery and the Wilkes-Barre train station.

The Scranton Lace Factory is a monument to the industrial age in northeast Pennsylvania. It stands in decay, a ghost of its former self; much like the Paulinskill Viaduct, which carried the trains from Scranton to Hoboken NJ. The Laurel Line and the Pheobe Snow are gone though there is talk of a revitalization of the rail systems in Northeast Pennsylvania, but it is unlikely.

Our heritage, our history is worth more than this.

Prologue

Rose McGill leaned over the kitchen sink, staring at the blood dripping from her trembling hands, asking herself why this man had turned on her so suddenly and without provocation. She poured a shot of whiskey, staining the bottle and glass with her bloody fingertips. Trying to pull herself together, she threw back the shot as a chill ran up her spine. Tying a knot in the belt of her black satin robe, Rose picked up the phone, and called the police.

Once she made the call, Rose took her bottle and glass to the living room and sat on the couch awaiting their arrival. Her mind filled with images of family, friends, and strangers, spinning counterclockwise in her head. She leaned her head back, her face throbbing, believing she heard the dance of raindrops falling on the porch steps. Rose listened to the rhythm, recalling tales told to her about her family, wondering how things might have been, regretting none of what she had become, adrift in a deepening gray haze.

Chapter 1

Mother Nature, Matchmaker

The September sky stood still. A storm front anchored by thick black clouds hung across the British Isles. From Dunmore Head to the English Channel and north to the Shetlands, thunderheads thrashed and rolled for six straight days. On the seventh, as if heaven sent, a string of light pierced the perpetual gray and bathed the streets of Belfast and into the countryside of County Antrim and east and south through County Down.

Matthew Flannery as he had each morning donned his brushed brown storm coat and swung his umbrella across his wrist anticipating the breach in the weather would not last. He made his way through the mud and standing pools of rain along Springfield Road to the small sundry shop he owned and operated. On this day, however, as he stepped about trying to avoid the worst of a most unpleasant mess, a woman wrapped in what seemed to be the remains of an Irish chain quilt brushed by him in a rush. Clinging to the edges of what must have been a fine blanket now bathed in mud and tattered; she lashed about through the mire, flinging great gobs of clay with each ill-fated step.

Matthew hastened his gait at the sound of thunder riding up behind him knowing this signaled another downpour. The clouds inhaled the rays of sun and gusts of wind bent back the birch and willow. He watched the ragtag woman stumbling in a pond size puddle then slip with a splash that rippled the waters in large unending circles. The rains had just returned as he plodded through the waters to where the women knelt. Gripping her arm and waistline, he lifted her to her feet and led her to an overhang just beyond the line of trees.

He pulled from the deep inside pocket of his overcoat a large white linen handkerchief, dampened it in the rain, and began to wipe the brown muck dripping from the woman's face. The notion of asking the woman why she was traipsing through the rain soaked streets in such a rush entered

Matthew's mind. He dismissed the question not wanting to pry, concentrating more on removing the mud spatters from her face that smeared as he wiped.

"Oh, thank you, thank you," said the woman looking down at her mud-stained clothes. "I must have been quite a sight, rooting around like a sow. I'm such a clumsy oaf. Quite a sight indeed," she repeated tossing back the wet heavy quilt and looking up.

Matthew had turned away to freshen the hankie in the rain, "Its fine now Mum," he began. Suddenly the words were stolen from his mouth as he gazed into her eyes, deep blue sparkling eyes, eyes like he had never seen before; warm, caring, calming.

"May I ask your name, Mum?" he said cautiously. "Nora Burns, good sir," she answered respectfully in a sweet subtle wisp of a voice.

"Ohhhh," replied Matthew introducing himself as he looked down the road. "You have the tailoring shop just past Haggerty's on the east bend and before Kil Pipers Hill. Mine is the sundries shop down by Pat Clancy's Pub along the west side."

Nora did nothing to acknowledge what Matthew said. She too found herself staring deep into the soft hazel eyes of a stranger who, for some reason, felt very familiar to her. A lash of rain invaded their moment. Their haven was now getting soaked and so were they. Matthew raised his umbrella and covered Nora's head. He was much taller than she was. Putting his arm around her, she snuggled in beneath him and placed her hand over his, as he guided her across a slick mossy incline to the gravel road keeping her dry until they reached her shop.

Nora opened the door as Matthew bid his goodbyes. "Could I see you later, for dinner perhaps?" he asked hopefully.

"You are a most bold young man", replied Nora. "Thinkin cus' you pulled me from a puddle I should be wantin to eat with ya. I must say! And what else would you be thinkin Mr. Flannery?"

A crack of thunder rumbled as the rain pelted and splashed about them. It seemed Mother Nature had not finished playing matchmaker when a flash of lightning and another crash of thunder boomed. Nora shivered and shook before saying, "I'll be having dinner with me sisters," and then paused. Seeing the look of disappointment in Matthew's eyes, she added, "but you are certainly most welcome to join us."

"That sounds delightful," exclaimed Matthew, "Around five then?" Nora agreed.

The rain played a steady beat upon Matthew's umbrella as he turned and dashed the distance to his shop. Two blokes in dark brimmed derbies where waiting in the doorway when he arrived. Their coats where soaked and dripping as they huddled beneath the small kelly green awning above the entrance waiting for the shop to open. Matthew shook the excess beads of water from his umbrella and turned down his collar while both men stared him down shivering.

"You're late Mattie me boy," one of the men said. His sandpaper voice cracking as he spoke.

Matthew dug the keys from his coat pocket and nudged past the men inserting the key and turning it as he leaned his shoulder to the door. Damage to the lock and knob occurred when vandals broke into the store a week or so before.

Matthew intended to repair it properly once the weather improved.

"Sticks a wee bit," he quipped shoving the stubborn door ajar.

The two men scrambled past him and scurried up to the old potbelly stove in the corner of the shop. The embers where barely lit. The first man took hold of the iron poker and stirred up the embers while the second man grabbed four small chunks of wood from the corner stack. He handed them to the first man one at a time who chucked them in and slammed the door. The dry bark caught fire quickly, soon after the logs were in flame warming the entire store.

Matthew hung his coat on the rack to the right of the stove and sat down on a rickety old chair beside the wood stack. He exchanged his damp shoes and stockings for a dry pair he left behind the counter and placed the wet items near the stove to dry. Matthew dried his feet with an old towel, pulled on the new socks and shoes and went behind the counter. The two men now warm stood before him. He recognized them as regular customers and was not bothered that they took it upon themselves to stoke the stove. The two men were brothers, twins in fact, but Matthew did not know their names. They came in twice a week, purchased two cans of tobacco, cigarette papers, a box of stick matches and a copy of the Belfast Newsletter.

"Well, you lads know my name," Matthew said taking the usual items from the shelf and spreading them out across the counter. "And who might you be?"

Both men looked quite bewildered. One removed his drenched derby, stepping sideways as the water dripped from its brim, to scratch his head. They stared at each other then back at Matthew who was himself perplexed by the looks on the men's faces. The men were much shorter than Matthew was. He leaned down to take a better look, studying the deep lines, crow's feet, and tough leathered skin, and peering into their simple brown eyes. Still he saw no one that he knew.

"Ya don't know us at all Mattie when we been cumin here twice a week since the day ya opened. We shoveled your walks fur ya when the winters felled heavy snow at your front door and bought ya more than one pint at Patty's place, we did!" one of the men snapped, more than a little annoyed.

"Sorry boys," Matthew answered, "I know I know ya, but I just never caught your names."

"Joseph and Dougy Lynch it is, Mattie," spoke Joseph as he introduced himself. "We thought ya know'd us since we been friendly to your family for so long. We lived down the road from you in Dungannon when your father had the apple orchard and me sister cooked pies with your Mum."

"Best apples north of Kilkenny they was," Dougy added. "Sweetest I had ever had, before or since!"

Matthew apologized profusely at not having recognized them sooner; or at all, pointing out that he was rather young at the time, and remembered so little of his early days in Dungannon.

"Don't think because your names escaped me, that I wasn't appreciative of the things you boys done to help me," stated Matthew, then tossed them each an apple from the wicker basket on the corner of the counter.

"Not as good as me dads, but not bad neither," he added, taking a bite from one himself.

A bang at the door and the quick stomp of the newsy dropping the bundle of newspapers inside the door ended the conversation. Dougy or Joseph, Matthew was not sure which, retrieved the lot and brought them to the counter.

"These er soaked," he yelled. "How will we read this pile of scraps?"

Matthew calmly removed the thin piece of twine holding the lump together and did his best to separate the pages. He placed what he could salvage by the stove to dry. After an hour or so, he had enough for a half dozen full newspapers. The rest he burned up in the stove. The twins took their copy, paid the bill, and went on their way. Matthew walked them out. As they exited the shop the sun burst through the clouds, dancing in flicks across the pools left behind by the rain.

"Maybe the storm has ended," Matthew, thought aloud. Joseph, or Dougy turned, "Looks to be true, Mattie. Be seeing ya."

Matthew returned to his spot behind the counter. His thoughts turned completely to Nora. He could feel her nestled in beneath his arm, her soft touch upon his hand as they held the umbrella together, the silk of her skin as he wiped the mud away and her eyes, "Oh God" he thought, those beautiful blue eyes.

Customers came in and out all day, buying one of this, a little of that. Nothing special, but it was a very steady day. The sun brought people out, needing things they would not weather the storm to fetch. During the entire day, Matthew's thoughts easily strayed to Nora. He flipped open the pewter pocket watch his father gave him as a teen repeatedly, longing for five o'clock to arrive. Not wanting to wait any longer, he locked up early, hustled across the cobblestone, and stood before Nora's door.

Despite a steady flow of patrons passing through the little dress shop that morning, Nora found herself distracted by thoughts of the impromptu date she had agreed to. The Haggerty family came in around midday; all thirteen of them, with their mother, Genie, needing new fall outfits for each child. The Haggerty's gave Nora and her sisters an endless flow of business. Genie Haggerty knew very well how to make babies, but had no clue when it came to dressing them. The children seemed well enough fed, though rumor had it, she had no talent for cooking either.

All the while, measuring, marking, and sewing, Nora rambled on about the young man she had met that morning.

"He was so tall and handsome, with soft hazel eyes and brown hair that curled around his ears. He was strong and careful as he held me and I felt safe with him, yet nervous all at once."

"Oh my," exclaimed one sister. "Quite the dandy," added the next, sharing a laugh amongst themselves.

Mary, the youngest of Nora's sisters, took Genie aside as the other sisters began measuring and logging each child's dimensions. From oldest to youngest, they made their way down the line, carefully exacting each aspect and logging it on cards headed by each child's name. Nora became annoyed when, in the middle of it all, Mary disappeared and did not return for quite some time. Once the rigorous detailing was completed, Genie lined up her ducklings, gave an odd little wink to the milliners, and marched her family out the door.

As the day passed Mary returned, immediately whispering something to her sisters, and giggling a slight little giggle as she peeked at Nora. Two of the sisters who were busy sewing, stopped at that moment to speak to Nora, who was confirming the notes on the Haggerty family. They whispered back and forth before saying what they had to say, cautiously considering how their sister might react.

"Nora, we feel ya should not have this gent to our dinner table this evenin," stated the first of her sisters.

This came as a complete surprise to Nora. She never believed her sisters would deny anyone a meal, especially someone of whom she felt rather enamored. Nora spun to face her sisters, not sure how to respond. She was not angry or upset. Rather, she was concerned, and mostly curious as to why they felt as they did. Before uttering a sound, young Mary skipped across to Nora's side, tugging playfully on her sleeve.

"Nora, please don't be angry," she started, looking back at her sisters with a mischievous grin. "We don't feel ya should have yourself a first date sittin at the dinner table with the likes of us. To be sure young Mattie Flannery wishes something else entirely."

"Why you bold little thing," Nora snipped, grabbing a piece of cloth from the counter and snapped it at Mary.

Mary dodged about, avoiding the swats of her sister. "You'll be dining at the WayFair, it's all been arranged."

The WayFair was the finest restaurant on the north edge of Belfast, and much too expensive for the Burns sisters to patronize. It was said, since they had no way of knowing for sure, to have white linen tablecloths and fine cut crystal glassware on candlelit tables in quaint private booths. Finely prepared foods and French wine with each meal, made the WayFair too rich for the more common of folk.

"Absolutely not! We can't afford such a thing," Nora replied in a huff. "Mind your business little one, 'for ya get yourself smacked!"

"It's already done, taken care of the whole lot," teased Mary dashing between mannequins, out of range of her sister. "Genie Haggerty took care of it for the price of a dress and new shirts for the mister."

The Haggerty's were quite a well to do family and Daniel Patrick Haggerty, the mister, was on the council of Belfast. He owned the land on which the girls small tailoring shop sat and as far south as the eyes could see. He was a generous man, and befriended their father when he was down on his luck. When their mother passed, their father turned to drink. At the advice of Genie, his wife, Daniel set them up in the tailoring shop and housed them in the small apartment above it. The girls paid a small rent and provided services to the family as needed, babysitting, cooking, and retrieving the doctor whenever Genie went into labor.

The two sisters, who had been hiding, came forward at that moment, holding out a long sky blue dress adorned with sheer white lace from the neckline to a point between the bosoms, and all down the back. There were dark blue satin roses embroidered in bunches along the pleats of the skirt, surrounded by leaves of forest green tipped in gold.

Nora knew the dress. A woman had brought it to them some months before in need of repair. The woman never returned, so they placed the dress on a form, covered it, and stored it in a corner. Hearing Nora going on about this chance encounter, and knowing she had nothing acceptable to wear, prompted the sisters to act.

Rumor had it that the woman who owned the dress had taken ill and passed away. Not caring whether the rumors were true or false, the sisters altered the dress, tearing away the simple high collar and large unflattering bow from the bustle, adding the lace, and enhancing the embroidery, turning what was a nice frock into something quite stunning. Genie dropped off a nice pair of shoes and an antique cameo necklace to complete the ensemble.

Mary took her sister by the arm and led her away to prepare for her date. She washed and brushed her sister's hair, letting the jet-black waves curl about her neck and down her back. After coloring her lips with the juice of a bilberry, Mary helped her into the dress. Nora wrapped a dark blue satin shawl about her shoulders, and gently eased her fingers into small white gloves, smoothing them about her wrists. Standing before the full-length mirror she smiled, delighted with the way she looked, blushing at the way she looked, frightened by visions of the events about to unfold.

Matthew fidgeted nervously outside the garment shop while staring anxiously at the face of his pocket watch. He never noticed the carriage coming towards him until he turned to find himself face to face with a snow white mare chewing on a piece of hay. Startled, he stepped back and nearly stumbled into a particularly muddy bit of water. Sidestepping the worst of it, he pulled himself together just on time to see Nora standing in the doorway.

Astonished by her beauty, Matthew stood still and speechless. He tugged at his collar and swallowed, unsure and unaware of what he should do next until the white mare gave him a nudge. Nora snickered just a bit and smiled, staring deep into Matthews's eyes.

"There's been just a wee change in plans. I hope you're all right with it?" Nora said wearing a rather coy grin. "My sisters arranged a more suitable evening as they see it, though truthfully, they never made mention of the carriage."

After helping Nora into the carriage, Matthew followed her in and sat beside her in silence. Nora looked at him in utter sympathy for the situation they now shared. After a few moments, she took his hands in hers and rested her head upon his shoulder. She could feel his heart beat slowing as they road along, watching the sunset melt into the trees.

Matthew finally broke his silence, "Nora, If ya don't mind me askin, where is it we're goin?"

"Down to the WayFair, if that's all right by you, Matthew?" she answered softly.

"The WayFair?" He questioned in amazement. "I can't afford the WayFair. You can't afford the WayFair. How are we going to the WayFair?"

"Relax, it is taken care of. It is all taken care of," Nora sighed.

Matthew struggled to feel calm, which made him anything but calm. He met a mud-covered angel on a stormy street this morning past, and was now riding in a handsome cab with a princess resting on his shoulder, heading to the most lavish and expensive restaurant outside of London. However, in that sigh, such a simple thing, Matthew found assurance, he heard peace; Nora had taken his heart, and he did not want it back.

The restaurant experience was exactly as they expected, with fine food and wine, their conversation as easy as two people who had known each other for years. They smiled, they laughed, and they endured the moments of silence. Nora explained how this night came together, by the conniving of her sisters and the generosity of Genie Haggerty who simply could not resist getting involved in this romantic plot. Matthew sipped at his wine, hanging on every word that passed through the loveliest lips he had ever seen.

Autumn winds made the ride home rather chilly, swirling leaves down upon them as they went. The coachman placed an orange and green plaid blanket across the young couple's legs. Matthew spread it neatly out, making sure Nora was sufficiently covered. He put his arm around her and she nestled up against him, finding warmth and comfort in the cool September night.

Matthew gazed into Nora's eyes, knowing that his deep desire to kiss her was very inappropriate. Nora shared the same thoughts and hoped Matthew would disregard rules of acceptability. She considered making the advance, but did not want to give Matthew the wrong impression. A woman kissing a man was so indecent, much more than a man kissing a woman.

As the carriage wheels splashed through the same puddle where Nora had fallen that fated morning, Matthew tossed aside polite convention and kissed her; a soft lingering kiss, full of emotion, his heart beating like the rolling thunder of the morning storm. Nora's pulse raced as she ran her fingers through the curls of his hair. He pulled her tight to his chest. She kissed his neck then returned to his lips and never left.

The coachman prodded the young lovers with his whip handle as the carriage pulled to a stop in front of the tailoring shop. Matthew and Nora separated lips as their driver turned away. Nora leaned forward and gave a tug to the sleeve of the coachman's coat. The slightness of it went unnoticed by the burly, robust, gruff looking man perched precariously in the driver's seat.

"Sir, I do not know your name," stated Nora in a whisper to the coachman.

"Jeffrey Haggerty it is Mum. Cousin to Daniel," he answered in a bearish deep voice.

"Please keep this to yourself. Would ya do that for me, Jeffrey?" she asked.

"Do I look to be the town gossip Mum?" he replied, rather offended.

"Some may view this as most unseemly," added Nora.

"I think it is a beautiful thing Mum," he answered. "Yours is safe with me."

From that day forward, Matthew and Nora spent every available minute together. They would walk along Springfield Road hand in hand, making friends of strangers, enjoying the autumn leaves and admiring the colored hillside. They spoke of hopes, dreams, and days gone by. As the winter came and the snow fell, their walks became short and less frequent. On the coldest of days, they would sit by the old potbelly stove in Matthew's shop. She would sew while he read the Newsletter or the occasional telegram from his best friend, David Addison, who lived abroad in New York City.

Big Jeff Haggerty wandered in every now and again to buy some little thing. He would smile at Nora and she would give him a wink and a nod, reassuring that their secret remained in safekeeping. His red rosy cheeks rounding out through his reddish disheveled beard, and the kindness in his soft brown eyes let you know that he was quite a gentle giant. Nora believed he was checking up on them; Matthew would smile and agree.

The twins made their regular visits, teasing Mattie a bit about his new girlfriend. Nora's eldest sister, Flora, frowned upon much of the affair and on occasion would chase Nora back to the dress shop with the pretense she was being neglectful of her work. This of course was untrue, however Nora humored her rather than arguing. She knew Flora's ill temper was really a mask meant to conceal her caring.

One snowy winter morning, Flora sent Mary to fetch Nora from Matthews shop. Dougy Lynch needled Nora who playfully tossed a fistful of snow at the twins. Soon snowballs flew everywhere and like children, they were caught up in an uproarious snowball fight that spread up and down the road. The Haggerty clan joined in along with Patty Clancy and his buxom wife Colleen who tossed a few good handfuls at their son Shamus, who had eyes for young Mary. Soaked and exhausted, the whole thing ended with hot cocoa for the women and children, and pints for the men.

Matthew asked Nora to wed on a warm April afternoon beneath a budding white willow beside the spot where they had first met. Bent on one knee he held her left hand, affixed on her face as one single tear ran down Nora's cheek and splashed on his hand holding hers. She leaned forward and kissed him. From the softest of voices came the loudest most resounding yes he ever heard. He rose to hug her and she squeezed him so tightly he could barely breathe. They kissed and kissed until the messenger carrier on his bicycle clanged his bell, ringing them apart.

"Oh my heaven, I near forgot," shouted Matthew, reaching into his pocket and taking Nora's hand again. He placed on her finger a thin gold Claddagh ring with small diamond chips adorning the crown and a heart shaped piece of jade at the center, held by two delicate gold hands.

"It isn't much of a ring," he told Nora, slipping it on to her finger. "It was me mother's. She gave it to me on her death bed and made me promise to give it with me heart."

"It is the most beautiful ring I have ever laid eyes upon, Mr. Matthew Quinn Flannery," Nora cried.

Nora rested her head upon Matthew's chest and he held her tight. Horse drawn carriages and carts passed by unnoticed. Time drifted like clouds in the sky as the day went on about them. The twins, Joseph and Dougy Lynch, sat off in the distance, checking their watches in harmony and smiling. The news ran swiftly along Springfield Road and people poured into the street, stopping their day, checking their watches, wondering how long the couple would hold their embrace.

It was only when they noticed the sun going down, that the couple broke their hold and started home. An explosion of cheers ran along the cobblestone streets and down Kil Pipers Hill. Some say that the cheers heard on Springfield Road that day, echoed in the halls of Belfast and Bangor castles and into the ears of St. Patrick himself. The truth in this one can only measure in what you believe. Love can be the cause of many strange things, as life will attest. And so it would be in the years to come for Matthew and Nora and the lives that they would touch.

Chapter 2

The Fates

Elation rained when Nora announced the news of her betrothal to her sisters. Mary dashed about the tailoring shop like a water bug on skates, while Cora and Dora took turns hugging their sister, listing all the things that needed doing before the big event. Matthew attempted to blend into the background amidst a line of wire mannequins, avoiding Mary, overwhelmed by the commotion the news had wrought. He never had sisters so he never imagined what the idea of a wedding did to a room full of women.

"What a circus," he thought, as the sisters turned their attentions to him.

Mary gave him a kiss on the cheek as she skipped by, with a wink and a gleam in her eye. Cora, who looked so much like Nora, hugged and blessed him under her breath. Dora stepped up with a giggle, hugging him awkwardly then eased back to hide behind her sisters. Now, they all stepped back to await the final test.

Flora, the eldest who up to this point buried herself in the shadows stepped into the light and bore down on Matthew. She swung her shillelagh a wild swing just missing Matthew's face. Her errant stroke struck the first in a line of mannequins causing them all to fall like dominos in a clatter upon the dress shop floor. Nora attempted to intervene, but her sisters held her back.

Flora approached Matthew, her eyes wild, her blood boiling. Matthew stood firm. Flora took her best shot and missed. He allowed her no second chance. They stared each other down like bitter adversaries ready and willing to brawl. Nora warned her man of Flora's wrath. Instructing Matthew that he needed to gain her respect or he would find himself at the wrong end of Flora's stick.

"Why is it ya think I should allow the likes of you to marry me sister?" Flora snarled.

"I love Nora. Neither you, nor will anyone, change the way I feel!" Matthew answered. "And if you love her, you wouldn't be standin in the way of her happiness."

"So that's whatja think is it Mr. Flannery," answered Flora, "That I'd be keeping my sister from being happy, havin kept her safe all her life as I have? And what have I done fur her if not made her happy?"

"I know you've kept her safe," replied Matthew, adding, "You've kept them all safe. I'll do me best to protect her as you have, if you'll allow me to do so."

Acknowledging Flora for protecting her siblings, shielding them, without help from her parents, gave Matthew the advantage he needed. He played on her pride, stroking the one thing Flora felt fiercely dedicated to. Matthew had played the right card, plucked the right string, now Flora needed to decide. Would she fold or fight on, opening a wound that might never heal.

Flora looked at Nora, seeing that she felt the same for Matthew. She pounded out a steady beat on the wood floor with her walking stick, determining whether to consent or blast this man to hell with her shillelagh. The sisters held tightly to one another, watching and waiting for their sister's verdict. When Flora stepped in and hugged Nora's beau smiles formed on every face and Nora rushed in to embrace her sister.

Cora disappeared into a corner near where she spent her days sewing. There, behind a shelf filled with various colored spools of thread, was a heavily varnished wood rack with many dusty cubicles. Cora pulled sleeve after sleeve of patterns from the rack and spread them out on a large table, weighting down the curling corners with burlap bags filled with buttons.

"Nora, come look here at these," Cora yelled, bouncing from foot to foot excitedly.

Cora secretly collected many designs of wedding gowns just waiting for the day that she or one of her sisters became engaged. Some of the gown patterns were of her own design, comprised from pictures she had found of royal weddings or historic women whose marriages made the news. From countesses and queens, first ladies and dignitaries, she studied styles from the United States, France, Spain, and Asia. Her excitement spilled over, snagging Nora by the arm and dragging her aside to view the various styles.

Nora amazed at the fine detail and artistry of Cora. Her collection too, was quite incredible, spanning years and continents, diverse in culture and style. Nora flipped over one and then another to the harmonized oohs and aahs of her sisters, while Cora stood over her shoulder spitting out ideas of her own like confetti from a canon. Nora wanted a more traditional, but elegant design to her dress. This disappointed Cora slightly but briefly as she removed more patterns from the rack.

Nora chose a few patterns that she really liked and made some changes that best fit her image of the ideal wedding dress, while Dora collected the scattered forms and returned them to their upright positions. Cora made some suggestions, as did Flora, which worked well with Nora's design, but she could already see a more extravagant gown forming.

All the while Matthew stood quietly in a corner, inconspicuously listening and longing to leave. Nora finally noticed Matthew and left the final details to her sisters. Taking

Matthew by the hand, she walked him out amid the bickering over veils and whether to use a chapel train or cathedral style. They said their goodnights beneath a new moon in front of Matthews's shop where he would spend the night sleeping on the counter, instead of hiking the few miles in the dark to get home.

The next morning Matthew and Nora made their way to the Sailortown district of Belfast. There they met Father McCormick, the portly old priest at St. Joseph's Church and the 'Chapel on the Quays'. Nora had only been to this church once in her life, as a child with her family one Easter Sunday morning, but she never forgot the beauty of this grand old Abby. This is where she wished to be married. No other church would do.

The city of Belfast boasted a wealth of fine architecture, but none where as unique as St. Joseph's. The Romanesque façade was made of sandstone shipped from Matthew's hometown of Dungannon, its steeples blessing the skyline along the docks for over one hundred years. Many an Irishman knelt before it's alter to say a final prayer before setting out to sea, wishing to return safely to their families with full nets and possibly a glorious tale to tell.

Father McCormick found a date available on his calendar that was much sooner than either of them planned. "Tis' a wondrous thing when two fall in love," said the good father, looking over the top of his glasses. "A fine, fine blessed unity of lives, it is. Oh my, oh my, we have an excessive bit ah schedule done already. Rather brisk time for our little chapel it seems."

The couple held hope for a date in early September, but the old priest made it clear there was nothing for them there. He flipped the pages forward and flipped them back again, thumbing through his calendar, saying no to each date that he found. Seeing something he hadn't expected, he removed his glasses and pulled a graying cloth out from under his left sleeve. He fogged up each lens with a huff of his breath and polished them clear.

"I do have a date, but it's sooner than later. That is to say, it won't give ya much time," he said despondently. "Second Friday a June, some six weeks less to the day! Ten in the a.m. is bout all I can do. Less you stall it til' the winter and even that's hard to say."

A deep, disappointed look took over Nora. Thoughts ran through her head of a rushed disaster of a day, instead of the beautiful wedding she had always dreamed. She hung her head down below her shoulders as she brushed the touch of a tear from her eye. She looked at Matthew, her deep blue eyes holding a sadness Matthew had never seen before. The weight of her pain wrapped around his heart until it ached in his chest.

Matthew stood up suddenly, without considering what he was saying or how it sounded, he shouted to the priest, "We'll take it! Mark our names in your book father."

Nora's sadness turned to shock, straightening up in her chair. "Matthew, are ya daft?" she questioned. "We can't put together a wedding in such a wee bit a time! What can ya be thinking?"

Matthew circled the room then stopped and stared out through the stained glass. A light rain pinged against the rose window as he watched the trees in the courtyard bending in the wind. Father McCormick rolled back in his chair and set the quill pen down beside his scheduling book. He peered down his nose with curious concern, wondering just what was on young Matthews mind. Matthew started again, circling, thinking, then knelt before Nora and smiled with a sigh.

"I don't want to wait, Nora. I'd wed ya today if we was able," peeking over with a hopeful eye at Father McCormick who quickly shook his head no. "We can get this done. We will certainly be in need of some help, to be sure. Your sisters will pitch in and Joseph and Dougy will too. I will make it fine for ya, I'll promise ya that!"

Nora tried to interrupt, but Matthew continued, "It's the fates Nora. They have designed it, don't ya see? There is only one day been left for us, Nora, it is there for us. Father's book had our names there, but we couldn't see em. Fate has chosen the day just as it chose us to be together. Surin you can see it, Nora."

Matthew's passion poured over every word. The heavy drops of rain on the stained glass told Matthew again that fate had a hand in the way they met. He knew it! He was never so sure of anything in his life.

Nora did see it. She believed in Matthew, she felt his resolve, "Mark it down father," Nora said with a smile.

"It's already done," replied the good father in a soft calming voice, placing the white feathered pen back in its stand.

Once they had made the decision, Father McCormick walked the young couple through the chapel so they might exit through the front of the church. As they passed through, Nora directed Matthews's attention to the baptismal font located to the right of the pulpit. Words between the couple were unnecessary. Matthew knew without saying exactly what

Nora had on her mind. Father McCormick noticed the looks the young couple shared.

"I've done many a baptismal service for the families of our parish, and look forward to welcoming your children to the church, when the time comes," stated the good father as they exited the sanctuary.

Outside the church, Matthew thanked the old priest with a firm handshake while Nora landed a soft kiss to the good fathers already flushed cheek. He bid them farewell and stepped back through the large dark wood doors, pushing them shut behind him.

Matthew and Nora stood beneath the large archway on the steps of St. Josephs. Matthew glanced up to watch the sun chase away the last of the storm clouds, admiring the aged sandstone façade. Its' unique and most unusual design, particularly the large engraved four-leaf clover just below the bell tower, fit perfectly with the spirit of the day. Fate, chance, luck, whatever one may call it, had come to play games with the lives of these two people.

Matthew felt it, but had no idea where it was going to lead them. He returned his attention to Nora who stood two steps above him, which put her face to face with Matthew.

Nora, speaking in a silky Irish lilt, poured her feelings out to her future husband in a way she had never spoken before. "Matthew I love ya with all me heart and in me heart we been married since the day we met. Since ya looked into me eyes and I in yours, you have been me husband and I your wife." She kissed Matthew softly, passionately, holding his head with her hands, weaving her fingers through his thick brown curls.

Nevertheless, a formal union was not only required it was Nora's desire. She had always dreamed of a fine church wedding in a beautiful dress with flowers in her hair and enormous brightly colored bouquets decorating the church. Her friends dressed in their finest attire there to celebrate. Nothing short of this would ever do. She told Matthew each detail during their walks along Springfield Road in the fall. Matthew remembered, wanting to have this for Nora as much if not more than she wanted it for herself.

"Well there you be again, and doin the same thing as I remember you doin," said a deep voiced man from the direction of the street.

They turned to see big Jeff Haggerty in his undersized coachman's uniform sitting in his carriage with his white mare Daisy leading the way. He stepped down onto the street, pulling from his large pouch pocket a small red apple, which he fed to the horse. Matthew strode down the steps to greet him, followed by Nora. Jeffrey wiped the horse spit from his big hand and reached out to shake Matthews's hand. Matthew hesitated, seeing the long streak of saliva rolling down the coachman's pant leg. Jeffrey grabbed hold of Matthews's partially extended hand and shook him about like a rag doll. Nora, chuckling, reached up and gave the big man a soft kiss on the cheek.

"Could ya help us out Jeffrey, my friend?" Matthew asked, wiping the horse spit from his hand with his hankie. "We'll be needin to get to the courthouse and the telegraph office. If you're not too busy, might ya take us about, please?"

"Say no more laddie," replied Jeffrey. "It would be my sincerest pleasure. Climb aboard. Me and Miss Daisy will getcha where ya be needin to go and take ya home agin."

The couple settled into their seats. Jeffrey, with a flick of a wrist and a whistle, nudged Daisy ahead. The streets of Belfast teamed with activity as they started along Princes Dock Street. There were barges and ferries unloading at the docks and many horse drawn carts and trolley cars filled with people jammed each lane. On Royal Avenue, the congestion stopped them more than once, as herds of pedestrians crossed at every intersection. At the courthouse, Jeffrey aided them in getting their wedding license filed since he was the councilman's cousin. The next stop was the post office, which was not too far from the courthouse.

Matthew hoped he could reach New York and his friend David Addison quickly. He wanted David to be his best man, but since the wedding was to be in less than six weeks, he had his doubts that David would make it back to Ireland in time. Nora knew how important this was to Matthew. David was his best friend. He spoke of him often and missed him greatly. Once he had sent the telegram, Matthew arranged for a messenger to come to his shop with a response as soon as it arrived.

During the ride home, Jeffrey voiced his concerns regarding the marriage ceremony and the choice of his friends to have it held at St. Joseph's Church. "Please Sir and Mum, I believe it is a fine and lovely thing, your marrying that is. And the chapel is a beautiful parish for such a beautiful event. Nevertheless, I worry about what might happen. There are many in Belfast that has no fondness for the Catholic Church, as well ya know. The thugs and ruffians of the street might take your blessed day and use it for ill."

"How do ya mean 'ill' exactly, Jeffrey?" Nora asked.

"Well Mum," continued Jeffrey, "They have been givin the poor father and his a rough time of it. Even knocked about the alter boys cumin to the church last Sunday morn."

"I'll not have me dream taken away from me by some hooligans!" Nora stubbornly exclaimed which did not surprise Matthew, knowing his fiancé and her sisters well enough at this point to know they backed down from nothing. This display did catch Jeffrey off guard, startled by the fire of this sweet, sensitive little woman.

"We'll not let no one nor nothin upset your day, Nora," interjected Matthew. "Isn't that right Jeffrey?"

"Surin and it'll be a fine day Mum," Jeffrey echoed, giving a snap to the reins as the carriage passed the WayFair and headed for home. From that moment on, he kept his misgivings to himself.

Early the next morning, just as Matthew reached his shop, a bicycle messenger rode up clanging his bell. Matthew at first thought nothing of it. The day before had turned into such a long, emotional and exhausting day that he had forgotten this messenger might be looking for him. He glimpsed over his shoulder as the boy on the bike swung sideways to a stop.

"Are you Mr. Flannery?" the boy asked.

As Matthew answered, the boy reached into his weathered leather saddlebag and pulled from it a yellow envelope. Matthew took from his green and gold plaid waistcoat pocket a sixpence. He placed it in the palm of the boy's hand taking the letter from him. The boys face lit up and he sped off shouting thanks in a cloud of dust. Matthew set his umbrella beside the entrance door and pealed open the top flap of the envelope. It was from his good friend David Addison as he suspected. It turned out the scheduling of the wedding perfectly coincided with a business trip. He would arrive in Belfast three days prior to the date and would be proud, and honored to be his best man.

However, he would need to know what to wear and have it tailored in New York prior to his departure because he would not have time to do this in Belfast. Matthew looked down the road to see if the messenger, who had peddled away so abruptly, was still in eyeshot. He was not, but Matthew noticed his bike resting against the hitching post near to the gate of the Haggerty house. He raced to the spot and caught the boy just as he straightened up his bike to leave.

"Hold up, young man," Matthew yelled to the messenger. "I need ya to take back a telegram for me. Can you do that, boy?"

"Well, yes sir," the boy answered nervously.

Matthew asked the boy to come along with him, turning and stepping quickly to the tailoring shop and tapping on the door. Flora answered brandishing her large oak walking stick. Her salt and pepper hair sticking out in all directions made her quite a frightful sight to see. The boy turned to run, but Matthew caught him by the collar and held him in place. Flora stared fiercely at Matthew before saying anything.

"It's too early to be knockin at this door, whether ya be wedding me sister or not sir," Flora barked. "What brings ya here before breakfast, and it better not be to kiss me sister good morning?"

"Flora," began Matthew, "I'll be needin to know just what I'll be wearing and me best man too, for the wedding, if you could be answerin me that I'll not bother ya further this morning."

Nora and Cora came up behind Flora, whose broad shoulders filled every inch of the doorway. They could not see around to know who was in front of her, but Nora recognized her fiancé s voice and tried to push Flora to one side. She remained immovable, deciding whether Matthews answer rang true. A determined Nora squeezed beneath her sister and stepped between Flora and Matthew.

"Nora," Matthew shouted, still gripping tightly to the collar of the young boy, who struggled desperately to get away. "David needs to know what he should be wearing for the wedding day. He can make the day, but he needs to know. The boy will take the message with him and David will get his clothes made in New York before he leaves."

Nora pulled the telegram from Matthew's hand and read it over. Cora had already retreated to the design rack and was pulling out men's suite patterns along with swatches of material. The girls gathered, quickly dispensing with pattern after pattern, basic black silk suit . . . no tails, since it was a morning wedding, with a simple white linen shirt to make it easy for Mr. Addison. The collar would be high and stiff and the jacket would be longer, not a frock coat, but below the hip to mid-thigh with a split tail curled around at the top. Broad satin lapels and a black tie with a gold tie chain and black shoes, easy enough, and formal enough to accent Nora's gown.

"Well you've dressed him right down to his knickers," Snipped Flora, tired of it all.

Nora wrote everything out while Cora drew perfect sketches of both the back and front, sending these along with the telegram. Nora folded it carefully and handed it to

Matthew who added a note of thanks to his friend. Placing the paperwork back into the large yellow envelope he had brought with him from the store, he handed it to the boy with another sixpence. The boy thanked him again and lit out as fast as his peddles would move him. The sisters, including Flora, invited Matthew in for breakfast. They retired to the second floor apartment for a cup of tea and fresh made scones. Together over breakfast, they formulated a plan to get everything done by the second Friday of June.

Flora took charge of the guest list, which was not going to be that extensive. So much of both their families had passed in the famine or migrated to the United States. Genie Haggerty provided Nora with some delicate parchment and Cora, who had excellent penmanship, wrote out the invitations. Big Jeffrey, along with Mary, rode across the countryside to deliver the invitations by hand to cousins in Monaghan, Louth, and Dublin counties to the south and west as far as eastern Donegal. Those who lived further south or west, were mailed invitations, but these were just a handful.

As each day moved past Flora made sure, she checked something off the list. The invitations were done, check. The neighbors up and down Springfield Road volunteered to provide the food, check. Cora worked with Dora on Nora's dress, while Flora, Nora, and Mary combined their talents on Matthews's suit. Fittings occurred at the end of each day, Matthew's in his store, and Nora's in her shop, until wedding gown and groom's suit were completed; check and check.

Nora gave a shopping list of flowers to Joseph and Dougy to gather and bring to her shop. However, Genie Haggerty intercepted them before they even got started. She insisted that she would take care of the flowers. Genie had one of the finest gardens in Northern Ireland, roses where her specialty. She would not hear of anyone else doing the arrangements.

She took the list and with her line of children following close behind, marched directly in to the dress shop.

"Nora Burns you insult me," began Genie. "You know very well that my flowers are the finest in all of Antrim County, yet ya don't come to me for your wedding! I always thought of you girls like family. Not only shall I be doin your flowers, I expect the reception to be in me gardens on the north patio and I'll hear no more of it!"

Nora was stunned by the forcefulness of Genie Haggerty's generosity. She rose from the high stool were she had been repairing the hem of a customers dress. She removed the pins she held between her lips and stuck them in the green pincushion that already resembled a porcupine and wrapped her arms around Genie.

"You are my dearest friend," Nora said softly. "Your generosity to me and mine has been overwhelming. I did not feel comfortable asking for more of ya, since you've given us so much already."

"Nonsense," replied Genie. "Sides, I had a hand in the bringin of you and that fine looking young man together, so ya can consider this me gift to ya now and that be that."

Nora took the time to hug each of Genies thirteen children as they exited the store, right down to the youngest, Ryan, who gave her a light kiss on the cheek. Nora kissed him back, just above the deepest dimples a child's cheek could hold. Then she ran a hand through the head full of gold curly locks that framed his delicate china doll face. Genie was the last to leave the shop, insisting that if they needed anything more Nora should talk to her first. Nora nodded and thanked Genie again before saying goodbye.

Flora spoke up, "God bless that woman. She has the most generous heart of any person I've ever known."

The days, filled with nervous anticipation went by quickly. Matthew had not heard from his friend across the pond and hoped everything remained on schedule. Invitations with happy responses from cousins and friends that looked forward to sharing in this grandest of events returned from all parts Ireland. Nora and her sisters worked diligently, insuring that each stitch of clothing, including the tiniest of suits to be worn by little Ryan, were completed on time and perfectly stitched.

Jeffrey Haggerty, still uneasy about the recent conflicts between Protestants and Catholics in the streets of Belfast, went to see his cousin Daniel. His concern was not only for his friends, but also for his cousin and his family, knowing they would all be under the same roof during the wedding. Daniel had the same concerns and had already begun taking steps to help insure the integrity of the day. Daniel felt that the less attention paid to the church and the event, the lower the possibility of an occurrence.

"Something with more importance than a simple wedding would create a distraction," Daniel thought.

Jeffrey agreed. They devised a plan to create just that effect. The men swore to secrecy the plans they made, agreeing that no talk of it was to be shared amongst anyone. This included the bride, groom, and especially Daniels wife Genie. Genie, as mothers are, was very protective of her children and the idea that they might be put in harms way would have her canceling the wedding entirely, even though it was not her place to do so. If the plan worked, no one would be aware of anything happening beyond the church walls.

Chapter 3

Lost at Sea

David Addison was supposed to arrive the Tuesday before the wedding, but he had not. Matthew had heard nothing from his friend in weeks and was now very nervous indeed. "If David couldn't make it, he would surely have telegrammed," thought Matthew.

Wednesday around noon, Matthew closed up shop and made his way to Sailortown and to the docks, accompanied by Joseph and Dougy Lynch. Matthew knew from David's telegram, received weeks before, the details of his friend's schedule. He was crossing aboard the Majestic, a fine steamer built in Belfast by the Harland & Wolff Company. The ship would arrive in Liverpool on Monday. He then intended to ferry across the channel Tuesday afternoon. That had not occurred. What altered David's plans, Matthew did not know. His hope was to get answers at the ferry office and that his friend was safe and on his way.

Clarence O'Dea managed the ferry office for the White Star Line, which was the operating company for many of the ships traveling across the Atlantic. Clarence knew David Addison by name since he had many trips abroad working for the Belfast Lace Company. After some research, Mr. O'Dea determined that the steamer delay was due to some inclement weather conditions and fallen a few days behind schedule. He could not tell Matthew if the Majestic had reached Liverpool yet, or when it might reach port.

Matthew anxiously paced the docks along the waterfront with Joseph and Dougy keeping step. He was not only worried who would fill the shoes of his best man, if need be, but how he was going to break the news of the last minute change to Nora. Dougy and Joseph stopped for a second, lit a cigarette, and then began again. They strained to keep up with Matthew whose pace quickened with every purposeful stride. Dougy finally gave up and sat down on a barrel, his back pressed against a post, gasping for air. Joseph did the same at the next barrel and post, chasing away some seagulls that were perched there.

"Mattie, me boy me thinks we should slip into that pub over there and have a wee bit of a drink," stated Joseph as he rolled another cigarette. "What would ya be sayin to that my friend?"

Matthew stopped and gazed across the choppy waters of the harbor, peering out to where the breakers met the horizon. He watched as the white foam blended into the heavy gray sky, straining to see beyond his sight. His hopes rose and fell with every large swell he mistook for a ship breaching the skyline.

"David Addison was many things," thought Matthew, "A womanizer and a sneak, but not one to let a friend down." He knew something was wrong and his worry strengthened with each lost minute.

Matthew turned to his friend and nodded, agreeing with Joseph that a drink sounded like an excellent idea at that moment. Gathering up Dougy from his barrel, they made their way across the docks to a small bar called 'The Gulls Nest' for a pint. The first ale went down quickly, the second lingered as Matthew pondered his predicament. Joseph and Dougy sat quietly on either side of Matthew wondering how they might help their friend when all at once Matthew ordered up three Irish whiskies. The twins offered no argument to that idea. The clock was ticking, however, and being bellied up to the bar drinking was not finding a solution.

When the three men emptied their shot glasses and set them down on the bar, Joseph took charge of the situation, "If ya don't mind me sayin so Mattie, we needs to be heading back. There still be a bit a work to do and Miss Nora will be needin ya, to be sure". Dougy echoed his brother's thoughts and added, "Mr. Addison will be there. Don't ya ask how I know, but I feel it with all that I am Mattie."

Matthews's eyes opened wide, hearing spoken what a part of him believed, but in his anxious state, had forgotten about. "You're right Dougy," Matthew exclaimed, "It's the fates. We need to get home, it's true, and I won't be surprised to see David standin beside me come Friday morning."

A mouthful of ale remained in their mugs and none of them had a mind to leave behind a bought beer. They gulped the last bit of foam, feeling a bit more settled with the situation. Matthew stepped out on to York Dock Street followed by his companions, stopping to take one more, long look across the harbor. "He'll be here," he said then turned his back to the water and headed for the cart.

Night crept up and gathered in the trees as the three men made their way back to Springfield Road. Matthew had very little to say, lying down in the cart, counting off the cracks in the gray sky as they went. The air smelled of springtime and reminded Matthew of his mother, hanging the linens in the breeze. How fresh they smelled on his bed afterward. He closed his eyes and found himself back in Dungannon, the sweet scent of apple blossoms drifting on the morning air.

They reached Matthews house by nightfall. Joseph and Dougy bid their friend a good night and headed down to Clancy's Pub for an early nightcap, or two. Sitting at the end of the bar, Dougy removed his derby, looked inside, and then scratched his head. Filled with confusion he turned to his brother. Joseph recognized the look as one his brother always got when he did not understand something, but waited to find out the cause, hoping not to have to come up with an answer.

"Joseph", Dougy began, "What do ya think Mattie was meanin when he spoke of the fates?"

Imitating his brother, Joseph removed his derby and scratched his head, "Well, I don't truly know, but I think Mattie feels there be more things at play then meets the eye," pointing at his eye.

To Dougy's mind, or to Joseph's, that wasn't the best of explanations. With this on their mind, they each rolled a cigarette, struck a stick match on the barstool, and poured down another pint. The twins continued to ponder the fates while watching Colleen Clancy wash out the glasses and listening to Pat playing his fiddle in the background.

Early Thursday morning Matthew awakened to a knock on the door. He sat up in his bed, stretching his arms wide and then reached for his pocket watch which he had set on the nightstand. "4 a.m.", he mumbled to himself still half asleep. He slid his feet into his slippers, stood up and pulled on his robe. The knocks at the door grew louder and more persistent. Matthew shuffled to the door full of hopeful expectations for whom he would see standing on his porch stoop. He threw open the door to the sight of nothing, but a light fog hanging in the darkness. He looked left then right and left again before telling himself that he must have been dreaming.

As he was about to close the door and returning to bed, a familiar voice shouted his name from behind a crop of scrub oak down along the roadside. After a few seconds time his friend, David Addison, stepped out from behind the bush buckling up his pants. Matthew rubbed his eyes, still not completely focusing the silhouette in the mist. Nevertheless, he knew the voice and that was good enough to send a feeling of relieve to a very anxious mind.

"Surin if it isn't Mr. Addison, who we all thought lost at sea," Matthew joked. "Ya dopey bastard, where the hell a ya been?"

"Matthew, what kind of greeting is this to be givin to your best man?" replied David, reaching into a tree and pulling down a long white linen bag.

He moved toward Matthew and handed the bag to his friend. Matthew turned and draped the linen wrap over the back of a high wooden chair in the corner of his sitting room. By the time he turned around David had stepped inside, placing a gold and brown patterned carpetbag on the floor and shutting the door behind him. Matthew shook David's hand, wrapped his left arm around his neck and releasing a large sigh of relief.

"Matthew, you worry too much," David exclaimed pushing off his good friend. "Ya knew I'd be here; have ya no faith in your old friend? This marrying thing got you skittish as a schoolgirl."

Matthew poured them each a double-shot of Irish whiskey as David explained what had happened to make him so late. A storm at sea forced the ships captain to alter course, going further to the south than was originally planned. Although they managed to miss the worst of it, the steamer still needed to battle rocky seas, high winds, and lashing rain. The ship docked in Liverpool harbor around sunset Wednesday, just as the ferry across the channel was set to depart. The captain of the Majestic persuaded the ferry captain to hold just long enough for David to board.

"It was a slow go to be sure, crossing the channel in the fog, but it was at the docks that perplexed me most", began David. He took a short snort of whiskey and continued. "I gathered me things and stepped lively down the gangplank and wouldn't ya know two little fellows in dark brimmed derbies stepped outta the fog. Two most odd characters they were, blocking me way in the darkness."

Matthew scratched his head in amazement, asking, "And then what happened?"

"The first of the pair, who smelled strong of cigarettes, asked me my name," David answered. "I asked what business it was of theirs who I might be and refused to tell em of course. The second man who looked exactly like the first asked if I knew you. Moreover, if I wasn't worried enough, they asked together if I was David Addison! Well when I acknowledge that I was, those two little men broke out a jig, dancing around me like two silly bastards. Being tired from the trip, I thought I met meself a couple a bloody leprechauns. Too many pints I imagined and tried stepping around them."

Matthew at this point was laughing, listening to his friend's account of the evening's events. He wondered how Joseph and Dougy managed to be waiting for the ferries arrival at the dock, and more so, how they knew Addison would be aboard. It all seemed very strange. He continued to listen, refilling their glasses, and then leaning back in his chair to relax.

David continued. "They grabbed up me luggage and escorted me to a cart just a few steps off York Dock Street. After exiting the city limits we rode through the fog along a ghostly trek with the sound of dogs in the distance and trees swiping past on both sides. They stopped in the middle of what looked like nowhere and said that we had made it, but I was mystified as to where. Those boys pointed your house out through the murky night passing, helped me off with me bags and then went on their way."

"We gonna be needin some rest, David. I'm sure you're spent," said Matthew in a yawn. David agreed and curled up on the sofa, as Matthew returned to his bed.

A sliver of sunlight found its way between the window frame and faded blind that covered Matthews's bedroom window, slicing a line across his eyes. Matthew always arose before the sun, but not today. He had overslept, mostly because of David's late arrival. The slim piece of sun startled Matthew awake. He reached for his watch. Discovering the time, he leaped to his feet, yelling to his friend David.

"I'm very late, David," Matthew began. "I should have opened the store a half hour ago."

"Do ya need me for anything this morning?" David asked.

"No, but come round the shop this after and we'll discuss tomorrow," Matthew answered, tugging on his shoes.

David agreed to do so, rolled over, buried his head beneath his pillow and went back to sleep. Matthew raced out the door and down Springfield Road without a second thought. He never noticed James and Dougy Lynch sitting in a horse drawn cart just beyond the scrub oak in front of his house. Matthew ran a quarter of the way to work before he realized the twins were riding along side him. Matthew stopped and bent forward to catch his breath. Dougy pulled up the horses, bringing the cart to a stop beside him. Matthew sat down quietly as Dougy snapped the reins, motioning the horses forward again.

Matthew and the Lynch brothers shared a long silence until Matthew opened the shop and hung up his coat.

"Too warm for that coat today, Mattie," Joseph said. Dougy agreed.

Matthew pulled the usual items from the shelf and spread them out on the counter top. "No charge boys," he exclaimed. "You gents have been there so much for me of late, and how did ya know to pick up David last evening? That still got me scratchin me head."

The Lynch brothers explained that as they were sitting at Pat Clancy's pub after dropping Mattie off at home, pondering the fates. They overheard a man requesting one more pint before he headed down to the docks to meet the last ferry of the night from Liverpool. Putting two and two together they determined that if they understood the fates correctly, then this was surely a sign. Therefore, they borrowed Mr. Clancy's cart, which they were fixing to return momentarily, in the hopes that Mr. Addison would be on board, which, as the fates would have it, he was.

Matthew shook the twin's hands, thanking them for their help in getting David from the docks. As Dougy headed off to return the horse and cart, the newspaper carrier arrived with the morning bundle of newsletters. Matthew carefully clipped the twine and picked up the top paper. The news made him very nervous. The bold headlines read **'Protestant—Catholic Clash in Streets of Belfast'** with a photo of men fighting on the steps of the courthouse. The subtitle beneath the photo stated 'Battle over Home Rule Charter Rages' as unionist attempts to petition parliament fail.

Matthew became worried, not knowing how Nora might react to the headlines. Her grit and determination made Matthew sure she would not cancel the wedding. His dread over the past days events in Belfast had him unsure about the safety of their wedding day. He chose not to mention anything to Nora; resolving to only make conversation regarding the unrest if she brought the subject up. He went about the day's business as if nothing had happened and hoped that Nora would do the same.

The busyness of the shop came as no surprise to Matthew. People along the street, aware of the store closing the following day, stocked up on essentials to get them through the weekend. Matthew sold tobacco and cigarette papers, personal items and toiletries. Sugar, flour, and coffee went too. Many of his customers would be at the wedding, but those that would not congratulated him in advance. He cared for each customer with patience, showing no nerves despite everything that was racing around in his head.

David arrived just about closing time as Matthew tallied up his receipts and balanced his log for the day. Matthew handed him the last of the newspapers, which he had hidden beneath the counter for himself. David glanced at the headline, seemingly unfazed by the news from downtown Belfast. He flipped through the pages while Matthew finished his end of day chores, uninterested by everything he read. David closed the paper, rolled it up, and tucked it beneath his arm as they exited the shop.

Matthew locked the door behind them and the two walked up Springfield Road to the bank, so that Matthew could make his daily deposit. The conversation stayed light, with David asking how the day went, Matthew asking how David slept, and how nice the weather has been. Matthew pointed out some of the shops along the road and David pretended to be interested. Nothing stressful or thought provoking until Matthew saw Nora crossing the street and walking towards the two men as they exited the bank.

"Well Matthew Quinn Flannery, I've seen nor heard nothing from ya all day," Nora snapped, half in jest.

"I thought we weren't to see each other before the wedding," Matthew replied, leaning to give her a kiss on the cheek.

"A kiss on the cheek is it," she bellowed. Nora grabbed Matthews face and laughingly planted a kiss firmly on his mouth. "I didn't embarrass ya now did I dear?"

"And this must be Mr. Addison," she voiced, slipping her arm around Matthew's waist as he wrapped his arm around her shoulder.

"Matthew told me you were a scoundrel, but he did not tell me what a handsome scoundrel you are!" Nora added.

"Guilty on both counts I'm afraid," David replied. Stepping up, he took Nora's hand and touched it to his lips.

"Now I see what's got Mattie's head turned," added David.

"Well, gentlemen, if you will excuse me, I need to make me deposits before the bank closes. But don't ya go running off," Nora said, slipping away and into the bank.

"Don't show her that newspaper David," Matthew exclaimed anxiously. "She'll not react well to it."

David twisted the paper tightly and stuck it into the inside pocket of his coat. Nora returned to them quickly, stepping between them and taking each by the arm. They strolled down Springfield Road to the tailoring shop where Nora introduced David to her sisters, Flora, Cora, Dora, and Mary. David almost laughed, but held it back, respectfully.

Introductions cut short at the sight of Jeffrey Haggerty standing on a bench in the middle of the room. His big red bearded face was as unruly as the mop of hair on his head, sticking up from a high white collar, which looked to be strangling him. On his legs, he wore nothing but his long underpants with his large hairy feet sticking out from beneath them. His large knuckled hands he had crossed just below the waist, covering his crotch, which was in no way exposed.

"Jeffrey what are ya doin up there?" Matthew asked, trying hard not to laugh.

"The sisters be fittin me with a new coachman's suit," he growled. "Miss Flora says the one I been wearin don't fit me correctly and it was not acceptable for yours and Miss Nora's wedding." "Well, I find it best not to argue with Miss Flora," replied Matthew.

Matthew, David, and Nora stepped back outside where they enjoyed a laugh at poor Jeffrey's expense. They walked together for a while enjoying the fine spring day. Nora and Matthew explained the plan for the church service. They reviewed how they would get to the church and to the reception in the Haggerty's garden. David, unconcerned for the details, feigned interest and at his earliest opportunity, bid the couple ado, allowing them time to themselves.

Matthew and Nora walked for a short time when they realized they were standing at the spot where they had met. Matthew kissed Nora softly then stepped in amongst the golden rod, bitter cress, and violets. He lifted a large rock from the weeds, carrying it with both hands and set it along the roads edge, centered generally between a willow and birch tree. Nora curiously watched her fiancé, unsure of what he was attempting to do. Once Matthew set the stone in place, she figured it out.

"Nora," Matthew began, "this stone will forever mark this spot. When time has changed or taken much of what we know and love, this stone will remain, reminding us of the times before tomorrow and what brought us to this place in our hearts and lives."

Nora leaned down and reached into the crop of wildflowers. Tugging out a handful, she spread them about the rock saying, "You are my rock, Matthew Quinn Flannery, and I am your flower."

Nora kissed Matthew softly, just as she had the day he asked her to marry her, just as she had the night on the carriage ride home from the restaurant. The way she believed she would for many days and years ahead. They parted then and there, Matthew made his way to his house, where he would share a light dinner and a drink or two with his best man, David Addison. Nora returned home to her small apartment above the shop. She too would enjoy a nice meal with her sisters while talking over the details of her wedding.

Genie Haggerty put together many large flower arrangements and sent them to the church to adorn the pulpit. She also had flowers and white sash buntings on each pew and on the sides of every cart and carriage that would transport guests to the church and back to the Haggerty house for the reception. Her husband Daniel had three exquisitely accented carriages, each drawn by two fine horses. The entire family piled into these to make their way to the church. The Haggerty carriages led the caravan. Nora road alone in Jeffrey's carriage, with the carriage containing her sisters following directly behind.

Matthew and David dressed at Matthews's house. Joseph and Dougy waited outside in Clancy's cart. The four men arrived at the church traveling unescorted ahead of the caravan. Many friends and family had already filtered in and greeted Matthew as he entered the chapel. Matthew and David took their places at the left side of Father McCormick to await the arrival of the bride.

A commotion outside let the wedding goers know when the bride's carriage appeared. A long white carpet rolled the length of the isle, signaling the organist to play. Twelve of the Haggerty children entered two by two followed by Genie who walked down the aisle holding the hand of little Ryan. Once the family settled into their pew the rest of the party entered. Nora's four sisters came next, each attired in unique and extraordinary dresses. They sat in the pew behind the Haggerty family. The organist ceased and the church was quiet.

The congregation arose in unison and the music began again when Nora entered on the arm of Daniel Haggerty, who had agreed to give her away when all efforts to locate her father met with failure. Daniel was a large, heavy-set man, much like his cousin Jeffrey, but unlike his cousin, he was clean-shaven with a large round face and kind eyes. Ahs from friends and family greeted Nora, seeing her in the most beautiful of wedding gowns.

The high collar of the gown turned down into a perfect V just beneath her delicate chin and was laced with white beading then clipped together with miniature white roses that spread on beaded vines around and down the entire gown. While white lace slightly revealing her fine narrow shoulders, they were draped with a satin shawl which tied in the front with a long ribbon festooned with beads and rose buds. On her head rested a crown of miniature white roses attached to a sheer lace veil and cathedral train, embroidered with many more of the tiny white flowers. She held a bouquet of white roses offset by cream orchids and sprigs of deep green.

Matthew found himself breathless, incapable of turning his head or blinking as his beautiful bride approached. David nudged him to no avail. The sight of Nora had turned him to stone, lost in the vision that now stood before him. The organist stopped and the wedding goers took their seats as the good priest began the ceremony. The only words Matthew managed to utter were "I do", which is when his lungs began to function again. Claps, cheers, and tears poured from the throng of onlookers as Matthew raised the veil and sealed the ceremony with a kiss.

Outside the church, Jeffrey kept a watchful eye on the avenue. Princes Dock Street had the normal amount of traffic, but remained quiet. However, activity around the courthouse stirred tempers to a fever pitch over the Home Rule Charter. When another vote on the newly revised petition failed to push through council, cheers and jeers turned into a brawl between unionist Protestants and Catholics. Jeffrey could hear the noise of the fighting in the distance and checked his watch. He then peeked over his shoulder through the open church door to view the ceremony. Matthew was just raising Nora's veil and Jeffrey looked down at his watch again.

The couple strode arm in arm quickly from the church and into the waiting carriage. Jeffrey, now perched on his seat, dressed in his fine new coachman's uniform, readied to lead the caravan back to Springfield Road and to the reception at the Haggerty home. It was up to him to veer the caravan away from the courthouse and get them home safely, that is just what he did. Across Duncairn Gardens then left onto to York through midday traffic, which was sparse by most measures. He turned them right and then left and then right again, until he reached the Divis and Falls Road split and the intersection with Springfield Road. The sounds of the row faded behind them as the caravan swung toward home.

At the Haggerty house, Nora and Matthew entered to await the arrival of their guests. They went into the large sitting room where Matthew found a bottle of Scotch with a note attached. Daniel had left it for Matthew, believing Matthew would need a good snort to get him through the day. Nora was afraid to sit down for fear of disturbing the flowers on the gown. Matthew stooped down and repaired some of the roses that had come loose on Nora's train. She had him remove her shawl and as he did so, their eyes met. All the nerves and stress of the day, which weighed so heavily upon them, vanished into thin air.

Music began to play in the garden as Jeffrey opened the large French doors from the sitting room onto the patio. Nora stepped out with Matthew delicately holding her hand. Little Ryan greeted Nora first, holding a fist full of mangled wildflowers he had pulled from his mothers flowerbed. Nora took them from him, lifted him up, and kissed him. Ryan hugged her head as tight as he could.

Genie eased her son away from Nora who went about greeting and thanking everyone present. Matthew went along, introducing his family and friends, giving special introductions to his two favorite cousins, Cathy Callaghan and Meggie Calpin from County Monaghan. Matthew explained to his wife how they had spent a great deal of time at his home in Dungannon helping his father in the apple orchard at harvesting time.

"And many a Christmas day," added Meggie, "when the roads where clear enough to get there."

"Strange he remember Meggie and Cathy," thought Matthew at that moment, "and not the Lynch brothers."

When the young couple finished speaking to and thanking their many friends and family for sharing in their day, they located Genie to express their heartfelt gratitude for her immense generosity. As they walked along the fieldstone pathways that wound through Genie's flower garden Nora noticed the rose bushes had no blooms. She question Genie, hoping that she had not used up all of her beautiful buds for her wedding. Genie assured her that this was not the case. She pointed out that it was much too early for roses, even with the beautiful stretch of weather they had been enjoying.

Genie led the couple further along the path until they reached a large house made entirely of glass. Matthew and Nora stood in awe, never having seen such a thing. Although Nora admitted she had heard of one, but she never imagined she would ever come face to face with a greenhouse. Genie opened the glass door inviting them in to the scents of many beautiful varieties of blossoms. The couple admired the red and blush roses, the huge fragrant lilies, and delicate orchids lining each side of the center aisle.

As they made their way along, sniffing flower after flower, Nora noticed a pot set away from the others. Curiosity tugged at Nora and she gravitated to it like a bee to honey.

"Genie", she asked, "what is that put back in the corner?"

"That's very odd," replied Genie, "your sister Cora asked the same question not minutes ago."

"It began as a red rose," Genie explained. "As bright and bold in color as any, but soon the color began to drain from it. The petals turned as black as coal. Funny thing though, usually this occurs when a flower withers and dies, but this one is still full of life. I put it away from the others thinking it might be sick and I did not want the disease to spread. But, now I am thinkin it's just a black rose, if there can be such a thing."

"It's so unusual and haunting," said Nora.

Nora noticed something else about the rose. A spot of red liquid, smaller than a teardrop and similar in shape, dripped from the edge of one of its petals. Nora eased her hand towards the plant when Genie stopped her. Nora, surprised by Genie, awakened from the spell she had fallen under, unsure of where she was or what she was doing.

"I don't recommend you touch it," Genie said to Nora. "Cora come through with that fine young man David. She too admired this flower. She reached for it and pricked her finger quite badly. That be a bit a her blood there on the petal."

As Nora beheld the black rose, a chill ran through her and she became very disturbed and frightened. She latched onto her new husband and asked him to take her back to the reception. Matthew guided her away cautiously, realizing his wife did not feel herself. He believed the pungent aromas coupled with the warmth of the greenhouse made her lightheaded. This may have been the case, but the black rose would trouble Nora from that day forward.

Pat Clancy arrived with his wife Colleen on one arm and his fiddle on the other. After a few ales, he hopped up on a large rock and began cutting a jig. The other musicians, who had been playing softly in the background, joined in, turning the elegant reception into a shindig. Genie Haggerty always portrayed herself as more refined. However, on this day she kicked off her shoes, hiked up her skirt and did a spirited dance with all of her children, including Ryan who sat smiling a broad smile on his father's shoulder.

The grand time continued until just beyond sunset when the crimson and purple faded from the sky. It was then that a messenger arrived at the festivities with a note for Daniel. The fighting on the steps of the courthouse had cascaded into the streets and down to the docks. Blood spilled in Victoria Square. The council chairman called for a special session to be convened Saturday morning and Daniels attendance was required. The news distressed the remaining partygoers, including Matthew and Nora.

Families wished they had left sooner and many who had booked accommodations in Belfast hotels changed their plans and head home instead. Worried feelings expanded to those who had departed prior to the news and headed to downtown Belfast to seek lodging for the night completely unaware of the trouble in the downtown. Clancy and some of the other neighbors invited those who had the farthest to travel to stay with them. Most declined, but were thankful for the invitation. Genie Haggerty extended the same invitation. None accepted, unsure of how far this might spread or if Daniel could be a target.

Daniel could not be sure either, fully aware that it was his plan that had set everything in motion. Jeffrey and Daniel exchanged a stressful glance before kissing the children and chasing them inside for the evening. He kissed his wife goodnight and then began to take steps to secure the house. Once his carriage drivers assured him they had locked up the stable he handed them shotguns and situated them at locations around the property to keep watch for the evening.

Matthews's cousins, Cathy and Meggie, stayed with Nora's sisters for the night.

Matthew tossed David the keys to his shop. "Sorry old man it is after all me weddin night and three is a crowd. There be a pillow and blanket waitin for ya. Help yourself to anything else ya might need," Matthew told David with a smile and a pat on the back.

David had plans to stay in Belfast, in one of the cities finest hotels and was greatly disappointed by the turn of events, but he understood. Nevertheless, he did not relish sleeping in Matthew's store. Genie Haggerty extended her invitation again, but David declined, aware of the house full of kids she had. The sisters watched him trudge across and down Springfield Road, entering the sundry shop and closing the door behind him.

Flora and Dora paid scant attention to David, except for a passing glance. Instead, they turned their attentions to Nora sitting along side Matthew in the Clancy's cart driven as usual by the Lynch brothers. Mary turned away next, leading Matthews's cousin to the tailoring shop where they would spend the night. Cora lingered, eyeing David every step of the way. Even after David disappeared behind the closed door of the store, Cora remained, until Flora called after her to come along.

Cora harbored thoughts of following after him, peeking over her shoulder as she walked towards the dress shop. She fantasized David opening the door and, from the shadows, calling after her to join him. She longed for it to happen, but it never did. Even as she dreamed, seeing the door crack open, awaiting David's invitation, again the door slammed shut. Its' bang echoing through her dreams, awakening Cora who found herself alone.

Rolling over, Cora hugged her pillow. Again, she drifted off to sleep, only to repeat the same dream, the ending unchanged. She spent the rest of the night struggling to sleep. She did all she could to clear her mind, but her thoughts always returned to David. Finally, after too many hours, she gave up the fight, climbing out of bed and taking a chair by the window to watch the sunrise. Laying her head back just as the first light of dawn sparked against the indigo sky, Cora fell into a deep undisturbed slumber.

Chapter 4

This Angry Place

Daniel Haggerty arose early the next morning following a very poor night's sleep. He scrubbed the dust from his eyes and ran a comb through his thinning red hair before making his way to the kitchen for a cup of breakfast tea. Genie sent one of the men guarding the house for a copy of the morning newsletter and had it waiting on the kitchen table for her husband to read with his toast. The news of the riots in the downtown covered the pages. Daniel distressed with every written word.

Many people were hurt in the streets of Belfast that Friday morning. There were even some young men killed. Daniel found the names of each listed in an article on the second page. He became overcome with grief at seeing the names of the lives he believed he had a hand in taking.

Jimmy Flannelly was the first name he recognized, stabbed on the courthouse steps by an unknown assailant. The next was Leo Carey, clubbed to death by the crowd. The names of the many injured took too long to read.

Daniel knew Jimmy as a rabble-rouser, often mixed up in disruptions of this sort. He had married his childhood sweetheart, Mary Pat Donovan, and left behind three children, two boys and a girl. Leo, however, was none of the kind. People knew him as a soft-spoken sot with a heart of gold. He left behind a brother and sister, but little else.

The article said that Leo died trying to safe a young boy who had been caught up in the trouble as it spread out through the neighborhoods surrounding the courthouse. The paper called him a hero in the midst of criminals. The last life lost was the most senseless of all. A trolley horse, spooked by the row, trampled a young woman by name of Theresa McCauley who had come to Belfast to visit friends that morning. No information was included about her background.

Before Daniel could finish his paper, two constables arrived at the Haggerty's door to protect and escort the council member downtown. Jeffrey traveled along with his cousin for added security. The ride into Belfast was a somber one. Entering from the west, they came across many carts and trolleys along the downtown streets still burning.

The five men made their way cautiously to the courthouse. A few dead horses remained in the streets, but little else. The bodies of the dead and injured men were removed, replaced by many of the Royal Irish Constabulary who moved from street to street securing each in their wake. The group heard the shouts of people arguing on a side street followed by many footsteps running towards the noise.

Seeing blood splatters staining the stone steps and walls of the courthouse, Daniel quivered and needed help from his cousin to get inside. Jeffrey and one of the constables guided him to his seat in chambers while the other officer brought him a glass of water. Jeffrey sat beside him for a short while, insuring he was all right, and then took a position back and to the left near a rear door. Jeffrey kept a watchful eye on his cousin; he loved Daniel like a brother and was deeply concerned for his health and well-being.

The slam of a gavel brought council to order. Senior council member, C.W. Langan took the floor. Calling the action of the rabble of Belfast, "reprehensible." He demanded a police action to, as he put it, "rout them from their holes, and arrest them like the common criminals that they are." Councilman Langan returned to his seat beside Daniel Haggerty amidst the loud muttering that went about the room fully expecting a harsh rebuttal.

The gavel dropped heavy again in an overdone attempt to silence the chatter.

Councilman O'Hara, who was a unionist and second senior member of council, voiced his side stating emphatically, "These people are not criminals, sir, but Irishmen who believe their rights are being denied them under law."

C.W. Langan leaped from his seat. "Irishmen indeed, Mr. O'Hara," fired Mr. Langan arrogantly, "This Home Rule is a pile of British dung being forced upon the good people of Ireland. A loyal Irishman would not stand for it, but against it!"

Members of The Irish Unionist party, which was predominantly Protestant, held large land rights across the country and favored a preservation of British rule in Ireland. They feared losing their land rights and subsequent wealth if the unity between the two countries was severed. Nationalists, such as C.W. Langan and Daniel Haggerty believed in a free and independent Ireland; one country from north to south and from the channel to the sea. This faction of the council, comprised heavily of Catholics, was in the minority in Belfast, but not in council.

Angry words fired back and forth across the council chamber, with the sound of the gavel hammering in the background as the head of council tried to regain control of the room. The head council member, Michael Deering, called the council to order threatening to remove anyone who broke protocol. He demanded Mr. Langan and Mr. O'Hara return to their seats, motioning to the chamber guards to have them removed if their actions continued.

"I will not have this chamber turn into what we witnessed in the streets yesterday," Mr. Deering shouted banging away with his gavel. "This council will take a short recess to cool our heads and get back to the business of finding a solution to these dire circumstances."

The room quieted as the council members settled back in their seats to deliberate with their friends and colleagues, when a young council member and unionist sympathizer by the name of Kevin Duffy arose from his seat. He moved methodically across the chamber floor. Daniel noticed him, but thought nothing of it, since he had known young Kevin's father, uncles, and brothers for many years. He thought he just might be coming over to say hello and to share his opinions on the morning's activities.

As Daniel turned his head to respond to a question asked of him by another council member who was sitting behind him to the left, Kevin pulled from under his council member's robe a pistol and opened fire. Panic reigned as council members rushed for cover. In an instance, the room turned to bedlam as bullets and blood flew.

Jeffrey barreled from the shadows and tackled the man in the middle of the chamber floor, but not before he emptied his colt pocket-revolver. A dozen Royal constables surrounded the gunman, handcuffed him, and dragged him out. The constables discovered shortly after, that Mr. Duffy carried a second handgun with the intention of shooting more members of council. Jeffrey's quick reaction kept this from happening. Once the constables excised the man, Jeffrey turned to check on his cousin, whom he saw slumped in his chair.

Two bullets had struck Daniel, one in the right side just below the shoulder; the second slug creased the right side of his head just above the ear. Jeffrey eased his cousin from his chair and down to the floor. He tore away his robe and shirt to expose the hole in his shoulder. Daniel's blood spilled out in time with every strangled gasp for air he took. Jeffrey ripped the sleeve from his own shirt and pressed it firmly against the wound, attempting to slow the bleeding.

Daniel pawed at Jeffrey with his left hand, grabbing a fist full of his collar. "What have we done Jeffrey?" he murmured languishing, "What have we done?"

"No way of knowing it would turn this way, Daniel," replied Jeffrey, glimpsing about to see if anyone could hear. "What's done is done. We just fanned the flames. We couldn't a seen it going like it did. Hush now, preserve your strength; we'll deal with it once you're able."

Once Jeffrey had settled his cousin down, he realized he too injured himself and was unable to stand. A sharp pain throbbed in his right knee and he could not walk. In tackling the gunman, Jeffrey had slammed his knee into the hard tile floor. When the medics arrived, they removed him alongside Daniel, explaining that he had fractured his kneecap in the fall.

Meanwhile, back along Springfield Road, Matthew and Nora invited David Addison, Nora's sisters, Matthews's cousins, Cathy and Meggie, and the Lynch twins, to a brunch at Matthews's house. Nora sent an invitation to the Haggerty house, but Genie respectfully declined which Nora fully expected considering the troubles that existed at the courthouse.

Matthew knew his house was small, too small for such a crowd, so he decided to take advantage of a beautiful June morning and moved the table out into the yard so that everyone would fit comfortably. The sisters brought with them an old piece of green and white checkered linen and pinned it to the table to keep it from blowing away in the breeze. They also brought a dozen or so of Flora's homemade grain muffins. The Lynch brothers arrived with a bag of fresh apples. Matthew cut these into quarters, seasoned the pieces with cinnamon and sugar, and then warmed the wedges on the stove. Nora made pancakes and coffee for everyone, while Matthew fried bacon together with potatoes for a side.

David dominated the conversation with stories from his and Matthews past. Seeing the girls, particularly Mary, were impressed with his exploits, he continued to regale them with the wonders of New York City, expounding on its style and grandeur. Flora had little use for such things, getting up and walking off in the midst of David's tales.

Cathy and Meggie took advantage of a lull in the storytelling to make their own announcement. They too were leaving for the states before the autumn and had booked passage on the Majestic. Matthew was pleased and disappointed at the same time. It had been so long since he had seen either of them and now they were leaving for good.

David Addison chimed in again with, "Maybe it's time you considered the states yourself, Matthew."

Although he had considered it a time or two in the past, Matthew told David he knew his home was in Ireland and there is where he chose to remain. Nora took his arm and rested her head against him. "Besides, I'm a married man now," he added. "Here is my place, here with my family."

"A toast then," David responded standing up from his chair. "To Nora and Matthew Flannery, may their love ever bloom on the hills of Eire."

While taking her children on their daily walk, Genie Haggerty overheard a conversation between several people standing in front of the bank. She could not be sure of what she heard, so she hurried her children along with her eldest daughter Shannon. Keeping her oldest son Aaron beside her, she returned to the group. At the sight of her approaching, they quickly dispersed. One man did not run away, however. It was the banker, Jasper Grandy.

"Well Mr. Grandy, a bit more spine than the rest, haven't ya now," Genie, said, in a higher octave than usual. "Tell what it is ya have to say and be quick about. I have my children to attend to."

"Well Mum, Mrs. Haggerty Mum," he stammered nervously, "There has been reports of a shooting at the courthouse."

"And?" Fired Genie as Mr. Grandy hesitated.

"It was on the courthouse floor and some of the council members they say are dead," he replied.

A look of shock ran over and grabbed hold of Genie. She threw her arm around her son, pondering in fear if this madman had killed her husband.

"What of my Daniel? What have ya heard?" she asked in a panic.

"I don't know anymore than what I told ya Mum," Mr. Grandy answered. "I am sincerely sorry."

Clutching her son's hand, Genie turned to run home. Half way there she gave Aaron instructions to take one of the horses and ride as fast has he could to Matthew Flannery's house and bring back the Burns girls along with Joseph and Dougy Lynch. Aaron ran off to the stable and did exactly as he was told, while Genie went home to prepare for the worst. One glance at her mother's face and Shannon shooed the children to their rooms as Genie threw herself into her husband's favorite chair and stared out into the garden.

Aaron rode swiftly, spurring his horse up a steep hill and into Matthews's backyard where the group was just finishing brunch. The sight of this large draft horse with this smallish boy clinging to its back storming the hillside surprised the party to its feet. The horse reared up briefly, but the boy was able to settle it, pulling the mare to one side in order to speak to the group.

"Something has happened at the courthouse, a shooting!" He yelled at all of them. "Mother asked for the Flora-Dora girls and the twins to please come to the house."

The girls began picking up as the boy continued.

"No word on me dad, but I think yawl need to be cumin along. Me Mum's real upset. I never in me life seen her this way. Please, please come help!"

Without a second thought the sisters piled into Mr. Clancy's cart, which the twins had borrowed once again and planned to return, momentarily, and started out along Springfield Road. Matthew and David lit out on foot trying to keep up with the cart, but could not. As they passed the stone marking Nora and Matthew's spot, Matthew noticed the weeds had been cleared away and replaced by many types of spring flowers. He did not stop, continuing along with David until they reached the Haggerty's front door.

Stepping inside they found Shannon, along with the Flora-Dora girls gathered around Genie, trying to calm her down. Genie was crying loudly, but beyond her sobs, and despite there being thirteen children, the house was silent. Genie asked the twins if they would go downtown and see what news they could gather regarding Daniel, and Jeffrey who had gone with her husband that morning. The two men were just starting out when a messenger arrived at the Haggerty's door.

Matthew took the note and inspected it first, making sure the news was not the worst. He studied it carefully before looking up at Genie. Terrified, Genie yelled for him to read it aloud. He did as she directed, but he preferred not to.

Matthew started by reading, "There has been a shooting on the courthouse floor. Council members C.W. Langan and Cyrus Mulvane have been killed, Council member Daniel Haggerty has been shot and wounded, however no other word on him is available at this time."

Matthew looked up at Genie before continuing, "Additionally wounded were Jeffrey Haggerty and the assassin Kevin Duffy, but it is reported that these injuries appear to be minor."

Genie asked if the letter said where they took her husband for treatment, but it had not. The messenger boy lingered by the door, listening as Matthew read the telegram. "I know'd where they been taken, Mum," he said calmly, quieting the crowd now stacked up in the Haggerty's sitting room.

The crowd parted as Genie bolted through, grabbing the boy by the arm. The boy's calm demeanor turned to fear as little Genie pinned him against the open door. Stepping up, Matthew wrapped his arm around Genies shoulders and gently moved her back, calming her instantly. The terrified lad took a deep swallow as the crowd closed in around him.

"They've taken both of the Haggerty's to the Workhouse, Mum," he chirped, and then made a mad dash for his bicycle, hopped on and sped off.

Matthew sent Aaron for a carriage and driver to take Genie to see her husband. Cora and Dora agreed to stay with the children while Flora, brandishing her shillelagh, chose to go with Genie. Mary and Matthew's cousins retired to the apartment above the tailoring shop, while the twins actually retuned Pat Clancy's cart. Nora clung to Matthews arm as they, along with David, returned to Matthews's house for the evening.

At the house, Nora instantly began tidying up while Matthew poured the men a glass of whiskey. Once Nora finished she sat beside her husband on the arm of his chair, took his glass, and had a large drink. Matthew was surprised. She did not cough, she did not flinch; she just swallowed the whiskey smooth and straight down. Nora, seeing the looks of surprise on Matthew and David's faces paused for a moment and then started to laugh. The men began to laugh too. Nora melted onto Matthew's lap where her laughter turned to tears. After maybe an hour, she excused herself, gave Matthew a soft kiss, and bid the men goodnight.

Matthew and David did not wish to upset Nora more than she was already; waiting until they were sure she was in bed before discussing the tragic incident. Matthew revealed to his friend that he knew this man and that he had come to Matthew's store numerous times. Matthew described Kevin Duffy as a pleasant enough bloke, respectful and courteous. How and why this man, who stood on the steps of a bright political career, could so boldly and brazenly gunned down two men was unfathomable. The whole thing seemed quite unbelievable to the men's way of thinking.

David, again, expressed his idea about Matthew coming to New York. "I fear the violence here is only going to escalate, my friend," David stated. "You are now a married man, looking forward to a long and happy future with this wonderful woman. Those expectations may be cut short if you remain here in Belfast."

Matthew had no argument. He found the recent events most disconcerting and worried deeply over the safety of those who were now a huge part of his life. He filled his glass one more time and took a drink, brooding over what would be a colossal decision. He had reached a crossroad in his life and his choice would influence many.

David finished his drink and then stretched his arms and back. He looked over at his friend, attempting to gage his way of thinking, seeing the worry in his eyes. Although they had not spent time together for some while, David knew his friend well enough to know he would do anything to protect and provide for his loved ones.

Trying to appeal to Matthew's sensible nature, David spoke up again "My friend, ya know there is more to it, Matthew, than just what happened today to think about. There is the future, a secure and successful future. You'll not be finding that here laddie, I venture to say."

Matthew agreed with David, but knew it could only happen if Nora believed it too. If Nora chose to stay in Ireland than that is where Matthew would be, alongside the most amazing and enchanting woman he would ever know, that he could ever know. There was no one in the world like Nora; he believed this with every fiber of his being. Matthew swallowed the last of his whiskey, said goodnight to David and went in to lie beside Nora. He wrapped his arms around her, feeling her heart beat next to his. Matthew kissed her alabaster neck and whispered, "I love you" and "goodnight" in her ear. He lay quietly until her even breathing told him she was sleeping, however, as the night wore on, he never did.

It was a quiet Sunday morning with a little touch of fog and light rain to dampen the somber moods a touch more than they were already. Nora brewed a pot of tea and split the last of her sister Flora's muffins between herself, Matthew and David. Sparse conversation about nothing important created an overtone of nervousness in the room. Nora talked of rearranging the furniture and adding some curtains to brighten up the place.

David finally informed them he would need to be leaving come Monday morning. Between the delays of his crossing and the unexpected tragedy at the courthouse, he had missed his business meeting and would need to report in at the office before heading back to New York. The Belfast Lace Company was on the other side of the city and David needed to be there before noon Monday. He then stepped outside to smoke a cigarette while Nora and Matthew cleaned up the kitchen.

Working side by side in the kitchen that morning, Matthew decided the time had come to speak with Nora about migrating to the United States. During all their walks along the road in the fall, Nora spoke of many plans for the future with Matthew, but none of these involved America. It took him some time to gather the courage up to say what he wished to say. Not wanting to pressure her or alarm her anymore than she already was, but he felt in his heart that this would be the best thing for them both.

"Nora, can we stop a minute and talk?" Matthew asked meekly.

Nora put away the last of the cups and dishes from breakfast, pushed the chairs in around the table, and removed the white apron she had tied around her waist, folding it neatly and setting it on the counter.

"Of course; we can always talk Matthew. Why would ya be thinkin you should be needin to ask?" she responded, gently grasping Matthews's hand.

"I've thought heavily on what David said about us moving to the states and with all the troubles, I think it is a good idea," Matthew told his new wife.

Nora looked away, wringing her hands anxiously, not sure at all what to say. Stepping to the window, she looked out across the hillside and green fields that blended into the fog. Matthew moved to look over her shoulder, knowing what she was thinking; admiring the beauty, which was Ireland.

"Oh, it is such a grand place isn't it Matthew," Nora said faintly, resting back against her husband.

"It is the finest most beautiful place on earth, I expect," he replied. "But, I do not feel safe for you here Nora. Nor do I feel safe for our future. It has become a dangerous place and it won't be long before it finds our front door."

"I feel it too, Matthew," Nora answered. "There is a dread, like something is on its way and we'll be caught in it, surin we will!"

Nora felt a dread coming from two directions. She feared the political unrest spreading across her country, but it was not all she feared. The first of many nightmares disturbed her sleep that night. This too plagued her as she looked to a future through uncertainty eyes.

Matthew wrapped his arms around his new wife, like a blanket, trying to say he would protect her. In his heart, he was not certain that he could. "We don't have to decide right now Nora," Matthew uttered, adding "we can talk about it a while and bide a wee, and see what we think after that."

Nora agreed that reflecting upon the subject would be the wisest thing to do, rather than making a rash decision based on current events. Nevertheless, she knew they were leaving Ireland and there was no way around it. Matthew was right. There home had become a dangerous place. "Sad to believe," Nora thought, "that someplace so beautiful could hold such hatred."

The next day, David packed his things and caught a ride with the Lynch brothers, who were picking up some supplies for Pat Clancy in his cart, into downtown Belfast. From there he took the trolley to the lace factory. After a day long meeting with his bosses, he would spend the night at one of the hotels nearest to the ferry launch, so to catch the first boat out in the morning.

Matthew wished his friend farewell, as did Nora, Dora, and Mary. Cora held his hand and kissed him goodbye, wondering if she might ever see him again. Exasperated, Flora gave her a clout on the ear. All but Flora waved him goodbye as the cart went round the bend and out of sight, disappearing into the trees lining Springfield Road.

The days ran into weeks and soon summer faded, giving way to the arrival of autumn. Jeffrey Haggerty's injuries left him with a limp, but healed well enough. Daniels recovery time lasted through fall and into winter. Physically he slowly heeled, but his mental torment over the horrible incident and the circumstances surrounding it would linger with him for years to come.

A cold hard winter gripped the British Isles with temperatures reaching record lows. Matthew and Nora moved their bed into the sitting room to be closer to the fireplace. Something good came from the frigid weather; there were no conflicts. The cold was too much for even the most devote rebel to take to the streets. The months of summer and fall saw many occurrences of unrest, with more frequent and increasingly violent confrontation spreading throughout the countryside. The cold of winter had brought a cease-fire, but not by choice. Once the weather broke, the hostilities would resume. Matthew and Nora knew it, they feared it, feeling the pot was about to boil over.

Matthew and Nora made their decision cuddled up beneath the blankets, their eyes fixated on the flames dancing in the hearth. Matthew would sell the house and shop and pool his money with Nora's considerable savings, which were more than he had imagined. Their intention was to book transit aboard the same vessel David had crossed the Atlantic on, the Majestic, as early in springtime as they could.

Since they had made their plans, Nora needed to speak with her sisters. She knew it would be a difficult conversation to have and wanted so much for them to join her and Matthew in America. The choice ultimately would be theirs to make. She could only hope it would be to leave Ireland.

Nora found reason upon reason to delay speaking with them regarding the decision Matthew and she had made, sure, that it would be ill received. She anticipated a frightful argument, particularly from Flora. Matthew knew this too and believed it best that they speak with the girls together. Nora felt it was her place and no one else's and she would do it when she felt the time was right. Matthew remained patient while secretly arranging the sale of his two properties.

February brought a false spring forcing Nora's hand. The abrupt, although short lived, warm spell brought forth multiple incidences of violence in both Belfast and Dublin. Tensions ran high throughout the Emerald Isle. No one felt safe, hearing stories of assaults occurring on an almost daily basis.

Genie Haggerty staunchly held to her daily schedule despite repeated warnings to the contrary. She always took her children for their walk around noon. She made her stops at the bank and Matthews's store, or the market and the cobblers. The string of children swung by the dress shop and then back home. The security guard her husband insisted on hiring brought up the rear of the line.

One warm afternoon as the troop began its march along Springfield Road, a cart with four hooded men came out of nowhere. Genie frantically urged her children off the road. The guard grabbed little Ryan under one arm and the youngest daughter, Autumn, under the other and ran them to safety. The men pelted Genie and her innocent children with rotted potatoes and stones, yelling profanities and threats as they drove their horses past in a gallop. Heather, the third youngest of the litter did not get clear of the cart in time. The right front wheel struck her a glancing blow and threw her to the side of the road.

Aaron noticed his little sister first and ran to her aid. Genie had fallen, stumbling on the cracked cobblestone. Seeing her daughter lying motionless in a heap on the street, she began to scream. Matthew witnessed the brutal scene from his shop window and, grabbing a blanket and some bandages, leaped into the street and ran to Heather. Aaron reached Heather first, but did not know what to do. Matthew yelled for him not to move her. Kneeling down beside her, Matthew inspected the child's wounds before touching her. She was unconscious and her left arm and leg appeared to be broken. She bled profusely from a gash on the side of her head. Matthew bandaged the cut and with the help of Aaron carefully wrapped the blanket around Heather.

By this time, Genie made it to her child. She wanted to take little Heather into her arms, but Matthew stopped her fearing that moving the child might cause further injury. Colleen Clancy, hearing the ruckus in the street, came from the pub brandishing a shotgun. She ordered her husband to get the cart then chased the bar patrons into the road and locked the door.

Genie sent the rest of her children back to the house with the security guard. The Flora-Dora girls met them half way and escorted them inside. Pat Clancy pulled along side Matthew, hopped from the cart, and took a board from the back. Matthew eased the injured child up just enough so that Clancy could slide the board beneath her.

When Matthew was much younger, he had worked at the local hospital as an orderly. There he learned many things about treating injuries and the one lesson he never forgot was not to move an injured person without taking precautions. Doing so could risk inflicting greater damage.

Genie continued to cry as the two men loaded the child into the back of the cart. With the help of Matthew, she climbed in next to her daughter and signaled for the guard to join them. Matthew cautioned Genie to keep her daughter warm and still as the cart pulled away. Pat Clancy turned the cart around and headed down Springfield Road to Doc Mullins's office across from the WayFair. Doc Mullins was the Haggerty's family doctor and had brought each one of her thirteen children into the world. Genie knew he would do everything humanly possible to save her daughter's life.

Matthew and Colleen Clancy went across to the Haggerty house together. Although it was an unseasonably warm day, Matthew noticed that Colleen was chilled. Before going to the Haggerty's he went back inside the store and pulled another blanket from the sales rack. He bolted up the shop and draped the blanket around Colleen's shoulders. She thanked him then adjusted the blanket to where she was comfortable, realizing she was inappropriately attired to be amongst children.

They reached the front door to find Flora standing guard with her shillelagh. Colleen replaced her at the front door still brandishing her shotgun. Matthew and Flora entered into the sitting room where Nora, Cora, Dora, and Mary were comforting the children. Daniel, still not fully recovered from his injuries, was lying down in an upstairs bedroom completely unaware of what had just occurred. Matthew agreed to accompany Aaron to his father's room to deliver the bad news. Aaron's courage and spirit impressed Matthew. The boy displayed maturity beyond his years, but he knew his father would not take this well.

Aaron remained calm as he entered his father's room and sat down beside him. Matthew took a step inside and stood still as Aaron laid out the facts as they were. Daniel sat up in his bed. One long tear ran from his eye. He put his large hands on the boys' shoulders and pulled him to him, burying his face in the boys' chest. His body jerked as he cried into his son's shirt. Aaron rested his arm around his father and glimpsed over his shoulder at Matthew. Matthew nodded and left the room.

As Matthew began down the steps, Shannon was leading the line of youngsters up the stairs. Shannon stopped at Matthew, giving him a hug as if to say thank you and then continued with her siblings. Matthew watched her usher the children to their rooms. She gave them each a pat on the head and nudged them into their rooms closing the doors behind them. She then walked down the long hallway and entering her father's room to join Aaron.

Matthew thought about the Haggerty children, how respectful, well mannered, and well disciplined they were yet he never once heard their parents yell at or punish them in any way.

Matthew rejoined the sisters in the sitting room. The temperature began to dip as the sun went down. Flora was stoking the fire in the fireplace and Nora was pouring tea. She glanced up at her husband as he entered the room, asking how it went and wondering how Daniel seemed to be. Matthew did not answer at first, lost in the thought of leaving this angry place and never looking back.

"Matthew!" Nora said feeling something more than the recent accident was bothering her husband.

"Daniel is upset, as you might expect" Matthew answered. "Shannon and Aaron are with him now."

"We need to have the talk with your sisters Nora," he added, "We should do it now."

Nora set the teapot down and gave Flora a slight tug on the sleeve.

"I'm listenin," snapped Flora, brushing aside her sisters hand, "and I think I know watcha be wantin to tell us, but go ahead with it. Surin we might be thinking the same thing."

Nora sat on the sofa between Cora and Dora. Mary, who had been sitting in Daniels high back chair beside the French doors, moved across the room and sat in a seat nearest to Matthew. A cold wind howled outside and rattled the panes of glass in the front windows. Mary looked out to see the last sharp strand of light settle into the foothills to the west, leaving behind a purple and orange glow that blended into the leafless, shivering trees.

Colleen Clancy, who had been standing guard outside at the front door, came in from the cold. She set down her shotgun, shook out the blanket, and reconfigured it around her shoulders. She took up a spot beside Matthew until she noticed the conversation had abruptly stopped and the sisters were staring at her. Colleen noticed the awkwardness. She excused herself and went to the kitchen for a drink.

Nora clutched Dora's hand. "Well Matthew and I have decided to move to America," she stated directly.

She waited for a response, but none was forthcoming. She looked up at Matthew standing by the sitting room door. Then she felt Dora squeeze her hand, and Cora slid her hand over the top of both of them. Nora turned to Cora whose face was a glow with the colors of the fire. Flora continued to prod the embers with a long twisted wrought iron poker, unfazed by Nora's confession.

A smile crept onto the corners of Mary's mouth as she arose from her chair. In the fires radiance Nora noticed her baby sister had grown up. The playful kid from just the year before was now a tall slender young woman.

"I will speak if no one else will have to it," she said rigidly.

Flora set the poker back in the stand beside the hearth with a loud and noticeable clang. She stood up straight and stretched her back, glared at Mary, then sat down in a small wooden chair beside the fireplace. A deathly silence filled the room. The sisters expected Flora to go off with the anger and spit she used so well. To their astonishment, she did not.

"Speak your mind, kitten," Flora said calmly.

Kitten was the name Flora used for Mary every time she showed a little more spunk or spirit to belie her childish appearance. Flora too noticed her little sister coming of age, but would not openly admit it. Mary's fire was undeniable, not by Flora or anyone else.

Mary continued, "We've all been talkin about it ever since Matthew's friend Mr. Addison was here, and Meggie and Cathy heading off on their own. Nothing seems right. Surin we cannot even cross our own street now without watchin for punks and hooligans around every tree looking to do harm to even the innocents. If you and the mister will have us we'd like to be joinin ya on this adventure."

Cora and Dora smiled and nodded. Flora still said nothing. Her brooding scowl seemed to deepen, her eyes affixed on her sisters. As happy, as Nora was with their decision she stilled worried, anxious for Flora who never did well with change. This was a huge step in a new direction. Everything was about to change. All the sisters knew it. Flora feared it most of all.

Chapter 5

Goodbye My Friends

Spring came earlier than usual to the British Isles. The normal morning fog lay heavy across the moors. However, many sun-filled afternoons offset the damp misty mornings. The buds on the trees and the bloom of butterburs, lady's smocks, primrose, and bugles colored the fields and hillsides with life renewed. Ireland was as beautiful as it had ever been.

Matthew booked passage for the group some months in advance. He sold his sundry store to the cobbler, Tom Cooley, who planned to combine the two business interests. He saw Matthew's spot as a premium piece of real estate with high visibility. "Much better", Mr. Cooley believed, "than the small hidden away place he had at the end of the business district, just beyond Barrett's post". Matthew did not see the profit in Mr. Cooley's idea, but he was willing to pay top dollar, so who was Matthew to disagree.

Pat and Colleen Clancy purchased his house on the hill, popularly known as Flannery's hill, book ending the section of Springfield Road to Barrett's Post. They had been living in the apartment above the pub for more years than they wished to count. Their son Shamus went away to school in England so they thought this little change might be nice as they got older. Matthews's house was up high enough on a hill to provide beautiful views of the summits and glens that rolled off in all directions. "A relaxing and beautiful spot," thought Colleen for them to live out their final years.

Pat and Colleen received the keys on the day Matthew, Nora and her sisters left. Although they were happy to get them, the sadness of seeing their friends leaving made the day a bittersweet one.

Pat Clancy shook Matthew's hand, but then pulled him in and gave him a huge bear hug as tears welled in his eyes. He moved over to Nora next. She kissed him softly, the way she always kissed to make a man blush. Colleen hugged Matthew, who could not help but feel her large breasts mashed up against him. She held him long and tight, uncomfortably lingering on his lips when she kissed him. Nora stepped along side them, clearing her throat, prompting Colleen to break her embrace.

"Sorry, Miss Nora, but I've always had a fondness for your man here," Colleen stated without shame.

"I don't blame ya none at all," responded Nora. "I feel the same way."

Pat Clancy gripped his wife's arm, tugging her out of Matthew's embrace. Colleen, pulling easily out of her husbands hands, slapped old Pat in the chest. Matthew and Nora stepped out the front door and closed it behind them, putting an exclamation point to this sentence in their lives.

Jeffrey Haggerty waited at the end of the path that led up the hill to Matthew and Nora's front door accompanied by his white mare Daisy. Matthew helped his wife along the slippery slope and into the carriage and then followed her in to sit beside her. Matthew wrapped his arm around his wife who was wiping away the last drips of tears from her eyes with Matthew's hankie. Matthew nodded to Jeffrey and the big man gave a flip of the reins nudging Daisy forward.

They had traveled only a short distance when Jeffrey pulled the carriage to a stop. Matthew stepped down from the cab, taking Nora's hand and helped her down beside him. They were at the spot where they had first met once again. A much larger stone, surrounded by four smaller stones, had replaced the rock that Matthew had set in place as a remembrance.

Someone had cut the grass and trimmed the trees that lined both sides of the street. Many colorful spring flowers now circled not only the stones, but also decorated the base of every tree that lined the road. Joseph and Dougy Lynch stepped out from behind the trees looking work weary.

"We hopes you don't mind, but we thought this might make a fine goin away gift to ya," Joseph said struggling with each word he spoke.

"Did ya see what we done on the stone?" asked Dougy.

Nora stepped to the stone to read the engraving the twins had made. In Gaelic, they had carved 'Gradh An Faigh', 'Love Is Born', To Matthew and Nora Flannery.

"Would ya be liken it Miss Nora?" asked Dougy.

Unable to speak, Nora buried her tear filled face in Matthews's chest. Matthew put his arms around her. "It's very beautiful boys. Thank you!" answered Matthew.

With tears rolling down their cheeks, they hugged their good, good friends and bid them farewell. Jeffrey helped both Nora and Matthew back into the carriage. They stopped at the Haggerty's where the sisters were sharing a somber goodbye with Genie, Daniel and their children. Genie and Nora held each other for what seemed like forever, crying copiously as they said their heart-wrenching goodbye.

Daniel had Aaron prepare a larger carriage to take Matthew and the girls into Belfast. As Nora gave Daisy a soft kiss goodbye the horse turned its head and pawed at the ground with its hoof. Everyone smiled and shared a good laugh, giving their hearts a lighter, happier memory to take with them across the sea.

Before Nora climbed into the carriage to join her sisters, who had taken their seats, Genie handed her a gift. Once again, Nora hugged her and thanked her. Matthew helped his wife up the step between the large wheels of the ornate carriage. Jeffrey gave a snap of the reins spurring the horses forward. Nora held the present in her lap as she leaned against Matthew. The Flora-Dora girls waved goodbye as the carriage disappeared, vanishing in the trees.

The group shared many moments of silence gazing out across the rolling hills, soaking up its scenery, admiring their lovely country for what they fully expected to be the last time. As they reached the downtown, they were more aware of the architecture they had previously taken for granted, as if they were seeing it anew.

Jeffrey stopped the carriage at St. Joseph's Church, where father McCormick descended the polished stone steps to bless them and wish them a safe journey, before continuing to the ferry.

They were nearly to the docks when Nora remembered Genies gift. She pulled the paper off to find a fine wooden box with a note attached to the top. She read the note aloud before opening the lid.

"Nora, my dearest friend," it began. "I will so miss you and your sisters, more than you could ever imagine. You have a fine man in Matthew and I hope and pray that you are as blessed with children as I. You may not want thirteen, but I would not give back even one. You will never be forgotten in our hearts or in our lives." She then added, "As you so admired this on your wedding day, I cut and preserved it in water for you. It will remain as it was forever, much as that day will live in our memories, some bad, and some good. Cherish the good, never discourage over the bad, enjoy each day of life, for as we saw with our poor Heather, you can look away just for an instance and it is gone. All my love, your friend, Genie Haggerty."

Tears fell like the rains of September past. Hard as he fought, Matthew could not hold them back. Big Jeffrey didn't even try. His large body shook the entire carriage as he guided it through the streets of Belfast to the quay. Nora carefully removed from the box a water globe containing the black rose from Genie's green house and held it up for all to see. Once it was fully admired, she returned it to the container, secretly wishing her friend hadn't given it to her.

The ferry had just begun to board passengers when the group arrived. The sisters stepped down from both sides of the cart with Matthew assisting on one side and Jeffrey the other. Jeffrey removed their bags from the cart and with Matthew's help, lugged them up the dock and onto the ferry. The group chose to travel light, feeling the more they took with them the more they would have to drag about.

It was on the dock where they would say their final farewells to Jeffrey, the gentle giant whose part in their lives had a much more profound influence than they would ever know.

Jeffrey hugged each of the sisters in turn, even Flora who allowed it grudgingly and wished him well. He offered Matthew a firm handshake and a request.

"I want ya to make me a promise Matthew me lad," said Jeffrey. "Keep the lassies safe and if ya ever have the chance, come back and see your friends along the road."

Matthew agreed to do so, but deep down he knew his eye would never see Ireland again.

He saved Nora til last. She managed to get her arms less than half way around the big man. Stretching up on her toes, she brushed the touch of a teardrop from his cheek, and then kissed him gently on the lips. Red faced, Jeffrey gazed into Nora's eyes wanting to say so many things, but he could not. One last time, she swiped her soft fingers across his cheek and turned to Matthew.

Jeffrey loved Nora. Not in the way Matthew did, but for the kindhearted, beautiful friend she was to him; she was to everyone. Jeffrey crossed the gangplank and paused on the dock as the gangplank retracted. He watched as the ferry became smaller and just before it became too small for them to see each other he raised his big hand for one last goodbye, and then they were gone.

Flora scanned the coarse and fragile faces of the passengers filling the ferry. Always the protector, she strained to determine which to be leery of, keeping herself and her shillelagh between her family and those she mistrusted. Despite her past misgivings regarding her brother-in-law, she trusted Matthew to help her if no one else would.

Matthew and Nora stood holding each other, watching their large friend growing smaller, fading into the blurred remains of Ireland. The sisters too peered over the rail of the ferry as their homeland blended into the horizon and was gone. Once the water of the channel was all that remained, Matthew turned Nora and the girls away from Ireland to face the new direction they now headed.

"Embracing the future," Matthew told the girls, "will make it easier to put the past behind us."

Chapter 6

Bound for New York

The trip across the channel seemed a long one to the group, but was actually the shortest step in their journey. It took just over eight hours before the ferry docked in Liverpool. Matthew arranged suitable lodging for the group in a boarding house on Chapel St. not far from the landing stage since their ship did not leave until the following morning. They ate dinner at a small eatery near the docks and stocked up on food for the trip at a nearby grocers shop. The combination of nervous anticipation over sailing into the unknown and the overwhelming sadness of leaving behind their home and friends meant none of them would sleep this night.

Many tired eyes saw the first light of morning. Matthew led the girls the few blocks to the landing stage. Around the final corner the girls jaws fell open, astonished by the first sight of the steamer, Majestic, its huge stacks pushed up through a cobwebby morning fog. Men in white slacks and dark blue jackets moved supplies up the gangplank and great wenches lifted bundles of cargo to the upper deck. Crowds of people toting all types of luggage congregated on the landing stage awaiting the call to board.

Matthew navigated through the scores of people and things, clutching Nora's hand, as Nora clutch Cora's hand, and down the line. Flora, her shillelagh swung over her shoulder, brought up the rear. They wove through the throng like a snake, dodging umbrellas and big hats, barking dogs and belligerent children, attempting to get as close to the gangplank as possible. When they could maneuver no further, they formed a circle and set their bags down in the center. Dora sat down on her suitcase, twirling her hair with her fingers and looking around nervously. Cora placed a reassuring hand on her shoulder as they awaited the call to board.

Minutes passed slowly, hours slower still. The sea of restless, eager, and apprehensive people jockeyed for position near the gangplank. When the call came, the first class passengers boarded first shoving aside the unpleasant peasants, which they regarded no higher than flies. This took the longest due to the amount of things that went along with them. Trunk upon trunk, bags, birdcages, even large carved wooden headboards went up the gangplank. Matthew, Nora and her sisters watched each piece pass before them anxiously awaiting their turn.

The second-class went next, boarding much quicker than their more affluent and overburdened traveling companions. Last, to embark was steerage, or third class. This group consisted of a melting pot of European society. From the frugal commoners who could not or would not, for one reason or another, afford the style and luxury of the upper class accommodations, to the less fortunate and dregs, who barely managed to scrape together enough money to make the crossing at all.

Most of these carried little more than the clothes on their backs.

Matthew and the women had pooled together enough money to book a second-class passage. They chose not to feeling the money better spent once they reached America. Once the final feet stepped off the gangplank and onto the deck the bridge rose and, with a resounding clang, the gate locked in place behind them. The whistle of the ship sounded, a puff of smoke came from each of the two large stacks, as the ship weighed anchor. The voyage had begun; bound for New York to what all hoped would be a much brighter future.

On board the steamer, the sisters taught Matthew to sew. They planned to open a shop in New York with Matthew as the tailor and the women doing what they do best. Having Matthew at the forefront eliminated the issue of gender. A woman operating a business was most uncommon. Matthew's good business sense and great salesmanship were useful qualities as the group entered into this new venture. He stood tall and straight and spoke in a way that made people listen. He was very sure of himself, answering questions without hesitation, confident without presumption.

During the first eight days of the cruise the weather conditions where quite inconsequential and, for the most part, pleasant and without incident. Some rocky seas and a brief storm on day two made up the worst of it. Conversation and pleasantries kept the feeling light despite the overcrowding.

Games of chance, a young man with a guitar and moments of laughter made the time go by easily. Flora stood guard with her shillelagh, keeping a watchful eye on the surroundings. She even donned a smile when some young lassies found space to turn a jig with a fiddler sawing strings at their side. She pounded her stick with the beat on the floorboards and hooted at the miss of a step.

A thousand or more bodies packed into steerage, making space a high commodity. After a few days, the heat and unsanitary conditions became appalling. The stench of human existence sickened the girls, particularly Dora who struggled mightily with the overcrowded conditions. Mary and Cora took turns walking with her above deck, finding the least occupied areas so that Dora could sit and breath. Flora went directly to the captain with her complaints.

"Too many people," Flora told the captain, "being packed together like animals, makes them start to think and act like animals. Dangerous situation you are creatin down there.

You'll know it when it happens if you don't stop it before it does."

Flora's rant did nothing for the conditions, but did land her an hour in the brig. The captain didn't know Flora and was not aware that this was her normal disposition and not a product of the condition. He thought it best she cool off, thinking she might start trouble herself in the mood she was in, and it was trouble he wished to avoid.

Flora's broad shoulders and permanent scowl gave her a tough appearance. Her long salt and pepper hair was now mostly grey, with just a few strands of black to remind her. She kept it pulled back and tied with a piece of green ribbon. The skin of her face stretched tight across her high cheekbones and pointed chin. She rarely took her hands off the heavy oak shillelagh, which she polished with a bone every night before bed.

Just about dusk that very same day, Dora and Mary decided to go above deck to catch a view of the sunset on the sea. They asked permission of Flora before heading off. Flora was fine with them going and told her sisters she would join them, saying that a good stretch might be nice to have now that her temper had settled. She told them to go ahead and that she would meet them on deck shortly as she rolled up a blanket and stowed it away. The girls went down the hallway and through the heavy metal doors that led to the stairway to the promenade deck.

Suddenly, as Dora and Mary started up the steps, four hooligans came at them from the shadows. Two of the boys dragged Dora into the corner of the first landing. Mary fought like a wildcat before being smacked in the head and knocked to the floor. A boy grabbed hold of her wrists, but not before Mary clawed the left side of his face just missing his eye.

The one boy tore open Dora's' top and was sucking and fondling her ample soft breasts. The other dug his fingers deep up inside her. He laughed and asked her how it felt; belching foul, disgusting air with each word he spoke. She screamed and squirmed, but she could not kick her way free. A third boy held Mary's arms tight to the steps while the final attacker pulled her skirt up over her head.

He loosened his belt and dropped his pants to his ankles. He was grabbing hold of himself when a loud crack echoed from the back of his head. In a daze, he spun round and a second blow took out what he had left of his teeth. The boy whom Mary scratched let go his grip on Mary and bolted up the stairs. Flora, her shillelagh in hand, lay waste the others before they could react; screaming at the top of her lungs as she rained blow after blow down upon them.

Matthew, Nora, and Cora, hearing the racket, ran down the hall and through the large doors to the stairwell. Two crewmembers also overheard the commotion in the stairwell and ran toward the noise. Nora and Cora covered Mary and led her into the hallway. Matthew and the crewmen pulled Dora out from under the two boys who now coward in the corner being pummeled mercilessly. The first ships mate restrained Flora, while the other took control of the two boys. The one with his pants down lay unconscious and bleeding at the bottom of the stairs.

"There was another boy," Flora yelled. "He ran up the steps."

Nora nodded to Matthew as she took Dora from his arms. Turning away from her, he flew up the steps, his long legs taking them three a stride with the ships mate at his heels. They burst through the doors that opened onto the promenade and into a crowd of people. The men looked about briefly, asking passengers if they had seen anyone exit from that door. No one had seen nor heard a thing and were annoyed that their good time had been so rudely interrupted. The other boy blended into the crowd.

The young ships mate along with a couple of deck hands, removed the remaining assailants from the stairwell, and deposited them in the brig. The captain questioned each at length trying to determine the missing boy's identity. The most they knew was that he called himself Luke and did not talk much.

Cora and Nora wrapped their arms around Dora and led her back to the steerage. Flora held onto Mary with a cast iron grip. Having predicted something like this might happen, Flora screamed at the throng that now teemed into the narrow hallway.

"Somethin could a been done, and should a been done, but the captain ignored it. He don't give a hoot about us. We're just cattle bein shipped across the sea," hollered Flora pushing her way through the crowd.

As they moved back down the corridor Dora whispered to Nora, "Is it wrong that I liked some of what them boys did?"

Nora, startled by the words of her sister responded, "Don't think nothin about it, whether ya did nor didn't. Don't think anything at all." Mary on the other hand, appeared quite unfazed. She shoved off her sister and straightened her dress.

"You're a tough little kitten, aren't ya little sister," Flora said to Mary, not all that surprised at the way she shrugged off the assault.

"Is Dora alright? If they hurt her, I'll kill em. I swear on our mother, I'll kill em I will," Mary screamed to Flora with fire in her words.

The boy had managed to ease his way unnoticed through the crowd and slip into a door at the opposite side of the ship, which led down to the boiler room. There after some deliberation, he stuffed a rag in his mouth and pressed the scratched side of his face against a hot steam pipe. The boy stumbled to the medic's cabin for treatment.

The ships doctor knew the boy. He had helped him in gaining passage aboard ship. Asking no questions he treated the boys wound, patching his face as best he could. The doctor falsified his log entry, stating that he had treated the boy for burns, a full day before the incident in the stairwell.

He then instructed the boy, "Keep moving, and go from deck to deck and one end of the ship to another."

The doctor stopped for a moment. Thinking he heard someone in the corridor outside his office, he stuck his head out. Looking in both directions and seeing no one he returned to his patient.

"The longer it takes em to find ya the better off you'll be," he told the boy. "And if they do find ya, act like ya don't understand. Speak little English and you'll get by 'til we reach the harbor. I'll say I don't know ya and I will show them me records. Then get off of this ship and don't ya never come back."

The boy toppled out the door and ran down the hall, doing exactly as the doctor told him, staying out of sight until the ship made port.

Matthew's friend David Addison awaited them in New York. At the age of fifteen, Matthew ventured to London. While there, he came across the young man, David Addison, taking a beating from three street thugs bent on rearranging his face. Turned out they were brothers defending the honor of their sister whom David had deflowered in the back of the livery stable. Matthew rescued David. Since then their friendship was as close as brothers were.

Matthew contacted him for assistance with a place to live upon arrival in New York. David agreed and told his friend he would be there to meet them at Ellis Island. In his letter to David, Matthew professed his parties business intentions with a hope that his friend might provide some assistance with this too. David agreed, telling his friend he would keep his eyes and ears open for an opportunity. This made Matthew nervous, knowing David did not always do things on the up and up, but he trusted his friend not to lead him into trouble.

The sight of the Statue of Liberty was breathtaking, rising up through the wispy morning fog. The cheers of thousands reverberated through the ship as people pushed to the rails to get a glimpse. Ten days aboard ship had everyone very tired and anxious to reach his or her new home. The tension of the next few hours would make them seem like the longest of their journey.

As the ship finally steamed into the New York harbor, small ferries slid up along each side and tied off. Gangplanks dropped and medical examiners began checking each passenger beginning with the first class and making their way down. The upper class examinations were brief and superficial, a steerage passenger endured greater scrutiny. Any indication of poor health or illness put the passenger in quarantine and possibly sent back to their country of origin.

No one wanted to come this far and be this close then be turned back.

The first and second-class passengers with all their possessions boarded the ferries first. Slender men in white outfits loaded trunks, suitcases, fine carpetbags, and racks of clothes onto the ferries to transport directly to Manhattan. The, more comfortable, well to do, did not have to endure the indignities of Ellis Island.

The examiners clipped nametags with assigned manifest numbers to the members of third class. Then they were loaded onto the tops of barges to be shuttled to Ellis Island. When their turn came to board, the surging crowd wedged in Cora and she was nearly left behind. "That's it, we're full," chirped the tug captain, hauling in the gangplank. Cora fell back into the raucous mass. If it were not for the persuasiveness of Matthew, the chaos would have swallowed Cora. Reuniting with her family seemed impossible. After a brief conversation between Matthew and the captain, the crewmembers reset the gangplank and Cora climbed aboard. Sobbing she rested in the arms of her sisters. They held tight to each other from that point on.

The last of the barges began to board when the boy came out of hiding. The medical examiners questioned the damage to his face. He pretended that he did not understand as two crewmembers, familiar with the attack in the stairwell, yanked him to the side. They summoned the captain along with the ships doctor. The doctor professed that he had treated the boy for burns a full day prior to the incident in the stairwell. Still suspicious, the captain requested that Mary and Dora come forward to identify him. Unfortunately, they had already left the ship on their way to Ellis Island.

"What is your name boy?" the captain asked him. At first, he did not answer. "Don't make me ask you again boy," the captain barked with the rasp of the sea in his voice. The crewmembers lifted and shook the boy. "Laguska Natanuski," he answered in a deep guttural Slovak tone. The captain looked about. Seeing only members of his crew present and out of sight of any passengers, the captain punched the boy with everything he had, knocking him to the deck.

"I know it was you, boy," growled the captain. The other crewmen lifted the boy to his feet. "And if I had the proof, you'd be getting much worse! Put this piece of shit on the ferry. Get him off my ship!"

The two crewmen who had gone to the aid of Mary and Dora tossed the boy down the gangplank and onto the last tug. The boy struggled to his feet, wiping away the blood from the split lip the captain gave him. Staring back at the captain, certain he had his full attention; he spit a mixed wad of blood and phlegm over the side and into the murky harbor water. He shoved his way through the crush of people to find a seat on the opposite side of the barge.

"Weather is not so different from home, is it now," Flora quipped, when a fine cold misty rain began to fall just as the group disembarked the tug onto Ellis Island.

With great efficiency, the immigrant's numbers were checked. Next, they were directed through the rear doors of the station and into the baggage room where immigration officers separated them from their belongings. They followed up a long, steep, winding stairway. At each landing, a uniformed man prodded them along while scratching notes on a small white pad. The girls held hands to keep together, Matthew brought up the rear. As the last of the group entered, the wind slammed the door shut behind them.

At the top of the stairs, they entered the registry room, a great expanse with high ceilings and huge windows. The din of a thousand or more voices echoing off the walls deafened the weary travelers as they pushed along through a maze of metal piping. First stop was a quick medical exam. Anyone found to be displaying unusual mannerisms was marked with a large chalk X, those who had possible health issues a P. One man, who seemed rather agitated, attempted to erase the X. A group of officers pulled him from the line and dragged him away.

The sisters worried for Dora. The noise and commotion had her shaky, fidgeting with her hair each time she had a free hand. The girls kept her close, comforting her as best they could. They hoped mightily that the medical examiners would not notice her rattled state.

Another uniformed man who looked rather important stood at a dark brown desk at the end of each maze. Flora was the first of the group to approach the desk. The officer eyeballed her then looked back down at some papers held by a clip. He asked her name, her occupation, how much money she was carrying and so on. Thirty-one questions in all where asked. Flora took objection with the interrogation and told the man so at the end of the inquisition. The man firmly stared her in the eyes, measuring her, then yelled, "Next!", and stamped her paper with a loud thud. Cora, Dora, and Mary went next, with Nora and Matthew last. After all had cleared, they reunited with their bags.

As each awaited their turns, Matthew and Nora gave instruction to Dora on how to act. The panic in Dora's eyes had Nora very worried that Dora could not get through this. Surprisingly enough she turned out to be a good student. Following Matthew's instructions, she answered each question calmly and honestly, only getting startled when the officer slammed his stamp down, approving her passage into the United States.

The next step along their way was the currency exchange. The girls found an unoccupied bench along the wall while Matthew gathered up each pound and pence the group carried and took his place in line. Despite the amount of people, this process went along efficiently and quickly to the delight of the girls, particularly Dora, who begged for relief from the overcrowded station. Matthew returned to the group within an hour's time. They then joined the river of people flowing toward the exit.

David Addison paced impatiently at the bottom of a long staircase separated into three sections. The sight of David birthed a feeling of happiness and relief to the entire group. They exchanged greetings, along with sighs of relief and tears of joy, feeling their journey nearing its end. After another short ferry ride, the girls stood in amazement, overwhelmed by the huge, bustling city that stretched out before them. The buildings, the car filled streets and the noise dumbfounded them. It was early spring 1898 in what was now the largest city in the world.

David eagerly wished to show Matthew and the sisters their new home. "Come along," he shouted with a smile grabbing onto Mary's hand. "We'll catch the trolley!" as he ran dragging Mary along with him. The group collected their things and scurried behind trying hard to keep up. David attempted to tell them all about New York while clutching Mary's hand. His passion and excitement overflowed as he pointed out landmarks and new construction at every corner. No one seemed to notice or care that the light rain had turned to light snow.

The sisters, however, did notice that Mr. Addison had not relinquished their young sister's hand. Flora disliked Addison. She knew his reputation as a schemer and a wolf that preyed upon the likes of Mary. Flora had raised Mary following the death of their mother, and their father became lost in the bottle. As the eldest, she felt a responsibility to keep them all from harm, but Mary was slight and delicate. Flora worried over her the most. Cora angered for another reason. David and Cora had danced at Matthew and Nora's wedding. They had walked amongst the flowers and David stole a kiss in the shadows under the trees. A kiss Cora never forgot. A year had passed, but she never forgot.

Dora thought his actions toward Mary rather sweet. She was a gentle, simple girl. A little dim in her perception of things, but with a kind heart. Unlike Flora who was tough as nails, and not like Cora whose harsh realistic impression of the world made her weary of it and its people. Both Nora and Cora had done well with the little bit of schooling they had and took every opportunity to further educate themselves. They looked similar in appearance, with dark flowing hair and blue eyes. They could have been twins, although Cora was a bit heavier.

Mary stood out from the rest. Her long wavy hair was a much lighter brown with highlights of red. Her skin was lighter and fairer. Though she stood just as straight, her shoulders back, her head high; she carried a slighter frame than that of her siblings. Her green eyes sparkled sharply, much like her tongue. She did not speak much, when she did her bold brash attitude overflowed. This characteristic Flora did not approve of not realizing her young sister had learned this from her.

"Well Mr. Addison will ya be done with me sisters hand soon?" Dora asked with a smile. Cora dug a sharp elbow into her sister's side. Both Mary and David blushed, staring sheepishly at the floor of the trolley. Mary let out a giggle and Addison let go. After a few moments, Mary reached down and took back Addison's hand. She kept hold for the rest of the day.

"We're here!" David shouted rising up from his seat. The trolley slowed and they all step down onto the street and hastened to the sidewalk. David, leading Mary by the hand, took his friends around a corner and half way down the block. On each side of the street were small shops selling such items as clocks and jewelry. Clothiers and butchers, even a confectionary passed by them as they went. David stopped suddenly to stare into a large empty storefront window. The group fell in behind him, peering silently into the large reflection of them in the dusty pane of glass.

"This is it, Matthew, your new store," he exclaimed, no longer able to bare his excitement.

David lifted from his pocket a set of keys and placed them in his friend's hand. "Go ahead open er up," he told Matthew. Matthew fumbled with the keys in his cold fingers. Nora wrapped her hands around her husbands and together they turned the key. Pushing the door open, they released a deep musty odor into the street. The wind blew in, tossing old newspapers and dust into a swirl across the floor. The group moved inside and David went about turning on the lights.

"Well, my dear friend, how do you like it?" asked David. Before Matthew could answer, David continued. "It has a large storage room in the back and two nice size tenements upstairs and it's all yours!" he shouted.

Matthew grabbed hold of his friend without speaking and wrapped his arms around him. "Thank you my friend, its perfect, better than I ever expected," replied Matthew. Nora and Mary joined the hug, followed by Dora and Cora, then Flora reluctantly.

"Whose hungry?" yelled David.

A resounding answer of approval rang through the store and out onto 34th street. David walked the group to a small restaurant at the end of the block. The sunset cast long shadows upon the buildings as they made their way along the avenue to get dinner. The sisters, except for Nora, had only ever eaten in a restaurant once. That was in Liverpool the night prior to setting sail for the United States. This was different.

"Much nicer then that grimy little dockside café," quipped Cora, "Don't ya think?" Everyone agreed.

Over a week had passed since Matthew, Nora, and the Flora-Dora girls had sat down to a proper meal. When the server handed them menus the girls gazed at it with bewilderment. Seeing their confusion David took it upon himself to order for the group, including two bottles of wine to the surprise and delight of the table. Warm rolls came first, followed by plates of chicken accompanied by fresh whipped potatoes and assorted vegetables. David ordered a fruit plate which the serve placed at the center of the table for all to pick at. Finally, for dessert David ordered each a large piece of chocolate layer cake covered in a thick dark chocolate icing and topped with a fresh strawberry.

Once everyone had eaten their fill and were sitting back contentedly, Matthew stood to toast his friends and the future. "May happiness be always with us, and good fortune light our way, as we face a bright new future. Lord embrace us and care for us as we face a brand new day." A complete silence fell over the room. "Or something like that," he added. The table burst into laughter. Raising their glasses, they shared in a most clumsy toast.

David placed a stack of blankets in the closet of the second floor apartment and prepped the old coal stove so it was ready to fire. He explained to Matthew that there was a coal burner in the cellar, but it needed repairing. "It has the capacity to heat the entire building when it works right," he explained. Once the party had settled in for the night, David said his goodbyes.

"I'll return in the morning and we'll head to the bank. Got some papers to sign, old Matthew, my friend," David said with a handshake.

He gave each girl a hug, even Flora, then leaned in to kiss Mary who gave him a cheek. She pushed him aside with a chastising glare. Matthew walked him to the door. With a wave goodbye, he stepped into the street and vanished in the evening air. The girls huddled close beneath the blankets, in the light of the coal stove, listening to the voice of the city howling through the night.

By the time David returned the next morning, the girls were hard at work. They found cleaning supplies in a closet in the storage area and some tattered old clothes, which they tore up for rags. David brought muffins, Nora brewed some tea, and they all sat on the broad sill in the light of the large front window and enjoyed a nice breakfast. Nora leaned back on her husband, Mary rested on David, Cora, and Dora sat beside each other, while Flora scowled in the corner.

Shortly there after, David stole away Matthew. They caught up to the trolley and rode it to the bank. David advised Matthew, "Simply sign all the papers, do not ask any questions and please do not act surprised. Be calm and businesslike; like it is just a formality. Put your pen to the paper, I'll explain it all later," David whispered to Matthew looking about as if someone might hear.

This made Matthew nervous, but he did as instructed. When he read down the contract, he was astonished at what he saw. So much so that he read it over again, and again, feeling he missed some crucial point. He had not. He was now the proud owner of a three-story building in the borough of Manhattan and he paid nothing.

Matthew glimpsed up at David who stared away, pretending not to notice his friend's hesitation. The banker too turned a curious eye towards David. Matthew put a lick to the tip of the pen, then signed each form and returned it to the banker who shook his hand and congratulated him on the purchase of the property.

David guided Matthew to a small tavern a few blocks from the bank. They bellied up to the bar and David ordered two whiskeys. Matthew stood speechless, nervous, and anxious to know what scheme his friend, unwittingly, dragged him into. As he did on the trolley, David panned the room as if someone might be watching or listening. Seeing no one particularly interesting he relaxed and ordered up two pints to wash down the shots. Matthews's frustration turned to anger, awaiting an explanation from his old friend. David knocked back his shot, took a large mouthful of ale, and then turned to Matthew.

"The building was owned by the Belfast Lace Company," explained David. "They were using it for retailing their merchandise and processed shipping through the office. It was not doing so well so they closed it up, booted out the tenants, and put the place up for sale. I did some fancy paperwork with my banker friend who owed me some favors and, well, now it is yours. It is all very neat. Just do not say nothing to nobody and if anyone comes asking just show them your papers. They are all very legal so don't worry at all."

Nevertheless, Matthew was worried and the worry would age him faster than time itself.

With all the extra money they now had, Matthew and the girls were able to clean and put a coat of paint on the apartments and store. They had the coal heater in the basement repaired, which as David had said, provided a nice even heat through every inch of the building. With the help of David, they purchased fabrics, of course lace at greatly discounted prices, and began, sewing and displaying each piece once completed.

The business picked up quickly as 34th street became the hub of the garment district in Manhattan. Matthew and the Flora-Dora girls, particularly Mary, enjoyed the excitement and prosperity that carried on for quite a few years. David and Mary became quite the item, dancing and dining at all the best clubs. Enjoying walks in Central Park during they day and along the shimmering avenues in the evening.

The announcement that Nora was with child brought happiness to everyone and prompted David Addison to his knees to ask for young Mary's hand in marriage. They wed at Christmas by a priest in the parlor of the third floor apartment before a grandly decorated tree. Mary wore the gown her sisters designed for Nora's wedding some years before. The gleam of the lights gave the white of the dress a halo affect, filling the room with a heavenly light.

After the "I dos" where spoken, champagne and whiskey filled many a glass. There was music and dancing, and loud boisterous laughter. Even Flora succumbed to a lighthearted romp; twirling her friend the shillelagh about the room with a grin. When the clock struck midnight, they passed about presents, and shared a Christmas toast to their friends they left behind on the road.

David and Mary left just as the snow began to fall. They made it to David's, trudging through bitter cold headwinds that lashed at their faces and reddened their skin. Despite their long courtship, Mary remained a virgin and David was anxious, but little did he know what was to come next.

David hung the damp coats along side the fireplace and lined up the wet shoes so they would dry overnight. Mary, very quietly, snuck up behind him. She wrapped her smooth arms around her new husband and squeezed him tight. Most suddenly and unexpectedly, she tore off his shirt, buttons flying in every direction. Mary yanked it down off his shoulders, gave a nip to his neck, and then dug her nails into his chest.

David turned now to face her, awestruck by her beauty, as she stood in the glow of the flames of the fire. Mary had taken some fine white lace and sewn a nightshirt that was shear and clung tightly to her curves and the tips her breasts. As David approached her, she attacked like a panther, driving him down on the sofa with the thrust of her hips. She kissed with a vengeance, she scratched, and she clawed him, and then pulled his pants away in an unbridled fit. She rolled with her hips, her legs wrapped around him, and she ate at his neck as if she had never been fed. After hours upon hours, they removed to the bedroom where they slept until midday when, again, she attacked.

Some time around dinner, they finally awakened. David stoked up the fire while Mary ran a warm bath. They ate by the window overlooking the street, which wore the white of the snowfall and the glow of the moon. Mary leaned in to kiss David who flinched at her approach. She kissed him softly and then sat on his lap. They watched as the snow fell, sipping tea by the window, not talking much really, just trying to relax.

Business slowed over the course of the winter, but picked up at Easter though there was still snow in the air. The girls used the free time to sew some new dresses, knowing they needed to get ahead of the spring sales. Nora spent less time sewing, feeling uncomfortable with her body as the weather warmed. At the doctor's advice, she spent more time resting, as the due date grew closer with the coming of spring.

David received a message to return to Ireland from the Belfast Lace Company and asked Mary to go.

"I shall not step foot on another ship to Ireland or anywhere else for that matter", she replied in that brash Irish twang she saved for such occasions.

David knew better than to argue. He left for Belfast in late March promising to return before Nora gave birth. Mary and Dora were the only two able to see him off. Matthew felt badly that he could not be there, staying home with his wife, while Flora and Cora worked in the store. Mary kissed him long and sensuously before releasing him to board the ferry.

"Somethin for ya to remember, Mr. Addison," Mary whispered, staring deeply

into her husbands eyes.

Mary and Dora watched as the ferry crossed the harbor and docked with the ship. The girls, hand in hand, walked from the pier without speaking. Mary showed little emotion as her husband's ship sailed from the harbor and out to sea. As they walked along the streets of Manhattan, Dora asked Mary how she felt about her mister leaving.

"After all the tearful separations we experienced when leavin Ireland, my hearts got no tears left for goodbyes," answered Mary. She tucked her hand into the crock of her sisters arm, gently squeezing, "Sides, my David will be back to me soon enough."

Dora understood to a point what Mary said, but thought it disheartening to believe that she bore no sadness and that her husband's departure effected her so little. Although she was not as bright as her sisters that did not mean she was not sensitive to the situation. She quickly dismissed her confusion, as Mary knew best despite a lingering feeling that something was not right.

Chapter 7

A Child is Born

David returned from Ireland prior to the birth of the child as promised. Traveling first-class, he bypassed Ellis Island. It had been a rough voyage with rain every day prolonging the trip. The harsh choppy waters had everyone sick, even some of the more experienced crewmen. When the ship steamed into the harbor the ocean settled, the cloud cover receded and the sun guided them in.

Matthew greeted his friend when the ferry docked in Manhattan, but Mary stayed home, more concerned for Nora. The sight of David dressed in a grey pinstripe suit, coming down the gangplank surprised Matthew. He wore a matching homburg and carried a small black suitcase in one hand and his old brown and gold carpetbag, which looked worn out and tired; across his wrist hung a beautiful brass handled umbrella.

"Quite the dandy, aren't ya now Mr. Addison," professed Matthew embracing his friend.

David, smiling, set down his bags and returned the hug. He looked puzzled at the absence of Mary not there to greet him, but understood once Matthew explained. "Probably for the best my old friend; we need to have a serious talk you and I. I don't think you'll like it all too much," exclaimed David. "Let's stop by the pub before heading home."

Matthew picked up David's old carpetbag, while David grabbed the suitcase. Together they did a bob and weave through traffic until they reached Kildaire's, a classically styled Irish pub not far from the pier. Matthew remarked about never having been to this bar or even having heard David mention it in any conversation. This to Matthew's mind was rather strange, since David spoke of every watering hole he had enjoyed. Particularly since this one reminded Matthew so much of old Clancy's place back on the road.

The place reminded Matthew so much of Clancy's that his mind ran back to his little sundry shop and the twins, Joseph and Dougy Lynch. He recalled many days sitting in the pub along Springfield Road, the sound of the carts on the cobblestone and how he would hear the wind twisting in the willows when the place wasn't too crowded and Patty left the doors open. He fully expected to see Colleen, her auburn hair pulled back in a bow, giving him a wink as she poured him a pint. "So many memories and too little time to reflect", he thought to himself as the present stepped in to interrupt his thoughts of the past.

They ordered a pitcher and took a table by the window. David inspected the glasses before pouring the beer. "Can't be too careful, got a chipped edge on a glass last time I was here. Put a nice knick in my lip, I'll tell ya that."

Matthew could see that something was amiss with his friend. David's hand trembled as he lifted the pitcher of beer. David filled the glasses and grabbed at the waitress.

"Bring us a couple of whiskeys, if you would please my dear," he said with a twinkle in his eye.

"Oh, Davey, haven't seen ya in a while. You're lookin very sharp," quipped the cute young server. "How's that wildcat of a wife? Don't see no new claw marks. Guessin you been outta town," she added with a coy grin.

"What in the world is she talking about, David," Matthew asked. "And what are you so shaky about? I never seen ya this way, even when those lads back in London were about to loosen your teeth when we was kids."

David brushed the foam from his beer, took a large drink, and paused. The server returned, leaning in to expose a substantial amount of cleavage as she set the shots of whiskey on the table. They looked into each other's eyes. David thanked her and slipped a tip into her hand. The girl smiled and nodded. It was obvious to Matthew that there was some history between them. What he did not know was how intimate and when the relationship had ended, if it had at all.

"Addison, what is goin on? I got a wife at home who needs me and you're flirtin around with some barmaid," snipped Matthew frustrated. "And another thing, you got a beautiful wife waitin at home for ya. She'd be really upset with what you're doin right here!"

"That doesn't mean anything, Matthew. We got more important things to discuss, right now," responded David knocking back his shot.

Matthew pitched back his whiskey and David ordered up another round. The young server smiled and winked again at David as she placed the second shots on the table. Another waitress breezed by and said hello to David with the same sexual undertone. David's wealth of popularity annoyed Matthew, having no patience for the frivolous wasting of his time when he had much more pressing business to attend to at home.

"Get to it!" snapped Matthew, "I need to be back with Nora."

"Now, don't panic Matthew, but a young bean counter in the home office by the name 'a Cleary been askin questions about the matters surrounding the sale of your property. He cornered me at one point, tryin to get some details, but I did my best to disperse with em. Pest! I think he has nothing, but a hunch and since you, the banker and me is the only ones who know the truth. I don't expect much to come from it."

During the entire time David spoke, he did not look toward his friend. When he wasn't peering out through the dirty window into the crowded street, or into his beer glass, he was ogling the young server who was going from empty table to empty table, wiping the tops with a yellowed rag. At each table, she threw back her shoulders and with an exaggerated lean forward exposed her well-shaped assets. None of it rang true to Matthew, not the words, not the glares and certainly not David.

Matthew slammed his hand on the table spilling his beer. "We're caught aren't we?" "Tell me the truth?" hollered Matthew.

Matthew rarely showed any inclination toward anger. He considered it a waste of energy, better spent on something more useful. David, however, tried Matthew's last nerve, causing an outburst David had never seen from his longtime friend.

The young server rushed to clean up the spill asking, "Is everything OK Davey?" "Oh, yes! Just an accident deary, no problem," Addison replied, smiling a deceitfully charming little smile.

David waited until the girl finished soaking up the spill and replaced the pints of ale before starting to explain. He scanned the bar one more time and cleared his throat then looked up at Matthew. Now he turned his full attention to his friend and the situation he had gotten them into. Though David had concerns, he believed wholeheartedly he could get them out of it clean. There was worry in his eyes. Matthew saw it immediately and braced for the worst.

"Alright Matthew calm down. It is sticky, but we're not stuck yet," David said in a low direct voice. "I think if you sell and get outta New York we can steer clear of it and make a good buck in the process."

"I got a pregnant wife and a full hen house, and you want me to pick up and move," Matthew snapped angrily. "Duck soup, Friday next soon enough ya think!" he howled sarcastically.

Addison stared down his friend. "You asked for my help, I gave it to ya, and I think I did a bloody good job," David responded. "Moreover, how much money has you and the Flora-Dora girls made? And I never asked for a penny or a pound. Hear me out and we'll get away from this before anyone's the wiser."

While David lay out his plan to Matthew Flora was returning from a doctor visit with Dora. Flora and Cora had taken notice that Dora had not been right. Dora was always a little slow and simple minded, the sisters realized her condition was getting worse. At times her clumsiness and confusion became such a problem the sisters feared leaving her alone.

Nora's doctor recommended a colleague who specialized in things of the mind. Flora protested, but Nora convinced her it would be for the best. After a lengthy session of question and answer with Dora, the doctor turned to question Flora. He requested some background information on the family, which Flora gave not understanding why it mattered, but she answered as best she could. Soon enough the questions aimed at Dora's symptoms, focusing on when the problem began, when Flora noticed it most, and when is it worst.

Flora took some time to reflect, remembering her sister's jitters on the pier in Liverpool. She recalled how the cramped quarters of steerage made her ill and her anxiousness in the crowded halls of Ellis Island. Dora's confusion and clumsiness increased when business in the store got hectic and she avoided going out when the streets and sidewalks were congested with people. Flora felt badly having to expose her sister to such scrutiny, but if the doctor could help then maybe it would be all right.

After some deliberation, the doctor concluded that Dora's mind was not strong enough to handle too many things at once. "New York," he pointed out, "has much going on all at one time and poor Dora is ill-equipped to deal with this constant activity. She is quite herself when she is alone with her family about her, as you've said, but the city is too loud and too busy for her." The doctor suggested moving Dora to the country, possibly an asylum were she could rest.

Gripping her shillelagh, Flora surprised herself when she did not knock the doctor out of his chair. She scanned the room thinking wild angry thoughts of separating the good doctor's head from his shoulders. Her temper boiled listening to his idea to put her sister away. Patiently she waited for him to finish his assessment. The doctor's nasal tone and patronizing attitude teased her temper to its limits. She arose from her chair with fire in her eyes, pounding her shillelagh on the desktop like a hammer.

The doctor, frightened, his face a ghostly white, pushed back from his desk. With a deep gulp, he clutched the arms of his chair. The flame in Flora's eyes seemed to rise up around him. His eyes bulged from his thin, smug face, trying desperately to recant what he had said, mumbling other options, which Flora vehemently dismissed.

"Thank you for your time sir," Flora said, biting her tongue. "We'll not be doin that to our sister. Have a fine rest of your day."

She exited the waiting room, swinging the door open so hard and wide that it slipped off its hinges. Flora gathered up Dora and departed. The remaining stunned patients stared in through the open door at the doctor. The good doctor eased back to his desk, putting his head down he realized he had wet himself. Uncomfortable, he stood up; not realizing his waiting room full of patients was gawking in at him.

When Flora returned Cora locked up the store and the three girls joined Mary at Nora's bedside. Upon entering the room, they saw Mary placing a cool cloth on Nora's forehead, trying desperately to settle her sister down. Nora was already voicing her desire to leave the city, tearfully upset by her troubled mind.

"This is just not a good place to be raising a child. It is much too noisy and far too frenzied a place. It's only gonna get worse you know, it's only gonna get worse!" cried Nora.

Mary stroked Nora's hand. "Calm down Sissy," Mary said, "We will talk to Matthew and David when they return. You know your mister will do what you want, and I'll take care of my David."

"But the store is doin so well and it means so much to Matthew," cried Nora. "How can I be askin him to leave with us doin so well here?"

Mary had no desire to leave the city. She enjoyed the fine restaurants, the crowds, and the excitement. She loved that high-class people with expensive jewelry in long cars came to their little shop to buy suits and gowns, and shawls made of the finest Irish lace. The noise played like music in her ears, a symphony that made her smile when walking along the avenue on the arm of her handsome husband. Nevertheless, she would do whatever her sisters, Matthew and David decided to do. She certainly was not going to be happy about it, but she remembered that she was not very happy to leave Ireland either despite her speech in the Haggerty's sitting room.

"It's about time we leave this damn city," Flora exclaimed. "Nothing here but blacks and dagos, and those Jews owning everything up and down the street."

"I miss the green rolling hills of home," Cora added, "and the sound of the birds singing in the morning. Don't ya miss that Nora?"

"I agree with Cora," Dora shouted and then went back gnawing on her fingernails, a habit that greatly annoyed Flora.

Flora slapped Dora's fingers away from her mouth. Cora went to Dora's side and put her arm around her sister. Dora looked up and smiled a simple smile, resting her head against her sister's hip. She did not like the city; that is all she knew. She missed the quiet little corner of the world they came from and never really understood why they had to leave.

"A bird can only choke on the fumes from them damn motor cars that fill the streets," added Flora.

Flora, still upset from the doctor visit, explained to her sisters what the doctor had said about Dora's condition. Cora held Dora close as she listened. Nora clung to Mary's hand with tears running down her cheeks. As Flora finished, silence filled the room. The sun, which had shone bright through the window, cautiously slid away behind a dark gray cloud.

Much as she had so long ago in the Haggerty's house, Mary spoke up. "We wouldn't ever do that to ya Dora, not ever! We will tell the gents straight that it is time we moved on. To some place green where we can walk and breathe fresh air and swim in a lake like when we was kids. How should that be for ya Sis?"

"That would be fine for all of us," Nora agreed as a look of distress came upon her.

"You relax Nora," Flora interrupted. "You're making yourself sick with worry. That ain't good for the baby and it ain't good for you neither."

Mary removed the cloth from Nora's forehead, wrung it dry, and dipped it in the cool bowl of water on the nightstand. She replaced the cloth on her head and sang to her sweetly a song that the girls shared when they were children. She began in Irish Gaelic, her sisters joined in when she repeated it in English. Cora ran her hand along Dora's hair as Dora rested her head upon her sister.

Éiníní, éiníní, codalaígí codalaígi

Éiníní, éiníní, codalaígí codalaígí

Codalaígí, codalaígí cois an chlaí amuigh, Cois an chlaí amuigh codalaígí, codalaígí Cois an chlaí amuigh, cois an chlaí amuigh

An londubh is an fiach dubh,

Téigí a chodladh, téigí a chodladh

an chéirseach is an préachán,

téigí a chodladh, téigí a chodladh

Little Birds, little birds, go to sleep, go to sleep,
Little birds, little birds, go to sleep, go to sleep.

Go to sleep, go to sleep,
Beside the wall outside, beside the wall outside,
Go to sleep, go to sleep,
Beside the wall outside, beside the wall outside

Blackbird and raven, go to sleep, go to sleep,
Female blackbird and crow, go to sleep, go to sleep.

Robin and lark, go to sleep, go to sleep,
Wren and thrush, go to sleep, go to sleep.

Nora did fall asleep, so did Dora, but only for a short while. A sharp pain followed by another awakened Nora. Mary and Flora had stepped out of the room when their sisters fell asleep. They hurried back to Nora's side hearing her harsh screams. Again, she cried out, grasping her round stomach as it hardened with a fresh contraction. Dora ran from the room, hiding in the farthest corner of the apartment. Mary did everything she could to make Nora comfortable, but she never delivered a baby. Flora had assisted with some of Genie Haggerty's children, but she had only been there to help. The doctor took care of the necessaries.

"Maybe ya should be getting the doctor now Flora," hollered Cora as the contractions became faster and closer together.

"Where is those two louts ya call husbands?" barked Flora grabbing her coat and shillelagh. "They should 'a been back hours ago, useless beggars that they are."

She kissed Nora on the forehead and promised to be back as quick as she could. Nora lay back in the bed attempting to find a comfortable position. Mary changed the cold compress again. Cora told Flora to hurry then went to check on Dora whimpering in the corner of the sitting room. Flora repeated her promise and flew out the door, slamming it behind her and running down the back steps.

Nora reached up and took hold of Mary's arm. A look of terror filled her beautiful blue eyes. Mary told her sister not to worry, that the doc was on his way and he would fix her up just fine. Nora moaned, as the contractions grew stronger and closer together.

"Mary," began Nora, "I saw the rose, the black rose in Genies greenhouse."

"You mean the one that's in the globe that Genie gave ya as a gift?" questioned Mary.

"Its petals dripped red, and there was death all around it," Nora cried fearfully.

"Just a dream it was Nora, not to worry," replied Mary. "It's still there on the mantle, as dark as the night."

Nora hadn't the strength to turn and look to the mantle. She clutched Mary's hand, holding tight from the pain. She begged to see Matthew, wondering aloud where he might be. Mary tried to console her, wondering the same thing. Mary hoped and prayed that the men would arrive soon. She begged the same of Flora and the doctor, not at all sure what she would do if they did not arrive soon enough.

The final bit of information David laid upon Matthew was that David's company wanted him to become their chief sales representative in London and David had declined. This resulted in his termination from the Belfast Lace Company. The company acknowledged the fine efforts of David and awarded him with a respectable severance, a fine suit, and a first-class ticket back to the states. However, they also informed him that Mr. Cleary, the accountant, along with some other representatives should arrive in New York sometime soon to review the state of the business there. David was to leave his portfolio with the office manager at their warehouse near the docks.

Seeing no alternative, Matthew agreed to David Addison's plan. This last bit of enlightenment meant the clock was ticking. They needed to get things in motion and quickly. His concerns now turned toward his wife Nora and the Flora-Dora girls. David believed he could handle Mary. Matthew seriously doubted that.

"The sisters as a group were a formidable force; stubborn, emotional, and a little scary," thought Matthew as they started out for home.

Matthew and David arrived at the store just after sunset. They had with them some fine fresh cuts of steak from the butcher shop on 34th Street and a bag of chocolates from the candy store just down the block. Both feared this confrontation thinking a good meal and some sweets might make the suggestion of relocating a little easier to swallow.

The men cut through the shop and climbed the back stair leading to the second floor apartment. In the darkness they heard voices coming up from behind them and hurried steps gaining on them. As David and Matthew reached the top step, they stopped and turned, peering into the blending of shadows. They could see two figures approaching on the poorly lit stairway.

Suddenly, Flora burst from the gloom, dragging Nora's doctor behind her. She pushed between Matthew and David, nearly knocking David over the rail. She traipsed down the hall and tossed the poor doctor into the room where

Nora rested. The voices of all the sisters mixed into a siren screaming, ringing throughout the apartment as Matthew and David came inside.

It terrified Matthew to hear is wife writhing in pain. He parted the gaggle and knelt at Nora's side. Matthew took her hand and immediately regretted doing so, when she latched on and squeezed it white. Amidst the sister's high-pitched chatter and Nora's painful shrieks was the soothing voice of the doctor followed by a whisper of a cry. The room turned quickly, spinning into a new direction. It moved away from one of panic, to one of delight with the birth of a beautiful baby girl whose soft cries now hushed the room.

"Such a joyous occasion", Matthew exclaimed, holding his newborn daughter in his arms. He kissed her soft brow, unable to take his eyes off her perfect face, amazed by her tiny little hands and little pink feet.

The arrival of the child brought calm to everyone. At the doctor's insistence, the Flora-Dora girls removed to the sitting room, except for Mary who, without a word, took David by the hand and dragged him out the door to the back stairwell. She pinned him against the door and kissed him hard. When she finally let him breath he tried to speak, but she kissed him again. Her hand slid down between his legs and grabbed him. Flora banging at the door with her shillelagh interrupted their moment of passion.

"We needs to talk," Flora hollered. "So put your tongues away and get in here. Damn it!"

The doctor completed his examination of Nora and handed Matthew a small baby receiving blanket. He showed the new father how to wrap the child. Once the baby was properly swaddled, Matthew brought the child back to Nora and sat down beside her. He set the baby gently in Nora's arms, kissing his wife, thanking her for the greatest gift he had ever received.

"What shall we name her?" He asked of his wife as they sat staring down on this precious bundle.

Nora softly replied, "We'll name her after our mothers Matthew. Elizabeth Grace she will be. How does that sound to ya, Matthew?" she asked. Thrilled, he of course agreed.

"Elizabeth Grace, what a perfect name for a beautiful child", he responded, aglow with a father's pride. The doctor, overhearing the name the happy parents had chosen, and having seen the baby, openly agreed.

Seeing they were alone, Nora took her husband's hand and told him the decision the girls made while he was off picking up David from the ferry. This surprising turn of events came as a great relief to Matthew. He questioned his wife generally, as to why they made the choice to leave Manhattan. Nora pulled baby Elizabeth to her, and, with a twinkle in her eye told Matthew, "This is why."

Matthew had no argument, not that he would have if he did. He did feel, however, that Nora left more out than she put in. He believed that the baby was not the only reason, but it was enough. Matthew kissed his wife and agreed to find them a new home, somewhere cleaner, quieter, and safer, better for raising a child.

The doctor finished packing up the last of his things. Putting them into his brown leather bag and securing the clasp. He returned to the bedside where Matthew and Nora cradled the new infant. The doctor asked how she felt, and gave the new parents some instructions before handing Matthew a prescription to be filled as soon as Matthew was able. Matthew kissed Nora again, and then stood to show the doctor out.

Many changes arrived all at once. They flew into the lives of Matthew and Nora, Mary and David and the Flora-Dora girls. They came from all directions and took many different forms, some very good, some not as good and still others had questions attached. The one constant with each was that it was time to move on and the group had little choice, but to do so, and soon.

Chapter 8

Changes Things a Bit

David wrapped his arm around Mary and led his wife back along the hallway to the sitting room. When they passed by the bedroom, David caught a glimpse of Matthew sitting along side Nora with the baby in between them. The doctor was putting his things away and voicing instructions to the new parents, who were not really listening. David noticed that Matthew had a very surprised expression on his face; even he could tell it was not the expression worn by a new father. He wondered what it might be as Mary yanked him away. Flora picked up the bags of food that Matthew had dropped in the hallway just outside Nora's door in his haste to get to his wife's side. She brought them to the kitchen while the other sisters got comfortable in the sitting room.

Once things settled down so did Dora, moving to the sofa to sit beside David and Mary. David put his arm around Dora, kissing her lightly on the temple. Donning a childlike smile, she whispered a faint welcome back to him. Cora moved from her chair across from Dora to stand by the window looking out over the street below. She did not bother to greet David. The years had not destroyed the memory of their walk in the garden. Rather time had fueled resentment towards David. She tried to dismiss it, but the knot that twisted inside tightened in his presence.

Flora returned to the sitting room with a bowl of candy, placing it on the table near Dora. She knew how Dora loved her sweets so she picked one up and handed it to her with a napkin. Shortly after, the doctor and Matthew exited the bedroom. The doctor gave him some final instructions. Matthew hung on his every word then shook his hand and saw him out. The group sat patiently, waiting for Matthew to join them. It took a few minutes before Matthew returned, having walked the doctor through the shop and out through the main doors. He stopped at Nora's room first to see if she needed anything before taking a seat across from Mary.

"Have you and Nora decided on a name, Matthew?" Mary asked once Matthew settled in his chair.

"Yes. Nora thought Elizabeth Grace after our mothers," replied Matthew.

Everyone agreed it was a fine name, regal and proper, honoring the memory of the mothers of both families. Matthew liked the name for its beauty and by the way it rolled easily off the tongue. David lifted part way off his seat, far enough to shake his good friends hand. When he did, Mary groped him playfully, annoying Cora and angering Flora, who told her little sister, "Leave that behavior to the low life's in the gutter." David grasped Mary's hand and sat back down, giving her a disapproving leer.

"Well, it has been a long time since we've heard the cry of a child, hasn't it?" stated Flora. "Changes things a bit, I'd say."

The girls and Matthew knew where she was going with this, but David did not. Flora held a long pause before continuing, "You lads have made some fine decisions and built me and me sisters a good life here in the city." Another pause as she gathered her ideas left everyone squirming in their chairs. Cora, who spent most of the time staring out the window, moved to Dora's side.

"What Flora is trying to say," interrupted Cora, "is that we ladies have discussed the matter and decided it is time to leave New York. I can't put it any clearer than that."

Relief washed over David. He had been trying to decide what to say to Mary, spinning words around in his head that might come together in such a way that would not prod her Irish temper. He heaved a long sigh, prompting everyone to turn and stare. Matthew, who was already grinning, wiped a hand across his mouth, facing away to hide a laugh.

Matthew stood up, as Flora sat back down in her chair. "Nora told me what you lassies have decided," he stated. "She gave me only a short version as to the why, which I'm sure will be explained to me in more detail in due time. In comin here today from the ferry, David and I had a similar conversation and, though we have made a nice livin to be sure, we concur. That is to say, yes, it is time to move on."

Mary, despite agreeing with her sisters, stared angrily at David for making a decision of this magnitude without consulting her. It did not matter that she had come to the same conclusion without consulting him. Infuriated, she rose from the couch, her hand gripping David's hand. She lifted him off the sofa and ushered him across the room into the hallway. She pinned his back against the wall when they heard the baby cry a whisp of a cry. Mary gazed into David's eyes. Her fire turned to passion, her anger to love. Holding David's face she kissed him softly, then harder, then harder still. He took her hand and they returned to the sofa beside Dora.

The anticipated row had not occurred to the surprise of Matthew and the sisters. A stunned hush hung over the room like a promise just waiting to be broken. When it was not, the group was happily confused, but sought no explanation. Mary leaned forward and took two pieces of candy from the bowl, feeding one to her and then one to David. They grinned as if nothing had happened, but a feeling remained that trouble was coming for Mary and David.

Seeing that things had calmed a bit, David took the opportunity to tell Mary that he was no longer an associate of the Belfast Lace Company, then braced himself. The tone of her voice, as it was known to do, rose a few octaves, when she questioned him why. He revealed to her and to her sisters the offer the company had made to him, explaining that he rejected it knowing that his wife would never agree to sail to London. His timing and reasoning avoided what could have been a very angry and upsetting confrontation with Mary.

Surprisingly Dora asked the question that welled up behind everyone's lips. Without hesitation she boldly asked David, "What shall you being doing with yourself now, David?"

"Mary," David began, turning to face his wife, "Do ya remember that New Years Eve party, the millennium party and the couple we met?"

"Surin ya know that I do," replied Mary, taking hold of his arm, recollecting on the evening.

"We was in the Chandelier Room at the Marquee Club. It was snowing outside, leaving a fine dusting on your top hat and shoulders, which glistened beneath the bright lights of the crystal chandeliers. The top brass button on your frock coat had come loose. I repaired it with a frayed thread from the edge of a tablecloth in the lobby to the amazement of some stuffy old haggis, who considered it much too common to do such a thing. I remember dancing, champagne, and the scent of different perfumes from each woman that passed by us as we danced. I recall the brightly colored fireworks that flashed through the French doors that led to the balcony overlooking the East River, and the ahs from the crowd at their brilliance."

"Do you remember the couple, Mary?" repeated David. "That we spoke with and shared a toast with at the stroke of midnight?"

"She was a wee bit of a thing, with long dark hair," Mary recalled, "And quite the chatterbox too, wasn't she now. The man was balding. I can still see the lights reflecting off the top of his head." This brought a laugh from the sisters.

"His name is C. R. Belin and the woman is Kerryn Long," explained David. "He is an associate of an up and coming lace company in a town called Scranton in the northeast corner of Pennsylvania, and Kerryn is the founder's niece. That evening Kerryn suggested I join their firm and Mr. Belin has made numerous offers to me since. I have declined up to now because it meant relocating and I know your fondness, Mary, for the city. Miss Long called it an open invitation, which I feel now I should accept."

David took a moment to give Mary time to think. She did not think long. Yes, she loved the big city, but she loved her sisters much more. If Dora needed to be somewhere else, than that is what they would do. In addition, of course there was Nora and the baby to consider.

"What do we know of this company?" Mary asked. Before David could answer, Mary added, "What do we know of Scranton, or of this part of the country? Is it goin to be right for our sister, and can we make a livin there? We'll need to be knowin before we up and go running blindly, wouldn't ya say?"

All agreed with Mary that these were questions in need of answers. None of them had ever heard of Scranton. The truth was they knew little of their new country beyond New York. What they did know they had gotten from newspapers and magazine articles, few of which carried anything noteworthy from this city or this region of the country. If they had, the girls paid little attention, never thinking they might end up there.

What they did not know and what David had no intension of telling them, this portion of his plan, the plan he had revealed to Matthew some hours before, was already in motion. David's relationship with Kerryn Long was more than just a chance encounter. He telegrammed her from London following his meeting in Belfast. Kerryn responded prior to David's ship setting sail, inviting him to come to Scranton upon his return to the states. David's shrewd manipulation produced a window of opportunity; opened wide by Mary.

After some deliberation, the group agreed that David should take the train and go to Scranton as soon as possible. Once his meeting with the representatives from the Scranton Lace Company concluded he would take a short tour of the area, finding out if this place would be right for all of them, with an emphasis on Dora's condition and the newest addition Elizabeth Grace. Cora wrote up a list of things for David to pay attention to while he was in the area. She handed to Mary, who relayed it to David. David agreed, feigning reluctance at taking on the task.

Once everyone was satisfied with the plan, Flora fried up the steaks Matthew and David had brought, along with some diced potatoes and they all sat down to a nice dinner. Matthew brought a dish to Nora, who ate only a few bites. Once Matthew removed her plate, he cuddled up beside her. She fed the baby and Matthew fell asleep. Mary and David stopped in to say their goodbyes to Nora and to get a final glimpse of Elizabeth Grace before leaving for home. Flora, Cora, and Dora straightened up the apartment, said their goodnights, and retired to the third floor for the evening.

Matthew and David went to see the banker first thing the next morning. The eight a.m. trolley overflowed with people heading to work that day, but David and Matthew were able to find a seat toward the rear. David tugged uncomfortably at his shirt collar. That is when Matthew noticed sharp red scratches across the back of his neck. Matthew recalled the comment of the barmaid the day before. David saw that his friend had noticed. Embarrassed, he made no attempt to explain, but instead changed the subject; focusing on how they would approach his banker friend with the proposition of selling the property.

Matthew's curiosity poked at him, longing to know how David received the fresh claw marks on his neck. Another side of him felt it was not his business, but David's and Mary's, and no one else's. The conversation between the men and the banker went as anticipated. David fully expected the banker, Mr. Burnbaum, would want some compensation. They agreed to fifteen per cent of the final sales price as long as the property changed hands prior to the arrival of the people from Belfast.

In addition, the names on the deed needed altering in such a way to erase any traces that might lead to Matthew. Mr. Burnbaum reluctantly agreed to the terms, knowing the possible implications if the bank found out what they had done. Since David received no compensation for the initial sale of the property, there could be no implication of wrongdoing on his part.

So how did David benefit from helping Matthew? This question plagued Matthews mind. If it weren't for everything else going on at the same time in Matthew's life, he would have pursued the question until he found the answer. Elizabeth Grace and Nora took precedence, followed by escaping New York ahead of the law. For a moment, he longed for his simple little shop and the stress-free life he left behind in Ireland, but he knew in his heart that, no matter what, his life with Nora and his beautiful baby girl was better than any fleeting memory of the past.

David left for Scranton on the following Sunday afternoon, on board the Lackawanna Limited passenger train heading west out of Hoboken. Mary saw her husband off just as she did a few weeks before when he left on the ship for Ireland. She disliked the ferry ride across the Hudson River. She bid her husband goodbye again, but she knew it would be fine and only for a couple of days. She gave him a hot, wet kiss to remember her by, ignoring the shocked expressions of the people on the platform. He boarded the train and with a long whistle, it began to move along the tracks.

Kerryn Long met David at the Scranton station that afternoon. They had an early dinner at a restaurant on Lackawanna Avenue not far from the station. David and Kerryn had an intimate relationship prior to David's marriage, but had seen very little of each other since, except for the occasional encounter at social events, such as the New Years Eve party at the Marquee Club. David did his best to keep the subject of conversation on business, but Kerryn had other ideas.

David never cheated on his wife up to now, despite many invitations and flirtations, but Kerryn was beautiful. She was part American Indian, which explained the long dark hair and tanned skin. She had haunting pale blue eyes that turned a man inside out with a blink and a nod. David knew he needed this job. It was an opportunity he could not pass up and resisting Kerryn's temptations could very well jeopardize getting the position. Not getting the job could get everyone stuck back in New York and possibly get Matthew arrested.

Kerryn took David to the Hotel Jermyn and booked him a room for the evening. She explained to David about the meeting with members of the board the next morning, insisting this was just a formality. She accompanied him to his room and ordered room service to bring up a bottle of wine.

David poured two glasses while Kerryn excused her self to use the bathroom. She returned wrapped in a hotel towel. Kerryn sat on the edge of the long low chest of drawers across from the bed and asked David to bring her wine to her. Kerryn wrapped her legs around David's waist and tossed aside the towel.

David and Kerryn made love through the night, until both were too tired to continue. When David awoke, he found himself alone. Sitting up he saw the reflection of someone he didn't much like staring back at him from the mirror. Kerryn left a note that she would see him at the meeting that day and congratulations on his new position, a word she underlined with a bold stroke.

David became physically sick with guilt, running into the toilet to vomit. Every justification that he used allowing him to betray his wife now failed him. He sat on the bed staring into the mirror, begging to God that it had not happened, but it did. He could not change it or erase it, nor could he turn back time, and replace one word for another or one action for the last. He now would have to bare the weight of it and keep it concealed. Mary would never forgive him just as he could not forgive himself.

The meeting with the executives included the owner of the company, Charles Belin Sr., his board of directors, and Kerryn's father, Samuel Long and Kerryn, along with some other less notables. The offer made to David exceeded anything he had gotten from the Belfast Lace company, including relocation expenses. However, he would not be working in the Scranton office. The company wanted David to headman a facility in Wilkes-Barre some twenty miles to the south of Scranton.

He would still do sales throughout the Eastern region; also overseeing production and shipping from the Wilkes-Barre facility and points south. This gave the New York territory completely to the company president's nephew, C. R. Belin. David quickly realized this was their plan all along, knowing David as C.R.'s main competition in the city. David agreed to their terms and signed the contract without hesitation.

Afterwards, David took a tour of the area and then caught the late train back to New York. On the train ride home his thoughts bounced from his regret and betrayal, to how incredible, sensual, and erotic the sex was with Kerryn. Those thoughts churned even more regret, even more guilt, even more dismay.

"How can I face Mary and not reveal myself?" David thought. He had never been able to hide much from her. No matter how he tried, she always saw through him. He could not let her see through him this time or he would lose her forever.

Mary met her husband when the ferry docked. She kissed him, as usual, with great aggression. They hopped on the trolley and road it back to 34th Street. David told Mary about the great contract offer and the company's expectations of him. He described the peacefulness of the area, which delighted Mary, thinking of Dora and her issues. She asked how the people in the area treated him and if his new bosses were nice folks. His thoughts ran quickly to Kerryn.

"They seem fine; very pleasant," he answered. "Talked to some strangers along the way; also very pleasant, I'd say."

"So we'll be living in a town called Wilkes-Barre. Sounds quiet enough", quipped Mary. "When do we need to be there?"

"They've asked me to be there and working in four weeks time," replied David. "Have there been any offers for the shop?"

"I know there has been, but Matthew been seein to that," Mary answered as the trolley reached home.

There had been offers, many extremely good offers, well exceeding their original asking price. Matthew waited until David's return to make any decision. Nora and her sisters wanted to hear about the area. They wanted to know if it had rivers and lakes. Was the area quiet, or crowded and could you raise a family their in peace. Once they knew these things and felt satisfied, Nora and Matthew decided to take the highest bid, pack their things and go as soon as they were able.

Nora worried about traveling with a newborn baby, thinking that it might be too soon to subject Elizabeth to such an ordeal. The doctors concern was more for Nora than the child and advised they postpone their moving, allowing Nora more time to heal. Matthew did not want to endanger mother or child, but knew that time was not a luxury they could afford.

David's news and description of northeast Pennsylvania delighted everyone. David and Mary left for Pennsylvania ahead of the family to find a place for all to live. Matthew, Nora and the sisters would follow once the sale of the property finalized. Matthew gave David a small sum of money to use as a down payment to secure the property if needed. David agreed to do so, and in two weeks time, David and Mary were gone.

They sold off most of the stock of inventory they'd accumulated during the years on 34th Street along with much of the furniture in the two tenements. The Belfast Lace

Company held the lease for David's apartment allowing David and Mary the freedom to depart upon David's termination. The apartment came furnished, so clearing out of there meant nothing more than packing their personal belongings and leaving. The dress shop, along with the two apartments needed everything when the group arrived. Now the rooms needed nothing, but to be emptied.

Just a few days before the group was scheduled to depart Nora received a telegram from Genie Haggerty. Nora had sent a letter to Genie just after the baby was born, letting her friend know about the arrival of Elizabeth Grace, rejoicing in her new child. Genie expressed her happiness for Nora and Matthew and wished them all the best, sending along a package full of baby clothes, made by Nora and her sister's for Genie's children in years past.

Genie regretted the addition of some sad news regarding the old priest at St. Joseph's Church, Father McCormick. His alter boys were attacked by some young rabble. The good father, attempting to intercede, was fatally injured. Jeffrey found Father McCormick on the steps in front of the church, but was too late to help him. He died in Jeffrey's arms.

Matthew took the telegram from Nora and wrapped his arms around her as she cried.

David found a place for Matthew in Ashley, a small coalmining town south of Wilkes-Barre. Although it had a nice storefront on the main street, the upstairs apartment was much too small for everyone, especially with the newborn baby. David and Mary decided that the sisters needed a place of their own anyway. They purchased a large house with a business front across from a church on Manhattan Street not far from Matthew and Nora's property.

When Matthew explained to the sisters what David and Mary had found for them, everyone felt comfortable with it, accept Dora. She became upset and saddened with the idea of her family breaking up and going in their own directions. Nora took her aside and held her, promising she would never be far away. Together they held and rocked the baby until Dora and Elizabeth fell asleep.

Chapter 9

David's Angle

During the train ride to Pennsylvania, Matthew had a great deal of time to think. That is when he was not caring for the baby so his wife could rest, or talking over ideas he had about the new store with Nora. Then there were the persistent distractions of the beautiful scenery. The mind could not deny the eyes. Still, time did exist for Matthew's thoughts to stray to a question that plagued him.

Matthew often wondered what David's angle was when he set up the deal for the property on 34th Street. What he had told Matthew was that Mr. Burnbaum owed him a favor.

"What kind a favor," Matthew asked himself, "Would make a banker in good standing jeopardize his job and his reputation?" There had to be something shady about the arrangement despite the perceived legitimacy of the paperwork Matthew signed some five years earlier.

Matthew knew very well that his friend was a schemer, not prone to do anything that he did not see the profit in doing. There had to be something in it for David and most likely for the banker too. Being caught in one of David's webs often meant skating the law which Matthew had no desire to do, wishing a much more stress free life. He believed wholeheartedly that there was more profit in living honestly. Matthew never shared his trepidations with Nora, since she never knew how the building became theirs in the first place.

Matthew could not even begin to unravel the mystery of it all. No money had changed hands, as far as he knew. David didn't get a kickback. He never asked for a share of the receipts from the business. The banker received no compensation; so where was the profit? Matthew's life had very little time left to spend building puzzles. The puzzle remained in the box, undone, awaiting a time when Matthew's idle curiosity might get the better of him.

Over the years, each time Matthew's mind pondered the question that lived in its corners something more pressing distracted him. Whether it was the day-to-day operations of the business, learning the latest trends of the garment industry, an industry he knew almost nothing about, or personal time spent with Nora and now Elizabeth Grace. Life provided many paths for his thoughts to follow. He fully believed the road to these answers was a sinister one, replete with many dangerous turns.

The risks of knowing the truth curbed his curiosity. Gaps in the distractions allowed these dangerous questions to walk forward and the train ride left many such gaps. The more the question came forward, the more the risks seemed to fade. Matthew watched the forests pass by his window, pondering cautiously David's motives. He knew it would take some investigation to expose the truth not sure, if it would be safer to find the answer or let the matter rest.

Matthew had no idea how criminal or dangerous David Addison's activities could be. Prior to Matthew, Nora and the sister's arrival in New York, David was involved in many shady deals. His sales job for the Belfast Lace Company earned him a nice living, but his side ventures netted him much more. Blackmail provided him the largest profit; keeping his ears and eyes open for any opportunity that might prove to be lucrative.

This is how he took advantage of the banker.

David was out one night, with the cute young barmaid from Kildaire's, at a seedy club along the Hudson River. It was a place, whose usual clientele consisted of anyone trying to make any easy buck. Between a pyramid of empty shot glasses, David spotted the narrow faced banker sitting in the shadows at the end of a long bar. He witnessed him drinking heavily and looking very distraught. Always on the lookout for a new opportunity, David thought there might be some advantage in knowing what it was that gnawed at the man.

After a few minutes and some disturbing promises, the girl agreed to help David with his sorted plot. He sent the girl to flirt with the banker, thinking some young attractive thing might get the man to loosen his tongue, providing David the means to a profitable extortion. The girl had no qualms with manipulating the man, but wanted satisfactory compensation, monetary and otherwise. Once they came to a suitable understanding, the girl unbuttoned a few buttons on her blouse, shook out her hair, and sashayed through the cluster of unsavory sorts that whistled and jeered as she passed.

The girl slid in behind the man. At first the banker paid little attention, more concerned with his torments than his surroundings. It did not take long before the girl took a bolder approach. As the banker reached for the next shot dropped in front of him by the bartender the girl snatched it away. Surprised by the girl's sudden action, Mr. Burnbaum straightened up to protest.

The girl peered into the man's weak pathetic eyes and then drank the shot, wiping the slight remains slowly and smoothly away with the curled tip of her tongue. The bankers mouth hung open, trembling he turned away. The barmaid pressed her body against him, whispering an obscene proposal into the man's ear. The timid little man blushed as she continued, punctuating it with a playful nibble of his earlobe.

Taking the man by the hand, she led him to a secluded booth in the darkest corner of the bar. He slid in first and she scooched in beside him, signaling the bartender to bring two more drinks. She again whispered in his ear and then began kissing and nipping his neck and running her hand between his legs. She grabbed hold of his small, stiff penis and squeezed hard. The banker squealed, lifting slightly from his seat.

She unzipped his pants; massaging him slowly, but firmly she began too ask him questions, telling him he might feel better and more relaxed if he spoke about what had him so troubled. She would keep his secret and he would feel much the better. She kissed him passionately as the stroking excited the man in a way he rarely felt. As he released his secrets poured out like his semen, telling her everything.

Watching between the swaying bodies and clouds of smoke, David admired the skill of this young woman. Although he couldn't see clearly, what occurred under the table, David grinned knowing by the motion of her arm and the expression on Mr. Burnbaum's face what she was doing and when she finished. David turned up a deceitful smile. Swilling back the last of his drink, he wondered what good bit of information would soon be his.

The girl licked her fingers clean, before kissing the banker on the cheek and waltzing away through the crowd. David met her at the back door of the club, where he greeted her with a kiss, and then took her to his apartment. She told him everything the banker had told her. Afterward David lived up to the first part of his bargain with the barmaid, fulfilling every sexual fantasy the girl had.

The banker it seemed had been embezzling from his employers for some time. Each bit of thievery worked at his conscience; the cost of living with an exorbitant wife who demanded things, having little if any concern for the cost. Mr. Burnbaum used his social position and married well up to a beautiful, shallow, and frivolous woman; spoiled by an over-indulgent father. For whatever reason he loved her, knowing full well she didn't love him and was only using him to support her lavish lifestyle. Following his last doctoring of the books, he realized he had pilfered some one-hundred thousand dollars and there was no way he could make up the deficit.

This was all the information David needed. The next Monday morning David arrived at the bank with the cute little waitress on his arm, asking to see Mr. Burnbaum about an important business matter. Interesting that David gained this trinket of knowledge just after receiving the letter from Matthew in Ireland, requesting his help in finding a location for his new business endeavor. Seems the fates had found their way to the United States ahead of the group and were waiting for them to arrive.

When David and the girl walked into the banker's office, Mr. Burnbaum nearly went into shock. David plopped down in the chair in front of the desk looking deadpan, knowing he had the banker by the shorthairs.

"Mr. Addison, what a pleasure it is to see you," said the banker trying to pretend that it was.

Mr. Burnbaum moved a chair from the corner for the woman to sit along side David. His memory of the night at the bar was sketchy, blurred by the unusually excessive amount of alcohol he had consumed. Taking a long look at the girl, he hoped he was mistaken, that she may not be the woman at all. All doubts ran away when she leaned in and took a nibble of his ear as he positioned the chair in front of her.

The banker took his seat behind the desk and poured a glass of water from the crystal pitcher, which sat on the farthest corner. His hands trembling as he did. He then pulled a starched white hankie from his inside pocket of his black satin waistcoat and dabbed the sweat from his brow.

"You're looking rather upset sir," exclaimed David, allowing the man time to squirm.

"I believe you know my friend," he added.

"I'm sure I don't," responded the banker.

Leaning back in his chair, David replied, "Do you really want to play this game?" looking from the girl to the banker and back again. "That is a game you have no way of winning."

The banker looked down at his desk, unable to face David or the girl. He had stepped into an inescapable trap built by his own frailty. He had two choices, turn himself in for his crimes and go to jail in disgrace or make a deal and fall deeper into the abyss. Weak and fearful of losing the wife he risked everything to keep he chose the latter.

"What is it you want?" he asked David.

"Now isn't that better," began David. "Yes, I want you to do something for me. It will be in the best interest of your career to do so and we will all profit from it in the end."

David explained to the banker about what he wished him to do regarding the property on 34th street, stressing that the entire transaction must be kept secret, even from the man taking possession of the property. Additionally, David demanded cash to still his tongue and for the barmaids silence. Having no choice Mr. Burnbaum agreed. However, something still bothered the banker about the arrangement.

"If you don't mind me asking", began the fragment of a man, "how is it I'll profit from this?"

David glared harshly at the man before answering, "Let's just view this as an investment in the future why don't we. When the property sells, it will be worth five times what it is now. We will take our cut then and it will be a tidy sum indeed."

"How can you be sure of such a thing?" asked the banker.

"Surin I feel it in me bones," replied David, the touch of a brogan slipping through his lips to the surprise of himself and Mr. Burnbaum.

"We'll just keep our secret and you stay out of trouble," added David. "And when the time comes, I'll be in touch."

The banker agreed, but refused to shake David's outreached hand as they concluded the meeting. David wrapped his arm around the barmaid who blew a playful kiss at Mr. Burnbaum as they exited his office. The banker closed the door behind them and then buried his face in his hands, feeling he had made a deal with the devil. He walked to the window, watching the couple exit the bank and cross the street, thinking he would be better off if he jumped rather than endure this ongoing nightmare.

David's prediction about the future worth of this property was spot on. The tailoring shop was a huge financial success for Matthew and the Flora-Dora girls. The girl's talents as designers and dressmakers attracted a rich and exclusive patronage. They started their own line of clothing, which they named "Snowflake" meaning that every garment possessed a unique quality, making each piece a one of a kind original.

This made little difference to David. The growth and development of the garment district in Manhattan made the location of their shop and the building worth more than all the suits, gowns, and shawls the dress shop sold. When the sale of the building finalized, the fifteen per cent taken by Mr. Burnbaum, Matthew viewed as a small price to pay if it kept him from jail. The banker split the money with David and the cute young barmaid from Kildaire's for their perpetual silence, or so he hoped.

This was David's last shady deal. From the time he took Mary's hand when the family arrived in New York David began to change. Mary turned David inside out, upside down, and sideways. She saw through every lie, blocked every scheme, and made him pay each time he stepped out of line. David was in love for the first time in his life, everything else seemed unimportant. She forced him to change, grudgingly at first, but in the end, he did it on bended knee. Mary tamed him to the regret of many women and the rejoicing of those he had been extorting from for so long.

Chapter 10

We're Home

Matthew signed the closing papers for the sale of the property the day before the group was scheduled to leave for Pennsylvania. The money from the sale, he transferred from his account immediately into a new account David had set up at the Miners National Bank in Ashley. Mr. Burnbaum, the banker, seemed quite pleased with the deal. Though everything appeared to go as planned, Matthew's nerves were getting the better of him.

Before heading back to the shop on 34th, Matthew stopped by Kildaires' Pub and tossed back a double shot of whiskey for breakfast. "So where's Davey hidin?" purred the sultry voiced barmaid from behind a stack of fresh washed glasses on the bar. Matthew remained curious about the connection between David and this woman and though he longed to know, he never asked. Matthew drank and left without answering her.

The next morning the group caught the ferry across the Hudson River from Manhattan to Hoboken. They boarded the nine a.m. train to Scranton. During the trip, the girls thrilled with the sight of the beautiful deep green forests that passed on both sides, along with the streams, lakes and ponds, and the occasional spotting of a deer between the trees. Cora brought a sketchpad and pencil, spending her time drawing as the scenic beauty flashed by. Everyone saw Ireland in the rolling hillsides and soft blue skies and recalled its aroma in the crisp morning air that poured through every window.

Despite many delays and bottlenecks slowing the train to a crawl at times, Matthew, Nora and the sisters arrived at the Scranton terminal by early afternoon. The scenery delighted the group so much that the three and one half hour ride seemed to go by in a blink. They found the ride so relaxing that by the time the train eased into the Scranton terminal they had nearly forgotten New York.

From Scranton to Wilkes-Barre, other than a long cart ride, Matthew, the Flora-Dora girls and baby Elizabeth had to ride the Laurel Line, an electric trolley line connecting the two cities. A short layover in Scranton before the excursion went south afforded the group an opportunity to stretch their legs. They walked along Lackawanna Avenue, seeing what Scranton had to offer. The streets bustled with people going in and out of stores all along the avenue. Matthew described the city as a small town trying hard to be big; everyone agreed.

Matthew assessed Scranton accurately. The strength of its rail system fed a growing metropolis anchored by its huge iron furnaces and a diverse manufacturing industry. It sat in the heart of coal country and equidistant between New York City and Philadelphia, making it a very profitable locale. These things and more attracted those that had money, and those that wanted it.

Unlike when they departed Ireland, the group brought much more from New York. Two packed freight cars accompanied them to Pennsylvania. The kelly green velvet living room set from the third floor apartment that Cora loved and Dora's bed, which she insisted she needed to sleep, made the trip. Also Nora's fine china, silverware, her best linen table clothes and photos of friends and family road the rails to Scranton.

Spools of brightly colored ribbon, thread, yarn, and all the finest Irish lace that remained after auction came along with them on their journey. In addition, five New Queen sewing machines, purchased as Christmas gifts for the girls that year shipped with them from New York. These machines were the finest in the industry at the time and were held back from the auction of goods when they sold off the shop.

These things and more would catch up with the group in Ashley. They were loaded onto a caravan of horse drawn carts to traverse the old roads south from Scranton to Wilkes-Barre. Mary and David awaited their families' arrival at the trolley station in Wilkes-Barre to take them by carriage to the Hotel Sterling, the finest hotel in the city. It was nearing dinnertime when the trolley reached the Wilkes-Barre station. The travel weary group longed for a good meal and comfortable bed. The Sterling provided the luxury of both.

When she saw her sister Mary, Dora ran across the trolley platform to greet her. She stumbled and nearly took a very bad fall, but David caught her just before she hit the concrete. Dora turned red with fright, burying her face against Mary who wrapped her comforting arms about her sister. Flora and Cora helped Dora into the carriage. Mary thanked David before turning her attention to Nora and the baby.

It had been nearly a month since Mary had seen her sisters or her little niece Elizabeth. She could not wait to see the child, amazed by how much she had grown in such a short time. Mary's eyes flickered with light as she held the baby in her arms. Elizabeth Grace smiled and laughed at Mary's attentions, cooing like a dove on a soft summer day.

Mary held Elizabeth for the ride to the hotel while sitting on David's lap. It was a tight squeeze getting everyone into one carriage, but Mary on David's lap and Nora on Matthews, everyone fit in relative comfort. The ride along River Street with the bright orange sunset blazing off the slow moving waters of the Susquehanna River brought an easy feeling to everyone. The group felt more at home than they had since leaving Ireland.

The hotel door attendant helped the women out of the carriage and summoned the bellhops to unload the bags and take them to the rooms. Each member of the group carried a single piece of luggage with them. Matthew and Nora brought one extra for the baby. The light of the sunset filled the lobby through a huge skylight, casting a peach glow on the elaborately detailed lobby. Marble pillars encircled the room, shouldering a second floor balcony with ornate cast iron white railings, decorated with cast lengths of garland and vines of flowers at each end. Heavily varnished and glistening wood accents ran along a beautiful winding staircase while fresh cut flowers filled large colorful vases, completing a most amazing entry hall.

Much like the elegantly adorned lobby, the rooms were equally beautiful and comfortable. The view of the river and the park filled with cherry trees in bloom caught Nora's eye from the window of her suite. She stood in the window, baby in her arms, and watched the last flicker of sun drain from the sky behind the spring green hillsides. Matthew joined her just at that moment, wrapping his arms around his wife and giving her a gentle kiss on the neck he whispered, "We're home".

Nora felt happy, looking out across the glistening river, but something about the sight of the cherry blossoms seemed familiar. She had seen them in a dream that cast a very dark shadow. Again the dread of the rose appeared, its black petals drawing her in, casting its bewitching spell. Nora shivered beneath the grip of Matthew's loving embrace.

The next morning the group rode the local trolley to Ashley. Matthew could see right away that the location for his new store was perfect. It sat in the middle of the block on the main street, three doors down from the Miners National Bank and right on the trolley line. The upstairs apartment needed work, but it was minor compared to the work needed on the New York location. This would be his sundry shop much like the one he had in Ireland. The girl's building housed a good storefront of its own where they could open their new dress shop.

The carts rolled in around noontime, with most of the cargo going to the dress shop. The furniture for the apartment came in first. The bolts of fabric, ribbons, spools of thread, yarn, and countless other items quickly filled the large storage room to the rear of the shop. The sewing machines came in last, along with box after box of Cora's designs. In all it took more than an hour to unload everything that landed on Manhattan Street that day.

Matthew and Nora took delivery of the bedroom set and baby's crib, but little else in the way of furniture. Nora's things remained in boxes. The apartment needed a good cleaning and a fresh coat of paint before. The carpeting and any furniture could be brought in. They decided to enjoy the luxury of the hotel until the apartment was livable, stacking their things in the store in the meantime.

The Flora-Dora girls chose not to return to the hotel, quickly arranging the sewing machines and reams of material to get the dress shop up and running. Matthew had a long list of venders that he had compiled over the month prior to leaving New York and found a few more in Scranton. He began sending out orders for stock as soon as he returned to the hotel.

Nora, Matthew, and Elizabeth Grace spent another comfortable night at the Sterling and after a fine breakfast, headed back to Ashley to beginning cleaning and setting up the store. Mary met them in Ashley so that she and Nora could split time taking care of the baby while they worked. Mary displayed a greater attachment to the child, more than the other sisters did. Nora realized this and became suspicious. She observed Mary while helping Matthew locate a sales rack behind the counter. That is when it dawned on her, shouting, "you're pregnant!"

Matthews grip loosened on the heavy wood rack, nearly allowing it to crash to the floor. He caught it just before it did so. Mary smiled, peeking up at Nora with a self-satisfying nod of acknowledgement. Matthew, completely confused by the sudden outburst, placed the cabinet to the side. He removed a hankie from his back pocket to wipe his brow before realizing what his wife had said. Nora rushed to her youngest sister's side, hugging her gently while Matthew pulled up an old wooden chair left behind by the previous occupants. He gave it a quick dusting and sat down. The chair broke into pieces and Matthews long legs flew into the air as he landed on his backside in a heap upon the dusty floor.

Mary laughed and passed the baby to Nora to help Matthew to his feet. He hugged her as Nora moved to his side. His wife asked him if he was all right, he said "fine" and recommended a break for lunch, which they all laughingly agreed to be a good idea, including baby Elizabeth Grace who let out a loud cry. They ate peanut butter and jelly sandwiches on the bench in front of the bank. Nora asked all the usually questions of her sister. Matthew, showing no interest in such girl talk, looked up and down the street. He greeted people as they entered the bank, wondering how his business might do at this location.

Before long, the store was in full operation. Business picked up quickly. The stores convenience and ever-growing selection made it the perfect little neighborhood shop. The dress shop, too, began well. Cora's designs brought women from all over the area seeking custom bridal gowns.

With its location directly across from St. Leo's Church, the store had a built in clientele. They began by selling wedding gowns, but soon enough they were getting requests for Confirmation and first Holy Communion dresses for younger girls, along with suits for men and boys. The extra work had Flora, Cora, and Dora struggled to keep up with all the orders since Nora and Mary were unable to help full time.

Mary began to show a few weeks after telling Nora and Matthew she was with child; just about the same time as David's first sales trip for the Scranton Lace Company. David headed south, stopping in Allentown Pennsylvania before several meetings in Philadelphia. Kerryn Long accompanied him to introduce David to the company's already established clients. In Philadelphia alone the company had a dozen stores and dress shops buying their products, not to mention a half dozen or so clothing manufacturers.

David visited every one of them, familiarizing himself with the employees as well as the bosses. Going further south, he visited textile mills in both Wilmington and Dover Delaware. Afterward the tour turned north with a short stop in Gettysburg followed by Harrisburg and back home again. David estimated the trip to take a little over three weeks. His estimate was correct, but he was still too late.

The day before David expected to return Mary caught the trolley from Public Square in downtown Wilkes-Barre and rode it to Ashley, stopping off briefly to see Nora before walking the few blocks to the dress shop to help the girls complete their orders. The day was warm, but comfortable with a light breeze keeping the bugs away. Mary worked with her sisters for a few hours before feeling a little tired. She sat and had a bite to eat with Flora, Cora, and Dora prior making the walk back to the sundry shop where she planned to rest and then catch the trolley back to her apartment on the square.

She turned the corner on to Main Street and felt a sharp pain in her stomach. Mary stopped for a moment until the distress subsided and then continued onto the shop. Another stabbing pain, worse than the first, doubled her over. Again she rested, trying hard to breath through the pain. Mary struggled to make the last few steps to the store.

Nora busied herself arranging a new window display at the store, when she noticed a large smug on the outside of the window. After completing the last touches on the new arrangement, she grabbed a wet rag and went outside. She immediately saw Mary struggling on the sidewalk and yelled for Matthew to help as she ran to the aid of her baby sister.

They helped Mary into the shop. Nora found her a place to lie down and Matthew fetched the doctor. The physician's office was one of the first in Ashley to have a telephone. The doctor instructed his nurse to ring the Mercy Hospital for an ambulance. By the time the ambulance reached the hospital Mary had lost the baby.

The Flora-Dora girls stayed with their sister the entire night and through the next day, much to the annoyance of the floor nurse. Flora made it clear that neither she, nor her sisters were leaving Mary's side, sternly tapping her shillelagh on the high polished floor. When David arrived home at the couple's apartment, he found a note telling him to go to the hospital. He entered Mary's hospital room to complete silence. The loss of their child devastated David. He took Mary in his arms and kissed her, looking into her eyes, seeing and feeling the anguish they bore.

Time went on steadily, quickening with every passing year following the loss of David and Mary's unborn child. The event prompted Matthew to get a telephone in the store, as did the sisters for the dress shop. The new method of communication dramatically increased business for both stores. David's sales also rose. His trips away became less frequent, allowing him more time to spend with his wife.

The young couple eventually moved from their downtown apartment, renting a house that overlooked the Susquehanna River. Mary enjoyed the view, but hated the quiet. David too found the more rural style of living less to his liking. They had grown comfortable with the noise of the city. After only a year, David and Mary returned to the apartment along the square.

Matthew and David purchased automobiles, which were wonderful inventions, but the roads remained brick or stone, or worse, rutted dirt treks built for horses not four-wheeled heaps of metal. Nora and Matthew used the car infrequently, mainly on Sundays after morning mass. They would take Elizabeth with them and park along the river, where they enjoyed a lazy afternoon watching the river flow.

Occasionally they took rides in the country to a spot with a view of the valley or to a lake in the woods where Matthew taught Elizabeth to swim. Some days they went with the rest of the family, making a day of it. Matthew and David built a fire along side the lake, roasting up chickens while the girls went for a swim.

The entire family embraced the community of Ashley, helping at church fundraisers and neighborhood block parties. Nora and Cora taught Sunday school at the church and Flora volunteered with the neighborhood watch. Matthew joined the Main Street Businessmen's Association. An organization designed as a lobby group for community improvements, but it in reality it did little more than allow the men a few nights a month away from their wives. Matthew, not feeling the same need as the other men, pushed the group to do what they were organized to do, with minimal results.

When Elizabeth Grace turned five Nora enrolled her in kindergarten at St. Leo's Catholic school. Even at a young age, she looked very much like her mother. Her long wavy black hair and deep blue eyes made her stand out from the rest of the children. She was a precocious child with a quick wit and pleasant attitude. Around this time, Nora spoke with her husband about buying a house with a yard, providing Elizabeth a safe place to play and so she could plant a flower garden. Matthew thought it a fine idea. The store was doing very well and the rent from the apartment would easily cover the mortgage.

By Christmas Matthew, Nora and Elizabeth moved into a new home along St. Mary Street beside Solomon's Creek on the most westerly edge of Ashley. The house had a large dining room with a big creek stone fireplace at one end and French doors at the other that opened into a broad entry hall. The ceramic tile in the hallway had diamond patterns formed by one-inch mosaic pieces of burgundy and gold, matching nicely with the polished cherry wood moldings. A large sweeping staircase led to the three bedrooms on the second floor. Every other room had hardwood floors with a highly polished finish covered by oriental area rugs trimmed in gold twisted tassels.

The entire family came to the house to celebrate the holidays. They were suitably impressed with the décor' enjoying the mix of grandeur and homey touches. Nora and Genie Haggerty exchanged Christmas cards each year since the group's departure from Ireland. This year Genie sent along a photograph of the entire family, including big Jeffrey Haggerty, her eldest daughter, Shannon, her husband and children and Aaron's family. Genie's Christmas card contained notes and photos from Pat and Colleen Clancy and the Lynch twins with their wives and children. Matthew would later have these pictures framed and hung in the hallway so that he could see them every day when he came home from work.

New Year's Day, Valentine's Day, St. Patrick's Day and Easter came and went, until the new buds of spring bloomed along the Susquehanna River. In the spring Nora planted her rose garden, using tips sent to her by Genie Haggerty. By mid-summer, the yard overflowed with their delightful aroma. Matthew set up some chairs and a table in the yard for he and his wife, allowing them to sit amongst the flowers and enjoy a lazy afternoon, with Elizabeth playing in the grass beside them.

The following spring David announced to the family that the company was transferring him to their new office in Baltimore, Maryland. The Flora-Dora girls could not bear to see their sister leave. Mary longed to stay, but knew her place was with her husband and said her tearful goodbyes with a heavy heart. She kissed and hugged her sisters for nearly an hour, sharing remembrances both joyful and sad before bidding her final farewell.

David and Matthew slipped away for a drink, sharing their own recollection of bygone days. They went to one of the local watering holes that occupied most corners of Ashley and sat down at the bar, ordering pints and shots of their finest whiskey. After a few good snorts, David asked a question of Matthew that he longed to ask, since his introduction to Nora and her sisters back in Ireland before the wedding.

"Matthew my friend can you tell why the sisters are named as they are?" David questioned. Matthew smiled. He finished his beer and ordered up another before asking David a question of his own. "Now why haven't you asked that question of Mary?"

Though David loved Mary, he feared poking her Irish temper. He did it once, a circumstance he would not share with Matthew and dared not repeating. He sucked down the last of his ale explaining this to his friend. Matthew raised an eyebrow and, with a hardy laugh, patted his friend on the back, sympathetic to his plight.

"Daniel Haggerty explained it to me a long time ago, when I and Nora first became a couple," began Matthew. "I thought the same as you; how comical it sounded. Shaun Burns, the girl's father, was a handyman, quite handy in fact. That is how Daniel met him. A nice enough man he was, much like his daughters, Daniel explained."

Matthew paused for a drink, wiping the excess foam from his lips with a napkin. David joined him for a swallow and requested another round. They kicked back the shots of whiskey, passing on a refilling. David knew he had a long drive ahead of him, a distance he had never attempted before, and wished not to be lightheaded behind the wheel.

Matthew continued, "Shaun met his wife Elizabeth, working as a barmaid in a pub in Dublin. After a short courtship, the couple wed and Elizabeth moved into Shaun's house in Craigavon near Lough Neagh. Shaun thought it a fine way to honor his own mother Lora, by naming each of their children as he did, starting with Flora."

"Then why did he name their last daughter Mary?" David asked.

"Let me continue and I'll tell ya what Daniel told to me," answered Matthew.

"Daniel Haggerty found Shaun a job with a construction company knowin he needed money to feed his children and his wife becoming upset with the hard style of living she'd married into. The job took Shaun from the family for near two months, but provided a nice paycheck. Some time just after his return,

Elizabeth began to show. To Shaun's mind the timing of it was off, which brought him to the idea that the child growin inside her weren't his."

Matthew took a short pause and began again, "Their father stewed in the belief that Elizabeth was unfaithful and began to drink heavily, givin the youngest daughter the name Mary cus' she didn't fit with the other sister and wasn't befitting his mother's name. Elizabeth passed from the fever less than a year later, swearing on her deathbed that the child was his. At that final moment, he believed his wife and begged her forgiveness.

Afterward, the combination of Shaun's grief and alcohol abuse consumed him. He lost everything, including his daughters. Flora did her best to keep her sisters safe. Daniel and Genie took it upon themselves to help the girls, taking them in and putting a roof over their heads. They never saw their father again."

Once Matthew finished the story, the two men returned home. There they found Mary sitting at the kitchen table surrounded by her sisters and young Elizabeth sitting on her knee. Elizabeth cried, begging her aunt and uncle not to leave. Mary promised Elizabeth they would return for the holidays, giving her their final goodbye hug. Elizabeth stood in the doorway, waving goodbye as their car sped off. Many years would pass before Elizabeth saw her Aunt Mary and Uncle David again.

Chapter 11

Love And War

Elizabeth Grace grew up much too fast to Matthew and Nora's way of thinking. One day she was catching fireflies in a mason jar in their backyard on a warm summer night or resting her head on Matthews's lap as he read stories to her beside the fire in the winter, the next she was a budding teenager entering junior high. The sisters of St. Leo's Church had grown very fond of Elizabeth over the years. She was a respectful, smart, and well-mannered child that simply loved to learn.

Everyone enjoyed being around her and she was a friend to everyone. She went to church every Sunday with her parents and helped in the store when school let out. To call her spoiled might be true. Being an only child not just to Matthew and Nora, but to her childless aunts and Uncle David too, who indulged her every whim. She never acted like a spoiled child. She never looked down on anyone and was always willing to lend a helping hand if she saw someone in need.

In September of 1914 before the turning of the leaves in autumn, Elizabeth and her classmates began seventh grade under an ominous cloud. War had broken out in Europe. The so-called Central Powers, lead by Germany, pitted their forces against the allied forces of Great Britain, France, and Russia, among others. At this point, no one could have imagined how this bloody conflict would shape history.

Many of the children had friends and family still living in the war torn nations and feared for their safety. The Priests and Nuns of the parish shared in their concerns and did all they could to help those members of the congregation through this horrible time. Matthew and Nora worried for their friends too, not knowing how their homeland would fare in such wide spread aggression or how many young Irishman might die.

It was during these troubling and difficult times that a new child joined the class at St. Leo's School. He entered Elizabeth's class on a Monday morning after the starting bell. Sister Agnes, who taught the seventh and eighth grades, introduced him to the class as Mister James McGill. Sister Agnes instructed the class to give him a warm welcome, which they did as a group. She guided him to a desk near the window and returned to the lesson, pausing just for a minute to ask James what school he attended prior to entering St. Leo's. It surprised her little when he responded that he had never been to school and she then resumed the day's teachings.

Over the next few months, James would prove to be a quiet boy, keeping to him self for the most part. He arrived in Ashley with his father to work in the coalfields and was only a couple of years removed from Ireland. To Sister Agnes he was a surprisingly good student despite having little formal education. Although he did not answer many questions in class, when he did, he was usually correct. Being incorrect angered him not ever wanting to be wrong. In checking into his records, Sister Agnes discovered James was a few years older than the other students in her class. This at first concerned her, but as time went by, she realized her worries where unfounded.

Sister Agnes had many boys like James pass through her school. Sons of immigrant families, struggling to make ends meet. They did not wish to be neglectful of the children, but in trying so hard to survive financially, the boys were often left to their own devices. The children easily fell into trouble, becoming bold and disruptive, causalities of a difficult and demanding economy.

Often the parents of these forgotten children would send them to Catholic school in the hope that the church would return them to a straighter path. In some cases this occurred, in some it did not. Sister Agnes did her best to educate and provide for these troublesome souls, but even she, with all her efforts, could not save the most damaged of them. These she could only pray for, hoping God would rescue them if she could not.

Elizabeth said good morning to James every day. James always blushed and turned a bashful eye. Finally, at the end of the school year as class let out for summer break, James responded to Elizabeth's good morning, with "Top of the morning" spoken in a heavy Irish brogue. Elizabeth stopped in her tracks, bending a smile to young James whose cheeks turned as red as fresh strawberries. Elizabeth's best friend, Amanda Collins, tugged at her sleeve and they continued on, leaving James to his embarrassment.

Amanda thought James was cute, but she considered many of the boys at school cute. Elizabeth looked for something more, not that looks did not matter. Someone who cared to keep up their appearance meant they cared. Cute need no such help. It arrived on its own, without any sense of purpose. Amanda had an adventurous spirit, providing a good compliment to Elizabeth who tended to be caught up in the "seriousness of life", as Amanda put it. Her joking, playfulness, and innocent flirtations kept Elizabeth in touch with the fun side of life, relaxed and carefree such as young people should be. The girls remained friends throughout their school years, balancing each with their opposite outlooks on life.

Amanda, too, was very beautiful. Her long blonde locks and soft blue eyes were in sharp contrast to Elizabeth's jet-black hair and deep blue orbs. Her sleek frame and long legs caught many a young boys' glance, which she played upon like a child on a swing set. Elizabeth enjoyed seeing her friend's lighthearted teases, but warned it might some day get her into trouble. Amanda knew well enough not to push it too far, but she did leave many a boy wishing.

Elizabeth grew straighter and taller during the summer, looking more like her mother every day. Her height she received from her father, along with her father's persuasiveness. She carried herself confidently, genuinely, never putting on airs or acting superior. As Matthew had said when they had given her the name Elizabeth Grace, it had a regal quality. It was hard to say if she was living up to the name or if the fates had come to play, knowing a regal person should bare a regal name.

The news of the war dominated the headlines, driving Americans to a seek distraction by rediscovering baseball. Baseball had been around since before the turn of the century, but its popularity grew with the rising death toll in Europe. People used baseball to feel good, muting the reports of hell on earth trickling in from Europe. Matthew and Nora celebrated their twenty-year wedding anniversary while American soldiers headed off to war. President Woodrow Wilson felt democracy would be the final fatality in the war to end all wars if Germany was not defeated.

Matthew and Nora told their daughter about Ireland and the civil unrest that led to their final decision to leave their homeland for the United States. This planted a seed in Elizabeth. She despised war and hatred, cruelty towards others pained her deeply. She was not unrealistic, however, understanding that sometimes one must fight to preserve the right things in this world.

Even at a young age, Elizabeth held no fear of voicing her opinions, basing them on facts and a good sense of right and wrong. She did not dismiss the opinions of others, acknowledging that, as individuals, each had their right to think or choose how they wished. Nora often called her daughter, "quite the politician", a description Elizabeth didn't like. She viewed politicians as self-promoting highbrows that never have the best interests of the people at heart.

Elizabeth Grace graduated top in her class, an accomplishment that made her parents very proud. Matthew and Nora, along with the Flora-Dora girls took Elizabeth to dinner at the Hotel Sterling to celebrate. Amanda Collins, her parents and Amanda's two siblings, a sister and brother, also joined them for dinner. Matthew liked having some male companionship for a change, to talk sports, politics, or to kick back a whiskey or two when the wives were not looking. Elizabeth was most disappointed that Mary and David could not attend, sending their regrets with a large bouquet of flowers. The years had flown by since Mary and David had departed. However, not a day passed that the couple was remembered in the thoughts and prayers of their family.

James McGill graduated also, which really meant very little to him. He was a coalminer just like his father and that is what he would be, diploma or not. On the Sunday following graduation James approached Elizabeth and her family on the steps of the church following the service. He requested quite properly of Elizabeth's parents, if he might walk their daughter home from mass. Matthew looked at his daughter and, seeing a wish for approval in her eyes, he agreed to allow James to do so. James held out his hand to Elizabeth and she slid her hand into his. Together they started for home with Matthew and Nora a few paces behind them.

Nora reached down, slipping her hand into Matthew's. He looked into her deep blue eyes, the eyes of the woman he had loved for so many years. Nora smiled, seeing the young man in the rain who came to the aid of a stranger and fell in love without question for the whole of his life. She pressed her head gently against his shoulder and they were there again, strolling along Springfield Road, young and so much in love.

Matthew's heart beat just a bit faster, sincerely hoping that his daughter would find the same joy that he and Nora had found and shared. Nora stopped and placed a gentle kiss upon her husband's lips, the streaks of silver in her long black hair sparkling in the morning sun. He put his arms around her and they were at the spot where they had met, watching Elizabeth and James walk further and further away.

Flora, Cora, and Dora observed from the steps of the dress shop across from the church. Dora took Cora's hand. Cora smiled at her sister, as the touch of a tear ran from her eye. Cora longed for such a love, but it had passed her by. She recalled the walk in Genie Haggerty's garden. How her heart leapt when David Addison kissed her. She never thought that moment would be the only such moment in her life. More than twenty years had passed. She was alone, longing so much to have lived the life of her sister. She wrapped her arms around Dora, holding her tight, she cried. Dora led her sister into the shop and poured them each a cup of tea.

Flora remained on the steps, paying less attention to Matthew and Nora, and more to Elizabeth and James. She had met James a few times and did not like him. It was not anything she could explain, more of a feeling, that he had a darker side to him. She tapped her old oak shillelagh on the walk, pondering the feeling that gnawed at her. He probably did not know it himself, as he had always been polite and respectful whenever their paths crossed, but Flora felt it and it gave her chills.

Business at the dress shop had slowed considerably during the war so Dora began working in Matthew's shop a couple of days a week. Cora picked up some hours in a silk mill in downtown Wilkes-Barre, while Flora helped at the church doing light housekeeping. The girls continued to put in hours at the shop in the evening just to give them something to do.

Some mean spirited children began picking on Dora one afternoon at the store when Matthew and Nora were not around. "Dippy, Dopey Dora," the children sang, giving poor Dora a very hard time.

Dora's sweet, simple way left her unable to cope with such senseless cruelty. She cried and swatted at the children with a broom, begging them to leave the store. Matthew came in through the rear door. He chased the children away and took Dora in his arms. She was shaking like a leaf and apologizing, but for what Matthew did not know.

He sat her down and locked up the door to the shop. In the distance he could still hear the voices of the children repeatedly singing, "Dippy, Dopey Dora." Once Matthew secured the store, he took Dora home with him. There he explained to Nora what had transpired. She took Dora into the yard and brought her a cup of tea, laced with a touch of whiskey to calm her nerves. Together they sat until sunset, listening to the birds and the sound of Solomon's Creek gurgling gently by.

That same day, Cora stopped at a small Italian pizzeria along Main St. by the name of Frankie's for a quick bite to eat before going home from work. The owner, Frank Letteri, served her a slice of pizza and a soda pop, striking up a conversation with Cora as he did so. Cora, flattered by his attentions, developed a soft rosy blush to her cheeks. Frank noticed her embarrassment and apologized for his boldness, which she told him was not necessary. He stated that he had seen her in church and asked if he could accompany her to mass sometime or possibly brunch afterward. At first Cora hesitated but seeing how cute this little old Italian man trying so hard to persuade her, she reluctantly agreed.

Brunch between Cora and Frank led to dinner. Then Frankie asked Cora to accompany him to the cinema and another dinner. Frankie's attentions made Cora feel good at a time when she felt this part of her life had passed her by. They had been dating for a month when Cora made a decision to take Frankie to bed. She put on her nicest dress and fixed her hair and make-up. Looking in the mirror, she saw the young girl from Ireland. Her blue eyes sparkled, her dark hair swam about her shoulders, and her lips were pink as rose petals.

Frank knocked on the door just before six p.m. Flora flung it open, greeting him with her usual snarl. Little Frankie Letteri stood on the porch afraid to move. Flora stared down upon the diminutive man, his thinning hair and olive oil skin, the crumpled fedora he gripped in his small wrinkled fingers, thinking what a sad case he was. She gave a yell for Cora then stomped her shillelagh on the floorboards, startling the little man. Cora came skipping down the stairs like a teenager. Frankie smiled as Cora approached him. Age had stolen some of Cora's looks, more than it had Nora, but she was still beautiful. It just took some attention to bring it out again.

The couple took in a movie. Afterwards Cora suggested they stop for a drink. They went to one of the many bars along Main Street that Frankie knew to have a pleasant atmosphere, one more suited to Cora. They shared a bottle of wine. Frankie talked about his late wife, with Cora listening, but thinking of the night ahead. When Frankie excused himself to use the restroom, she troubled the bartender for a shot of whiskey, hoping that it might help to calm her nerves.

He walked her home and she invited him in. Cora admitted to Frankie that no man had ever been in her bed, leading him to her room and easing the door shut behind them. They lay together on the bed in the glow of the lamplight and began to kiss. Pausing for a moment, Cora relaxed in his arms, but having had too much wine and feeling the comfort of his arms, fell fast asleep.

Frankie, being a gentleman, kissed her good night and left. As he passed the sitting room he heard a heavy tapping, like a branch banging on the siding of a house, but with a slow melancholy rhythm. He had his hand on the doorknob when curiosity got the better of him. He stopped and stepped back to look into the front room. There he spied Flora stretched out on the couch tapping the floor with her walking stick while gazing through the window into the night.

Flora, noticing the little man, sat up and covered her bare legs with her robe. He apologized for disturbing her and said goodnight, but Flora did not let him leave. She invited him to join her for a drink. He tried to refuse, but Flora was not one to take no for an answer. She guided Frankie in and sat him on the couch, giving him a drink from her glass. When he finished the drink, Flora picked up the bottle of rock n' rye she had hidden along side the couch. Refilling the glass, Flora stood in front of Frankie and took a long drink then hand him the glass. As he drank, she undid her robe and dropped it to the floor.

The old man sat speechless as she took the glass from his hand and pressed herself against his face. Yes, Flora was older, but so was Frankie. He did what she wanted. Then she wanted more, and he did that too. When Flora finished with Frankie, she warned him never to say anything to Cora or to anyone else. If Cora found out it would break her heart. Frankie dreaded what Flora and her walking stick might do to him and never spoke a word of it. Cora continued to date Frankie and eventually did sleep with him, never knowing of what had occurred between Flora and Frankie that night.

Elizabeth could have gone anywhere to college, but she chose to stay close to home. Her parents were getting older and felt her place was with them. Elizabeth decided to become a teacher, considering it a most admirable profession. Elizabeth, at the suggestion of Sister Agnes, enrolled at Misericordia College in Dallas, a small town just outside of Wilkes-Barre. It was a new facility and the first school of its kind in the Wyoming Valley and they were thrilled to have Elizabeth Grace as a student.

Her friend Amanda had very different plans. After one year at the local college, she transferred to a school in Florida. Her parents had taken the family to Florida on vacation some years earlier. Amanda fell in love with the beach and carried no fondness for the snow or the cold of Pennsylvania winters. When the opportunity presented itself to move, she grabbed it. She left the following summer, promising to return for the holidays, which she did.

Twice a year letters arrived from Ireland. As time passed, they bore the sad news that one of Matthew and Nora's old friends had passed away. First, it was Genie's husband Daniel, followed by Pat Clancy. The good news, if there was any, was that big Jeffrey Haggerty and Colleen Clancy had taken up after the death of Pat. Nora saw this as fine union. Matthew just smiled.

Dougy Lynch died of cancer, leaving behind a wife and four children. Joseph sent Matthew and Nora pictures of Dougy's family with the note. The sad news of Genie Haggerty's passing arrived just prior to Christmas, Elizabeth's first year in college. Their most generous friend was gone. Nora requested from the priest at St. Leo's that a memorial service be held in her honor. When she explained to him, the type of person Genie had been he graciously agreed. Colleen departed that same winter.

A letter arrived shortly after Colleens passing from Jeffrey Haggerty, informing his friends that she was gone and that Joseph Lynch, too, was laid to rest beside his brother. Matthew sat beside Nora on the couch in the living room, thinking of the friends now gone from this world as Nora read aloud Jeffrey's letter.

"Dear Matthew and Nora, my oldest and dearest friends, it is with great sadness that I inform you of the passing of my Colleen. The tears in my heart shall never be dried. As if there weren't enough sadness, and most regrettably, our good friend Joseph Lynch has succumbed to pneumonia, joining his brother Douglas in the grave. Of all, that I have known and cherished in my life it was the friendships of these fine people I valued above all. Matthew and Nora, I had always hoped you would return to us, but I too am in failing health and do not expect to see another autumn. Your love united all of us and taught us what it meant to love unconditionally.

I have missed you since the day you sailed from these shores and from my sight, but never from my heart. We will meet again on the chapel steps, as the sun clears the clouds where our friends await. God bless you both, your friend Jeffrey Haggerty."

There was more to it than the eye gathered, but the heart found easy to see.

Matthew and Nora held each other through the night, unable to express the pain they felt. Not only did they grieve for the friends now departed, but for themselves. The loss of their friends brought their own mortality into view. Nora could not bare the loss of her husband as Matthew's heart ached with the images of his life without Nora beside him.

They continued their daily walks, which had become shorter and closer to home with a necessary rest stop at the half way mark. Much as they had on their walks along Springfield Road, the conversations they shared spoke of days gone by and days ahead. They began to think that maybe a return home to Ireland would be nice, seeing Jeffrey and the old neighborhood and maybe take Elizabeth along so she could see all the things they had spoken about so often.

Winter faded into spring when the final sad letter appeared in the mail. The return address was that of Ryan Haggerty, Genie's youngest child. He wrote that his uncle Jeffrey Haggerty had died in his sleep. There was information on the service schedule, and where to send flowers, but little more regarding their friend.

Their large kindhearted friend, who shared their secret and knew better than any their passion, was gone. Though they had not seen their friend in what seemed like a lifetime, their feelings for this man remained as strong as their feelings for each other. To have his life summed up in a funeral schedule, Nora felt, was most unfitting.

Nora wanted to cry, but could not. She brought the note to Matthew who was resting in the backyard. She sat down on his lap and he glanced at the note feeling much the same as Nora. Flora, Cora, and Dora received the same message and made their way to Matthew and Nora's house. They found them in the garden, pulled up chairs along side the creek and listened to the birds singing as the sun slid low in the western sky, reminiscing about their friends.

Elizabeth returned home from school to find her parents and aunts in the yard. She kissed her parents then took a seat on the grass beside them. Elizabeth listened to all the stories, all the romantic moments, smiling and sighing and laughing at times. Cora reflected on Matthew and Nora's dinner at the WayFair, and Nora reminded Matthew of Daisy, Jeffrey's white mare, coercing Matthew out of his daze. They told stories of the Lynch brothers, Colleen Clancy, the snowball fight, and the grand wedding in St. Joseph's Church.

Matthew stood up and poured a drink for everyone to toast the friends that meant so much to him. He reflected one more time about the beauty of Ireland. Putting his glass to the sky, he said his final farewells, mentioning each friend by name. He then adding a blessing for Mary and David and threw back his drink. Taking Nora by the hand, he bid everyone good night.

The Sunday after the sad news of Jeffery's passing Matthew arose early, fixed his wife and daughter a nice breakfast, and then prepared for church. Nora helped Matthew on with his overcoat, calling after Elizabeth, seeing if she was ready to go. Matthew returned the favor, helping Nora with her jacket. He took his cane from the stand beside the front door and escorted his wife and daughter to the car.

Clouds rolled in just as church services ended, accompanied by a cool gusty wind. Elizabeth told her parents she was going for a walk with James, adding that she would see them later. Nora told her daughter not to be too late since she had planned a nice Sunday dinner with her aunts. Elizabeth promised to be there, kissed her parents, and walked off with her boyfriend.

Matthew suggested that he and Nora take a ride down to the river.

"I hear the cherry blossoms are in bloom," he told Nora, knowing how much his wife loved it along the river when the trees were flowering.

"Well, that sounds fine Mr. Flannery," replied Nora playfully. "I believe a nice walk along the river is just the thing for us today."

Matthew needed a cane to get around now, but still enjoyed his walks with Nora, although it hurt to walk for even a short distance. Nora held onto his arm as they meandered between the pinkish petals that blew about like snowflakes in the breeze. Matthew showed a twinge of pain so Nora guided him to a park bench for a rest. Matthew placed his arms around Nora, and stared into her eyes. He could see sadness and worry, prompting him to brush his fingers across the soft blush of her cheeks.

"I love you with all my heart Nora Burns Flannery", he whispered in her ear with his last breath.

"I love you Matthew, from the moment we met, I loved you," Nora replied as she too fell silent in her husbands embrace.

Their lives so tightly bound their hearts beat as one. Neither could exist without the other, nor did they want to. From the moment on a day in the rain when their eyes met, every fiber of their being intertwined and Matthew and Nora were united. They lived as one, they died as one, as much in love in that final exhale as they had ever been.

On that same Sunday afternoon, as Matthew and Nora rejoined their old friends in death, James McGill asked Elizabeth for her hand in marriage. Elizabeth happily said yes and rushed home to tell her parents. However, they were not there. She called her aunts on the telephone. Cora told her niece that they had gone for a ride directly after mass, but was not sure to where. Elizabeth then called her friend Amanda's father, asking if he had heard from them. He had not.

Elizabeth thought they might have gone to the park knowing the cherry blossoms were in bloom and that her mother loved to walk among them this time of year. Mr. Collins agreed to drive her to the park and to help Elizabeth find her parents. He arrived around two accompanied by his son Jacob. After a quick drive past the church, they turned and headed for the park.

They first saw Matthews car on River Street and pulled in beside it. They were not in the car. Mr. Collins scanned the tree-lined park, spotting them sitting on a park bench some ways away. He called to them as did Elizabeth, but they did not answer. Something was wrong, Elizabeth knew it, and so did Mr. Collins. Mr. Collins instructed his son to stay with the car.

Elizabeth and Amanda's father hurried to Matthew and Nora with Elizabeth, who was much younger and faster, arriving first. She knelt beside them, taking her mothers cold hand in hers and began to weep. Mr. Collins checked Matthew for a pulse. There was none. He did the same to Nora with the same result. Elizabeth rested her head upon her fathers lap as she had when she was a child and wept until her tears ran out.

Many knew and admired Matthew and Nora. His friendliness and her kindness touched all the hearts of the community. The parish priest at St. Leos called Matthew a true Christian gentleman and Nora the most beautiful soul he had ever met. Even the priest was overcome with emotion, choking on his words as he recollected Matthew and Nora. Cora held tight to Dora who cried through the length of the ceremony. James kept his arm around Elizabeth who tried to be strong, but the words of the pastor and the voices of the choir reduced her to tears.

Mary and David arrived as the priest began to speak. They slid into the pew beside Flora from the far aisle. Mary took Flora's hand to let her know she had moved to her side. As she looked into Flora's harsh weathered face, Mary saw something she had never seen before, a fragile softness. The hard, mean façade had come crumbling down, leaving behind a gentle face, much like her sisters. She resembled Nora and Cora, with their deep blue eyes and flushed cheeks. Flora had missed life while watching over her sisters, always believing since she was the eldest; she would be the first to go.

To have Nora, the person she had spent the whole of her live protecting put to rest, tore away the mask of anger that Flora had worn for much too long. She pained much more deeply for the loss of Nora, having been responsible for her for so many years. Mary put her arms about her older sister's shoulders. She felt her strength drain away as Flora collapsed into her arms.

Mary kept her arms wrapped around Flora through the length of the ceremony, kissing her gently on the cheek. Much like Nora would do to raise a bashful blush; a kiss that came from the heart, simple, loving, touching. Tears rained from every eye, saying their final goodbyes to the two people who had guided their lives for so long.

The window blew cold on cemetery hill as the caskets of Matthew and Nora were marched to their final resting place. Hundreds of friends and neighbors alike dropped roses upon their caskets, with Elizabeth being the last. She remained to say a final prayer over her parent's graves as the church bells of St. Leos echoed across the hillside.

A light rain began to fall when James led Elizabeth away and into the waiting arms of her aunts. Flora still distrusted James, but put aside her misgivings for a day. Elizabeth and James rode with Mary and David to what was now Elizabeth's house where many mourners where already gathering.

Amanda Collins met Elizabeth at the door accompanied by her parents. She directed her friend through the crowd and into the sitting room. Mary and David exchanged hugs with Flora, Cora, and Dora before joining Elizabeth to express their condolences. David instructed young James to get everyone a drink, which he did, but with exception. James strongly disliked being told what to do, but he did it for Elizabeth.

David called for a toast to his good friend as he poured an Irish whiskey and raised his glass. "Matthew Quinn Flannery was my oldest and dearest friend. There were times when I wondered why he remained my friend, but no matter what I did, he stood by me. The love of Matthew and Nora touched us all". He wanted to say so much more, but the words caught in his throat. He paused and silence filled the room. Finally, holding his glass as high as he could stretch, he mustered the strength to say, "Goodbye my friends." Mary hugged her husband then ushered him from the room to the clinking of glasses and many hushed goodbyes.

Mary and David remained in town for the wedding of their niece. Elizabeth invited them to stay at the house, which they did. Each night Mary sat, talking to Elizabeth after James had left and David went to bed. Elizabeth decided with a heavy heart to sell the house and the business. She felt the house held too many memories and she had no interest in running the sundry shop. James was a miner and had no desire to be a shopkeeper and she was going to be a teacher. Keeping the store she believed, would be more of a burden.

Her aunts agreed with Elizabeth's decisions and with David's help, she was able to get all the paperwork in order for the sale of both properties. David contacted the bank on her behalf and posted the properties with a realtor. There were no leans against either of them and all the bills were current and in good standing. David expected no less of Matthew, knowing him to be a most organized person and always on top of things when it came to finances.

"Even in death", David said to himself, discovering that Matthew paid for all the funeral arrangements in advance, leaving no burden or expense to their daughter.

Mary surprised Elizabeth when she informed her of having two cousins, Joshua and Michelle who were away at school. Elizabeth asked why her aunt had not told the rest of the family. Mary embarrassedly admitted that Joshua was not David's child. She explained to Elizabeth that she and David separated for a time when Mary discovered that David had been having an ongoing affair with Kerryn Long, his boss's daughter.

Although she had been fond of Joshua's father, he had no desire to marry. His father went off to war never to return. Years had passed before she took David back. Joshua was a toddler by then. Sometime during the first few months of David's return, Mary again was with child. "Michelle is David's daughter," Mary told Elizabeth. "David swore on his child's life that he would never stray again," Mary added.

"I love him as much as when we were young," Mary exclaimed, "but it took a long time before I could trust him again. Remember that with your James," she added. "Hold him to it. Be sure in his actions, do not presume from his words, and make him accountable. This is my advice to you". Mary paused for a moment, recalling her sister and Matthew.

"Your parents, dear, found something grand, they wished the same for you, but it is rare, so rare that I have only seen it once."

Mary spotted the water globe, which still held the black rose, fresh as it was on Matthew and Nora's wedding day. Taking it down from the mantle she gazed at it amazed that it was still in tact. A strange feeling came over her and she set it down on the table in front of Elizabeth. Mary poured a glass of whiskey from Matthews's decanter and sat back down.

"Your mother was haunted by this," she told Elizabeth. "The day you were born she awoke screaming, going on about the black rose. She believed it had some great darkness attached to it. I never learned what it was, and I guess now I never will."

Elizabeth knew some of what Mary spoke. More than once she heard her mother wake up crying in the night and her father doing his best to comfort her. Matthew wanted to dispose of it, rid it from their lives, hoping that would quiet Nora's mind. Nora would not allow it.

"There are two sides to everything," Nora would tell her husband. "Genie Haggerty gave me this as a remembrance of our wedding, that's a good thing. There is something better to it than that I expect, something beyond the dark dreams that trouble me so."

Matthew never understood, but did as Nora asked. The globe remained on the mantle beside pictures and trinkets of their time together. Elizabeth recalled her mother taking each piece down, recollecting the significant moment that went along with them, but never speaking of the black rose. She would dust and polish it, but talk of a little beyond the fact that it was a gift, given to her on the day she left Ireland. She said nothing more, though still insistent that it remained her most valued heirloom among her mementos.

"I suppose it is my possession now," stated Elizabeth, picking it up and inspecting it. "Mum wouldn't let me touch it, surin I never did know why."

Elizabeth looked fixedly at the dark black flower, marveling at the smooth and scalloped edges, which drew her in, mesmerizing her.

"Surin it is a fine flower now isn't it!" she said, this being the first time she had been able to really look at it closely.

Mary grinned and sipped her whiskey, "Never heard you talk with the touch of the Irish, Elizabeth," observed Mary.

Elizabeth smiled not knowing what to say. Usually, her Irish only showed when she got angry. An odd sensation ran through her, pins and needles in her hands and feet. She twitched and jiggled attempting to shake it off. Mary asked if she was all right. Elizabeth said, "Yes", and then excused herself claiming fatigue. That night both Elizabeth and Mary awakened in the night, disturbed by mysterious images of blood on a black rose. It was now Elizabeth's curse to carry.

Chapter 12

Elizabeth Grace & James

The war in Europe had ended. Many American solders did not return home, leaving wives without husbands and mothers without sons. Elizabeth lost parents, but found love in a dashing young man who proved to be strong and attentive. James continued to show his worth, comforting Elizabeth during her time of need. He knew how close she had been with her parents and shared in her grief since he too held a great fondness and admiration for Matthew and Nora. He empathized with her loss, remembering how he felt when his father died.

Elizabeth's aunts designed their niece a fine gown of satin and lace, with a delicate train made of the thinnest chiffon. Its simplicity made it beautiful, capturing the essence of the bride, subtle and demure, one of Cora's finest designs. Elizabeth chose to marry at sunset, loving the colors dusk draped across the hillsides. Though the sadness of her parents passing still lingered the day turned out to be the joyous celebration of a new beginning. Family and friends toasted a sad goodbye to Matthew and Nora and a warm hello to Elizabeth and James.

Following the reception Mary and David returned to Baltimore. The business and house sold to a Mr. William Kolb and his wife, whose name, surprisingly, was Dora. Mr. Kolb paid a decent sum of money, the deal arranged of course by David. Elizabeth placed the majority of the money in a trust for their children should they have any, leaving just enough for the young couple to buy and furnish a home of their own.

James did not approve, feeling the money better spent in the here and now. He never thought of children. Putting aside something for a possible future perplexed him. Having grown up in a world of poverty and in the shadow of war, James hadn't the ability to view life beyond the present. Nevertheless, it was Elizabeth's money to do with as she chose and that is how it would be.

Elizabeth and James McGill bought a double-block house along Main Street in Ashley. It was a very plain and simple dwelling with a white exterior and large front porch, a spacious living room and kitchen on the first floor, along with a small spare bedroom to the back just off the kitchen. The bathroom and two average sized bedrooms made up the second floor. The second apartment mirrored the first with a door in the living room connecting the two spaces. Elizabeth saw the potential in the big back yard, which at the time of the purchase was an entanglement of weeds. She pictured roses along the house and possibly a vegetable garden at the far end.

James did not understand and was not happy with Elizabeth's decision to live in such a humble abode, but Elizabeth insisted. "It is now our story to tell," Elizabeth said to James. "I've heard and enjoyed the tales my family told to me, and admired the beauty of their lives. This is our life to be and do, building memories we will share with our children and not to profiteer on the backs of our families," she added, "We will appreciate it, knowing it to be ours and only ours, when we look back on the path we've chosen."

James did not think in these terms, but he loved Elizabeth and believed she had their best interests at heart. He would do, be, and live exactly as his young wife wished. The house provided what they essentially needed. It was close to work for James and on the trolley line so Elizabeth could travel back and forth from school without an issue. It was within walking distance to a grocery store and pub, but far enough away from Elizabeth's aunts to keep them from stopping by to visit. James had no fondness for the old women, preferring to separate himself and his wife from them when ever possible. He loved Elizabeth and to him nothing else mattered, nothing at all.

Elizabeth reveled in decorating the house to her liking, using some of the items she had kept of her parents, and adding new pieces and trinkets that reflected her life with her husband. Initially, she placed the water globe containing the black rose on her nightstand beside her bed. She moved it to a table in the living room when her dreams became repetitive and increasingly disturbing. James did not hold much for memories, having little in his past worth remembering. The lessons he learned where all that remained of his parents. He did not cherish them; he lived them, which is why his parents taught them to him and for no other reason.

As newlyweds, Elizabeth and James learned much about each other. During the time they dated, they had fun, going to many of the nearby amusement parks. Elizabeth loved amusement parks since her Aunt Mary and Uncle David took her to Luna Park in the Nay Aug section of Scranton one summer afternoon when she was a child. As they crossed the bridge over Roaring Brook Gorge, Elizabeth delighted at the sight of big bouquets of colored balloons being hawked by colorful characters wearing bright cherry costumes, and rides trimmed in lights that flashed as they spun. The smell of popcorn and candied apples filled the air, while quartets of men in bright white suits and straw boater hats strolled along serenading the crowd.

James had taken Elizabeth to Rocky Glen Park on their first date. They rode the Laurel Line, which stopped right in the park. She kept souvenirs of the prizes he had won at the arcades along barker's row and shared a kiss for the first time in the tunnel of love. They kissed again on the ferris wheel as it stopped with their chair at the top. They rode the tilt-a-whirl, roller coaster and ate cotton candy, just before a brief rain chased them into the pavilion, smiling and laughing as they went.

Now, as husband and wife, Elizabeth knew right away that there was work to be done, joining two so different lives together. James left that to his wife. To his mind work was the mines and relationships, if he ever thought about it at all, were the reward for breaking his back all day. Elizabeth believed nothing of the sort. Their marriage, unlike her parents, required effort.

"Being happily in love did not mean things would take care of themselves," she would tell her husband.

James adored Elizabeth much the same way Matthew had loved Nora, but Matthew bore a sense of family. James had little experience in this area. His mother died when he was a child and his dad was a miner, cold and hard as the caves that surrounded him. He and his father became closer on the trip across the Atlantic. Emotions, beyond anger, his father did not share. Quite a different life then Elizabeth lived, whose family surrounded her with love and attention.

When it came to working the tunnels, James had few equals. His coworkers knew when James worked beside them that he had their back. They viewed him as trustworthy and dependable, highly valued traits for miners. His knowledge of the caves gave them a needed sense of security, feeling that if anything were to happen James would get them out safely.

Elizabeth too felt this strength. Her conversations with her husband when they spoke of his work impressed her. James knew all there was to know about life underground. He told Elizabeth, "The dangers are man made. A smart miner had little to fear." She loved him for his strength of will and fearless nature, but feared for him despite his words; she knew the unpredictability of the caves and that they could bury even a cautious man if something went wrong.

By the following November Elizabeth excitedly announced that she was with child. She sent a letter off to her Aunt Mary and Uncle David, insisting they come back to celebrate the holidays and to share in the good news. Mary responded just before Thanksgiving, regrettably informing Elizabeth that they would not be able to do so as David was ill and unable to travel. The Flora-Dora girls rejoiced with their niece, wishing Matthew and Nora were alive to hear such happy news. Elizabeth wished for this too, it saddened her to think they were not.

Cora took her niece by the hand, patting it gentle, telling her, "They are here with us, my dear. They know, they know."

James stood with his back to the door wanting to leave. Flora, the once fierce guardian of the family, kept a watchful eye on him. Her suspicious notions regarding Elizabeth's husband escalated with news of her niece's pregnancy. She still brandished her perfectly polished stick and though she was now a shadow of herself, still knew how to swing it if needed.

Dora put her arm around Elizabeth and smiled, asking her niece what she might want for Christmas. Elizabeth loved all of her aunts, but Dora's simple, kind way, always touched her heart.

Elizabeth kissed her on the forehead, "I think I have my gift for this year, Dora."

Dora smiled and responded, "I guess ya do deary."

Elizabeth and James spent the holidays with the Flora-Dora girls, though James had no desire to. He wanted to spend them alone with his wife, but kept that thought concealed, seeing how happy this made Elizabeth. New Years Eve, however, they did not spend with the old aunts. Instead, James took his wife to dinner and then to the San Souci dance hall at the San Souci Amusement Park. There they met Amanda

Collins and the young man of the day for Amanda. James was not much of a dancer, but he did his best to please his wife. Elizabeth appreciated his efforts, knowing her husband did not feel comfortable doing something he was not good at doing, recalling their school days and his anger at answering incorrectly.

Late that night, while the rest of the Wyoming Valley rang in the New Year, a fire ripped through the dress shop, which had not been open for sometime. The women got out alive, but with little more than the clothes on their backs. Cora attempted to save her collection of designs, rescuing a few, but getting her hands and face scorched in the process. Flora had a notion the blaze was no accident, deeply suspicious of James. Her accusations created a rift between James and Flora, one impossible to mend.

Flora lost something very important to her; her best friend, her companion, the one possession she cared for more than any she owned. Flora's shillelagh burned up in the flames. She spent little time mourning over it, finding a piece of wood to begin the process of shaping a new walking stick.

Following the fire Elizabeth contacted Mary, who now was getting up in years herself, asking for help as to what to do about Mary's elderly sisters. Elizabeth and Mary concluded that Flora, Dora, and Cora should join Mary in Baltimore. Mary sent her son Joshua to Wilkes-Barre on the train. Elizabeth met him with Flora and Dora so that he could escort them to Baltimore where they would live out their golden years together in a retirement home. Once Cora was well enough to travel, she would join them too. Flora strongly rejected the move, arguing all the way to the train. She ranted and raged, warning Elizabeth about her husband.

"There's something bad about that boy, I can feel it", she yelled repeatedly. "I can feel it in me bones. I don't know what it is, but surin there is blackness in his soul. I know'd it when he was a child, and I tell ya now, be wary of em".

Elizabeth did what she could to appease the cantankerous old woman, promising she would be careful. She hugged both her aunts with long loving embraces, hating to send them away, but knowing it was for the best. Cora said her tearful goodbyes to her sisters in the hospital. Old Frankie Letteri sat at Cora's bedside every day until her release. He accompanied Cora to the train some weeks later. She kissed him goodbye and cried with Elizabeth before Joshua took her hand and helped her aboard.

Prior to boarding Cora gave Elizabeth the few sketches, she was able to rescue from the flames along with a stack of notebooks held together by a dark blue piece of ribbon. The design of her mother's wedding gown was among the drawings and the notebooks chronicling every day from when she and her sisters were children. Each contained a photograph along with a letter, neatly folded and placed just inside the cover.

Her eyes swelled with tears as she glimpsed inside the first notebook written by her mother. Her father penned the second and both contained pictures that Elizabeth had never seen before. The Flora-Dora girls placed notes in the next three with another marked for Mary, but there was nothing there. David too had a page marked for him and there was none there either. Two more books remained, one marked for Elizabeth and a final, nameless, page, which said only "to be continued".

Cora explained to her niece Elizabeth that these things were to be handed over to her upon this fated day, when the real possibility existed that she would never see her family again. Elizabeth, feeling quite confused and upset, tried to refuse the books, promising her aunt Cora she would come to see all of them once the baby arrived.

Joshua stepped forward and handed Elizabeth the two missing letters from Mary and David. Elizabeth gazed at Joshua who spoke not a word. Elizabeth gazed at her cousin; her eyes pleaded for an answer. Joshua offered none. She placed the envelopes in their respective books and then returned her attentions to Cora.

"What is it Cora? What is this that you have given me?" Elizabeth asked of her aunt, desiring some explanation for this unwanted gift.

"We care for you very deeply child", Cora replied. "Each of us has a story to tell you. We have chronicled them here. Some would call them the self-indulgent scribbling of foolish people. You read them and see what you think and, hopefully, you and your little one will continue it for whatever it might be worth".

Cora then kissed her niece goodbye, said farewell to Frankie Letteri and left on the train to join her sisters in Maryland. Frank took hold of Elizabeth; watching tears slowly trickle from her sad blue eyes. For as much as she did not want to believe it she realized she would never see her aunts again. Frank helped her aboard the trolley back to Ashley. On the ride, he shyly told Elizabeth how much she resembled her mother and Cora too. She kissed him on the cheek, softly, gently and he blushed. They said their goodbyes on Main St. and Elizabeth went home to prepare dinner for her husband, who was hard at work in the mines.

Amanda phoned every so often to see how her friend was holding up, then sharing some outrageous stories of her latest fling. Elizabeth enjoyed hearing from her friend. Occasionally

Amanda would tease Elizabeth that she had settled down too soon and missed out on so many good men. Amanda pointed out how different men can be, boldly referring directly to their physical attributes. Elizabeth laughed off Amanda's obscene conversation, thinking how terribly funny she was for making such statements, while praying her friend was safe and hoping she was leaving at least a few boys wishing.

James rented out the other half of the house to a young couple by the name of Wells. They too were newlyweds, starting a new life together. Jeremy Wells made his living as a newspaper editor, while Bernice, Bernie for short, worked in the same silk mill that Elizabeth's aunt Cora had. The couple lived there only two months before buying a home of their own on lower Manhattan Street.

In the short time they were neighbors, Elizabeth and Bernie became good friends. The women shared recipes and tended the garden together. Elizabeth helped Bernie decorate their new home and they went shopping together when they shared a day off. James and Jeremy kept a civil relationship, not friends. James saw Jeremy as too different to his liking. Jeremy felt the same about James. They took a drink together at the pub across the street from the house, but that was the most they socialized despite the friendship formed by their wives.

All during Elizabeth's pregnancy, the Sisters of St. Leo's Church came to visit Elizabeth, usually when James was working. They talked with her and helped Elizabeth with housework and with her garden. Sister Marion, one of the older nuns at St. Leo's parish often sat with Elizabeth, discussing her expectations as a new mother. The Sister asked how James felt about the child within her, among other things. She advised Elizabeth to stay health and always vigilant, that times were changing.

"Children need a watchful and a strong mother to keep them safe", the nun told Elizabeth.

Elizabeth agreed and had concerns about her husband's ability as a father. She knew he had very little connection to his own parents and it would be up to Elizabeth to do the majority of the caring and nurturing. She loved James, but recognized his shortcomings, believing he would learn to be a parent once their baby was born. Elizabeth requested the nun's aid, not having any family left to help her. They gladly agreed and went about preparing for the child's birth.

Chapter 13

Working The Planes

The sun had not yet arisen on this warm humid August morning when the first of many men with hard hats and pick axes appeared on Main Street. One by one, they exited the dimly lit houses to join the march. The sweet scent of honeysuckle, which had laced the morning air, now paled beneath the stench of cigarette smoke and man sweat. From Newtown, Ashley, Preston from the north and the Sugar Notch and Warrior Run from the south, they descended upon the Huber Colliery. Though there were some who had cars, most would leave them at home and join the walk. It was a ritual held high by the miners, knowing and facing the dangers of their profession. Knowing that each day could be their last.

As the first speck of sunlight perched upon the hillside, a young man's voice rang out. Amidst the clatter of metal and the buzz and chatter of the morning the anticipated shout "All clear", echoed down from the mine entrance followed by another young voice repeating the same "All clear!"

The miners lined up before the supervisor's shack in the shadow of the breaker. The two boys entered through the side door with birdcages in hand. They placed the cages on the dusty table by the window. Chester the foreman, handed them each fifty cents and the boys ran off with a fading", Thanks boss", hopped on their bikes and raced back up Main Street.

Groups of men now poured into the caves and colliery, or made their way up the tracks to the planes. These were just the first of many workers that would arrive for the day as the shifts were staggered every two hours until eleven a.m. They numbered nearly 2,300 men and boys on the site and Chester bared witness to every one. Each man approached the desk to make his mark in the assignment log. This was a necessary formality, insuring all could be accounted for in case of an emergency. Days when changes to the log were necessary sat few and far between.

This day, however, was to be one of those rare days.

"Tis a fine mornin old Chester, my friend", spoke one of the miners as he bent to sign the log.

"Always a fine mornin when the canaries sing", replied Chester. "I'm puttin yas on the planes James, for the next few days", he added.

James had no argument with Chester's decision. Working the planes or the caves made no difference to him as long as his pay remained the same.

The planes were a system of rails set up to move the coal from breaker to breaker and over the Pennsylvania Mountains to points east. A barney truck with a large screw pushed the cars up three steep inclines until they reached Solomon's Gap in the town of Mountain Top. The barney attached to a cable that ran across pulley wheels set in the middle of the tracks. A steam engine twisted a large winch attached to the cable. Once the yard engines moved the loaded coal cars into place the barney was raised up from the barney pit falling in behind the loaded cars. The steam engine began to crank and up the mountain it went.

James McGill and Chester Lenore were long friends. Chester's wife, Eleanor Lenore, was the midwife to Elizabeth and was caring for her along with the Sisters of St. Leos Church. James appreciated the help and comfort they were providing his beloved. Although he was a proud man and not prone to accepting acts of kindness, he knew this was something he was incapable of doing. He hated leaving his wife's side, but he had confidence she was well cared for while he was at work.

"This way, when the time comes we can find yas and get yas home, if the need be", he told James, rocking back in his chair.

"I was there for my part, what else would I be needin to do", James answered with the touch of an Irish brogue still on his tongue. "I'm not the fathering type, I just want my Elizabeth to be happy", he would state firmly not only to Chester, but to anyone who cared to listen.

James was a hard man, but a good man for the most part. He was average in both height and weight, but he had disproportionately large forearms and hands with thick dark fingers embedded with coal soot. His nickname was Popeye as one might expect. He came to America from Ireland as a child with his father following the death of his mother. Onboard ship his father would teach him many things as his father saw them. All of which James took to heart.

His father taught him how to fight, to protect himself. He would say to his son, "Keep your eyes an ears open, It will keep ya alive and never strike a woman or a child James, for this is a coward's act, and if ya find a good woman hold on tight cause there's so few good ones to be had". All this and more James believed to be the truth and no one could ever tell him differently.

James had found a good woman in Elizabeth. The only thing that surpassed her beauty was her kindness. James had married up and he knew it. So did everyone who knew them. Questionable looks commonly fell upon them whenever they appeared in public, the refined statuesque Elizabeth, soft and demure, with the course gritty coalminer. Truly, this was a case of opposite attraction if ever there was one.

When those who were bold and curious enough to ask Elizabeth why she married James, she answered loud and sure, "He's a fine man who loves me with all his heart and does what ever I ask of him". This could not be truer of James. His wife was his life; he would do anything she asked without question.

She did have a bit of an Irish temper to be sure, although she rarely displayed it. This she inherited from her Aunts Flora and Mary and not from her parents. Elizabeth herself attributed it to a strong sense of right and wrong, claiming she only displayed it when things were not correct. This was not quite true, but James embraced this mood as he did the rest of his wife, in love with everything about.

"James Andrew McGill", she would holler and he knew he was in trouble.

What had he done? Usually something small, like forgetting to put the garbage out or sweeping the walk when it needed it. Maybe he'd had one too many shots of whiskey at the bar before coming home on Friday after work or maybe he left his dirty boots on and she'd chase him back out onto the porch to remove them. Nothing so serious really, but it kept James in line and that was fine with him; there was always a gentle kiss and hug waiting for him once he corrected his mistake.

James followed the track to the base of Penobscot Mountain where the coal cars were to be loaded and shipped east. His mind was on his wife and little else. The steam engines were already being stoked when he arrived. Two men exited the engine house and approached James. Behind them, the orange glow of the boilers cut through the morning shadows.

The first man coming towards him James recognized as Red Jamison. A pleasant enough old drunk who he'd shared ale with a time or two after the whistle. The second had falling in behind Jamison. Walking in Red's shadow made it harder for James to make out who he was exactly. As they came closer, he realized who was hiding behind Red, and with good reason. It was Lucas Nash. A man James disliked and had a run in with some months before.

Nash knew whom it was walking toward him. He too remembered the run in they had had, very well in fact. James had broken Nash's nose and knocked him on his ass right in the middle of Main Street with his wife and children watching. James witnessed Nash hit his wife and little boy. He had slapped her across the face and when his small son pushed at his father, Nash knocked the child to the ground and dug his muddy boot into the child's neck.

James McGill called after Nash, "Only a coward hits women and children!"

Lucas Nash was a slovenly man with a round belly that stuck out from beneath his dirty T-shirt. He had more than his share of chins and a balding-pitted head with two cauliflower ears dangling from either side. His left cheek, just below the eye bore a dark burn mark he had gotten as a boy. Nash stood some six inches taller than he stood and outweighed him by at least forty pounds. This meant nothing to James as he made his way down to where Nash waited.

James bellowed at Nash, "You're a coward fat man". James learned this lesson well from his father and believed it as strongly as any. Nash stepped forward and threw an off balance right towards James's face. James easily dodged the punch and stepped in, his huge fist landing square on the nose of Nash. Lucas Nash staggered back on his heels, catching his foot on the red brick that paved the main street. He landed on his ass at the feet of his crying wife and children. He struggled to his feet and charged at James who met him with another sledge hammer right.

Nash sat on his fat ass in the middle of Main Street, bleeding from his mouth and flattened nose. The crowd, which had gathered to witness the fight, dispersed quietly and Nash's family turned their backs on him and went into the house. James leaned forward and looked Nash in the eyes, "You're lucky I didn't use me left, ya fat bastard ya", then turned and went home to Elizabeth. Nash sat there wiping the blood from his face with his dirty T-shirt until a car came upon him. The driver beeped and yelled for him to move. Nash rolled to one side, spitting a large wad of blood and phlegm onto the brick, and then crawled across to the curb.

Later that evening, after many hours at the bar near his house, Lucas Nash returned home. He began breaking up the place and beating his wife and children with anything he could get his hands on. A neighbor, hearing the racket, phoned the police and Lucas Nash was arrested with great prejudice. After three days in the local jail, he was released. Returning home, he found his wife had taken his children and left. He never saw or heard from them again. Lucas Nash would not soon forget the run in he had had with Popeye McGill.

Red reached out his hand to James and they shook as Nash shoved past them, annoyed by the presence of McGill. "Popeye how ya been?" Red asked, "Haven't seen ya much at the bar of late."

"Elizabeth being due any time now, I'm tryin to be home with her as much as I can," replied Popeye. "Sides, we'll be needin the extra money once the baby comes."

Red agreed with Popeye, having three mouths to feed at home, and I wife that could out eat all three of them. Together they turned and went towards the head house just beyond the barney truck pit. James had worked the planes as a boy when his father was alive. Actually, he had done most jobs associated with the mines. He started as a canary bearer checking for gas leaks, did some sorting in the colliery, before coming out to the planes to work with his dad.

"Nash will be riding the barney up to Mountain Top once the cars roll in from Wanamie. You and I will scale the cars as they fill," Red told Popeye. "Seven ton they want from here a day, seven ton up the mountain," repeated Red. "You coal crackers been shoveling a lot a stone of late Popeye."

"Wanamie," James growled and spit, trying to displace the taste of it from his mouth.

"Ya need to let it go Popeye", Red answered. "What's it been now, ten years? Let it go Jimmy. Let it go."

Red knew well enough what upset James McGill. The Wanamie mines had a reputation as a dangerous place. No one except for Chester Lenore knew it better than James did. Chester knew it first hand. James knew what it had taken from him, with bitter recollection each time he heard the name.

Yes ten years had passed. James was just fourteen at the time, but he remembered it like it was yesterday. Spring had arrived early and the fields were a muddy mess. Anywhere you would step, your foot sank to where the mud crawled up around your bootlaces. He could still hear the sloshing of the men who came to speak with his father. He could tell they were not used to being in the fields by the way they reacted to their footsteps sticking in the mire.

"Mr. Andrew McGill is it?" The first man asked. His father kept on working, spreading ash around to provide more traction in the muddy conditions.

"Mr. McGill, we were hoping we could have a word with you," said the second man.

"So have your word, I can hear ya," his father barked not stopping to listen.

"Well, we'd like you to head up a crew for us at the Wanamie site," exclaimed the first man. "We feel we've found a new vein and need someone with experience to open it for us. Someone we can trust to do the job right."

Andrew McGill stood straight up and looked about until he caught sight of young James standing by the barney pit leaning on his shovel and listening as the men spoke.

"Are ya done boy? Cus' I don't think ya are. Maybe the shovel's broke," he yelled, then threw his shovel across the fresh spread cinders towards his son. "I know that one ain't broke, so get back to it."

The first gentleman, looking surprised at what Andrew McGill had done, spoke again. "We'll give ya an extra fifty cents an hour from now on if yas take the job and yas can return here once the coal starts moving."

This increased Andrew's pay to the most he ever earned, if he accepted. The Wanamie mine had a bad reputation, one McGill knew well. More than one tunnel had collapsed over the years. Though no one died, everyone felt it was just a matter of time before someone did. Then there were the rats. The Wanamie mine was a rat's nest, which really did not bother elder McGill, but he did not like it either.

He looked upon his son now shoveling ash along the track to the barney pit and thought, how much more he could do for him if he had the extra money. Maybe he could free James from this life, from having to break his back in the caves. Take away the blisters given by the pick and the shovel. Maybe he could have a happier life than his father had known.

"Alright, I'll take your job and except your terms," Andrew replied, reaching out to shake the hand of the first man. Andrew McGill squeezed the man's hand tightly and looked him in the eye. "But, I want Chester Lenore on this with me. I need someone at my back that I can trust. Make sure he gets the extra money too or I ain't doin it."

The men agreed and sloshed back through the fields.

The next morning and for many mornings after Andrew and Chester rode the barney truck down to the Wanamie colliery. They signed in with the supervisor there and headed into the caves. There where ten men in all assigned to work the new vein, but McGill trusted only Chester. Chester Lenore not only felt the same about his friend, he carried the same worries about Wanamie.

They had been at it some four weeks when the coal began to flow. McGill insisted the pillars be broader than was standard to provide for more structural support as the vein expanded. These pillars were made of columns of coal and stone, unmined expanses nearly forty feet wide, meant to support the surface from mine subsidence. Except for Chester, the crew disagreed claiming too much coal would be left behind if they did this. McGill, who was more concerned with getting out of the tunnels alive, told them leaving a little black rock were it was, was a small price to pay for their safety.

Andrew and Chester did not understand the attitude of the miners until they heard that some of the crew might be getting bonuses for every ton they sent up. That explained the cave-ins Wanamie had experienced in the past. He and Chester were not, and as far as he knew, the company had never sanctioned such bonuses because of the danger of over mining which reduced the tunnels integrity and caused it to collapse.

McGill realized the dangerous position he and Chester were in and could see the greed growing in the eyes of his crew.

The final day had come at last. The crew, under Andrew's direction opened the new branch. They laid the track and the coal flowed up from the tunnel. McGill and Chester spent the morning inspecting the farthest reaches of the cave. Once they were satisfied, they grabbed their lunch pails and picks and started back through the rooms formed by the pillars. The only sounds they could hear, was their own footsteps echoing through the pit.

At first this meant nothing to them, but as they walked they began to notice entire pillars missing, gone, removed; with nothing more than wooden poles left in their place. Rats began to pass between their feet and along either side of the newly laid rails. Faster they began to pace, hearing rumbling all around them as the walls and ceiling began to crumble. Chester caught his foot on the rail as the tunnel began to fill in behind them. McGill lifted his friend to his feet and dragged him forward.

"Another ten yards and we're outta here, Chester," McGill yelled. He pushed Chester ahead of him. "Run for it", he shouted to his friend and then he was gone. Swallowed up by the tunnel he had dug.

Chester leaped out of the dust and tumbled head over heals down the embankment that lead up to the mine entrance. His right leg was broken in three places and he suffered numerous bruises and scrapes, but he was alive. Andrew McGill, father of James Andrew McGill had died. His body was never recovered.

James waited by the tracks that led from Ashley to Wanamie until nightfall. He returned to the small four-room house his father had rented from the coal company and fell asleep in his father's chair. He awakened to the sound of sluggish, lumbering footsteps coming up the porch stairs. Two quick knocks and he knew it was not his father. Two more knocks rattled the glass in the old wooden door. This was followed by the voice of a woman.

"James, it's Eleanor, would ya be letting me in please? I have some news, sad, sad news, and boy; it's about your father. Please James, please open the door," said the woman. Three more knocks and young James opened to a see a tearful Eleanor Lenore wiping her nose and eyes with an overused handkerchief.

Sitting him down, she broke the news to James as directly as possible. He did not cry, he didn't even flinch, "Crying was fer girls and children," taught his father. "Hardship makes you tougher and tough is what ya needs to be in this world." He knew this lesson, as well as he knew them all.

Following the death of his father, young James would live with Chester and Eleanor Lenore. They knew they owed it to Andrew and to his son. Chester believed and rightly so that Andrew McGill had saved his life. If he had not stopped to help him and throw him forward at the last second Chester certainly would have died that day in the caves of Wanamie. Andrew sacrificed himself so his friend would live.

"One good friend James," his father told young James aboard ship. "One good friend's all you'll ever need."

"Wanamie," James spat again and walked off to the head house.

About the time the next crew arrived so did the two coal cars from the Wanamie mine. An old man with a conductors cap rode the barney car. A barney car did not require a conductor, but reports of kids playing on the cable made for an unsafe situation. The conductor's job was to keep the line and track clear. Other than doing that, he was just along for the ride.

"We need to take em down to the head house," yelled Red to the old man. "We need to scale em before sending em up the mountain. Seven ton needs to roll today so we need to scale everything."

As James and Red reached the head house, Nash and two other men were getting a full car ready for weighing. James checked the scale, recorded the numbers in the log, and handed the log to Red. Red double-checked the weight and initialed the log. The yard engine moved the car away.

"OK, bring in the first Wanamie car," Red barked. The men repeated the procedure and the yard engine pushed the cars in line at the base of the slope. The cable tightened, the barney rose from the pit and latched to the last car. Nash climbed up; his dirty butt crack prominently displayed much to the disgust of all the men present. The steam engines cranked and the load began to move steadily up the tracks.

Nash never spoke, not a word. The ride up the mountain would take half the day. Once the cars reached Solomon's Gap, the barney, which served to push the cars up the steep incline, would be released and the cars would fall along a gravity line into the White Haven shipyard where they would be loaded onto barges and sent to New Jersey.

"Perfect job for the fat man, wouldn't ya say James," Red joked as the line tensed pulling the cars forward. "We should a weighed him," James replied. "I don't think the lines gonna hold." The men shared a good laugh as the cars churned up the hillside into the morning mist. The sound of their laughter carried up the track. Nash, seething in anger, remembered well his run in with Popeye McGill.

It was on the third day of working the planes, about mid-afternoon, when a young man came running up the tracks to the barney pit. "James McGill," he hollered trying to catch his breath. "James McGill you're needed at home. Your wife, your baby, your needed at home," the boy repeated still gasping for air. James was trying to repair a rail in the pit, which had somehow come loose. "Calm yourself boy," James said as he climbed up from the pit.

Just as he did the screw car came out of nowhere and crashed into the pit. Red and some of the other men working close by came running down to see what had happened.

Two other miners came rushing from the direction the barney car had taken, with Nash following leisurely at a distance. The first young man, who looked barely old enough to work, spoke up.

"Oh my gosh mister, are you OK?"

The second man, who was not much older than the first, added, "We was fixing the loose cable when it got away from us mister. Jeez, mister we're real sorry! Glad you're alright!"

Red exclaimed, "I checked those cables and pulleys myself this morning, they weren't loose!"

"Nash says they was comin loose as he was makin it back down the mountain," answered the first young man. The second confirmed this with a nod of his head and they all turned to look at Nash.

Nash spit a large green gob of spit down on the rail. Speaking in a deep guttural Slovak tone, "They felt loose to me. No way for me ta knows sump in like this would happen."

Nash stared into the face of McGill, his right hand digging into his hip pocket. There was a fire building in Popeye's chest, tightening his grip upon the five-pound hammer he was using to fix the rail. Red Jamison stepped towards Nash while the other men eased back. Popeye flinched to move toward Nash, who braced himself.

"Mr. McGill," interrupted the runner, "Your wife, she's in need of ya."

James put aside his desire to beat the life out of Nash and hurried down the track toward home. The voice of Red questioning Nash faded quickly behind James McGill as his thoughts turned only to Elizabeth. The distress in the voice of the messenger boy weighed on his mind with ever tie that passed beneath his purposeful strides. The messenger tried to keep up, but finally, exhausted and bending for air, he stopped and watched James running from his sight.

Chapter 14

The Turning

James finally reached the house so leg weary he stumbling on the front porch steps before entering. He opened the door to the sight of the sisters of St. Leo's kneeling in the living room, chanting the rosary. A commotion coming from the upstairs bedroom immediately caught his attention and he climbed the steps two a stride. The stair rail shook as he grasped it, pulling himself up and forward. He stopped just before entering the room not sure what to expect. James moved the door open slowly, cautiously, to the sight of the doctor, his head barely noticeable beneath a sheet held up by his wives legs. Eleanor Lenore, held firmly by Elizabeth's grip, knelt beside his wife, trying to comfort her as she screamed in pain.

He stared in aw as the baby slid out with a gush of what seemed to be a mix of water and blood. The doctor caught the baby and flipped it over thumping the bottom of its feet lightly then rubbing it down with a blanket until it cried. He quickly wrapped the newborn while muttering under his breath, "There is too much bleeding." The parish priest came up the steps and nudged past James. He asked the doctor if he could help in anyway. "Pray," replied the doctor. The priest did so, kneeling down and reaching out for James to join him, but he refused. A touch of sunlight entered through a crease between the paisley patterned drapes, casting shadows that moved freely about the room.

When the doctor felt there was nothing more he could do he stood and began wiping his hands. He looked sad and concerned as he turned to James, putting together his thoughts, knowing how James felt about Elizabeth, how everyone felt. James looked into the doctors eyes. Panicked he moved to his wives side. Her, face drained of color, wore ghostly white and the sparkles that light her deep blues had disappeared. The priest knelt at Elizabeth's bedside, blessing her with the sign of the cross before giving her last rights.

Elizabeth spoke in a low weak voice that James could barely hear, "I love you my husband with all of me heart. Please promise me you will care for our daughter." She paused for a moment, struggling with each inhale, "I know this won't be easy for you, but the sisters will help. I have named her Rose Aileene. Remember always, she is the result of our love." He held his wife's hand until the light of this life that had shined so brightly faded into shadow, and was gone.

James promised to care for the child, but he did not promise to love it. The doctor patted him on the back, expressing his regrets, as did the priest. Eleanor Lenore wrapped her arms around James. She had known him for so long, caring for him when his father died, taking him into her home when he had nowhere else to go, but had no words to say to him that could ease his pain. Coldly James pushed Eleanor away and exited the room.

The doctor had called out for an ambulance, but not soon enough to save Elizabeth. They took little Rose Aileene in for observation. The doctor went along with the baby to the hospital, accompanied by Sister Marion, but James stayed home. He knew it was his responsibility to make funeral arrangements for his late wife, wishing to have died along with her.

The love of his life, the best part of him was gone in an instant; taken by something he never wanted. He wandered about the house aimlessly, picking up nick knacks and mementos that Elizabeth decorated the house with; memories she found pleasure in remembering. He choked on his heartache with every vision these bits of the past possessed.

James poured himself a tumbler of whiskey and sat on the front porch steps. His mind ran back to the days coming home from work, his beautiful wife greeting him at the door. He saw her smile and the sparks that flew from her deep blue eyes. He recalled the fire that only showed when she was angry, and the silk of her touch when they made love. He adored every glance, every breath, and every mood. Nothing else had mattered and now what would matter, what could matter. He finished off the bottle of whiskey and stumbled across the street to the pub. As he drank, he felt he needed to blame someone. His anger and pain consumed him with every glass he touched to his lips.

Someone bumped him quite accidentally and James shoved him to the floor. The bartender and some other gents who had heard the news of Elizabeth's death struggled to subdue him. Once they had, the men escorted him home. He plopped down in the big high back Victorian chair his wife had bought for him when they first moved in. Elizabeth called it the King's throne and would sit on his lap as he told her about his day.

James buried his head in his hands wanting to cry, but remembered what his father had taught him. He suffocated beneath the weight of a profound resentment. The room spun, his thoughts blurred, as consciousness slipped away. Without resistance, he lost himself, turning with every minute, transforming into the hard black stone that he mined.

Chester and Eleanor Lenore helped James with the funeral arrangements. Eleanor persuaded James to contacted Elizabeth's aunts with the sad news. He agreed to do so, though no part of him wanted to see the old crows. Maybe they had grown too old and feeble to make the journey, or so he hoped. The day of the funeral Elizabeth's family arrived in three chauffer driven black limousines. Even in the winter of their years, the sisters dressed impeccably in basic black with veiled hats and delicate white gloves.

Amanda Collins held the baby at the funeral, taking Rose about to show Mary, Flora, Cora, and Dora. Each of them took turns holding the child. David was in a wheel chair pushed by his daughter Michelle along side Mary and Joshua. Amanda handed the child to David, placing the baby in his arms so that he could get a better look at the infant. James paid no attention to the child or the sisters, preferring to stay by his wives side rather than mingle amongst people he did not care to see.

"She looks just like her mother," exclaimed David. "The spitting image of Elizabeth the day she was born back in the old apartment in New York."

The sisters agreed with David, returning the child to Amanda. The Flora-Dora girls expressed their sympathies to James who feigned acceptance, particularly from Flora. Cora asked about the books that she had handed over to Elizabeth, but James told her he knew nothing of them. Mary requested to go through Elizabeth's things to try to find them. James refused, but said he would look for them and return them to the women if he found them. This he never bothered to do.

Elizabeth, sometime after receiving the stack of notebooks from Cora, met with a lawyer. She placed the chronicles and letters in a series of safe deposit boxes with explicit instructions for these items to be giving to her child when it turned twenty, along with a letter from her and the value of a life insurance policy. When Mary arrived, back in Baltimore following the funeral there was a letter waiting for her. Elizabeth arranged with the lawyer to send this to her aunt in the case of her premature death. A black rose, its petals dripped in red, adorned the letterhead.

In the letter, Elizabeth told Mary of the nightmares she had been having since the night she took possession of her mother's water globe. The dreams became more vivid and more intense as her due date grew nearer. She professed to her aunt that she feared the worst, but not from James, describing him as a good man dealt a bad hand. Mary found this line most disturbing, knowing that her niece cared little for card play. Her making such a reference seemed far out of place.

Reading on, Mary learned that Elizabeth had confided in the Sisters of St. Leo's looking for some guidance to help deal with the troublesome dreams. The nuns insisted she destroy the globe, but Elizabeth refused stating, "There was some good attached to it, after all, it was a gift to her mother from her dearest friend." Mary had heard similar words from Nora, defending the continued existence of the damn thing to Matthew when she had awakened screaming in the night.

As time went on James lost faith in his father's words. The good woman he had found had left him despite how tightly he had held her; despite all his love, she was gone. He plunged into his work and into the bottle, trying to dull the pain that ate him up inside. He did as his wife had instructed him and took care of Rose, seeing that she was well cared for by the nuns or by Eleanor Lenore, but rarely by him. Together they kept the child healthy and safe.

One night when Rose was still a child, she awoke crying, complaining to her father of having a very bad dream. James grabbed hold of the little girl's shoulders, squeezing her tightly. He brought her to his face. She smelled the distasteful stench of alcohol upon his hot breath. His dark eyes flamed in anger.

"You have taken my beloved from me, and for that I'll never forgive ya!" said James to his daughter. "If ya waken me once more with your bellyaching, I'll stuff one of me dirty socks in your mouth and string ya to the bed." James dropped the child and she ran into her room to hide beneath her blanket where she cried herself to sleep.

The next day her father moved Rose to the small spare bedroom off the kitchen, wishing to distance the child from him so that he would not be disturbed again. The nightmares continued, but Rose never again sought her father's help or comfort. Hiding beneath her blankets provided little salvation from her dreams or her reality. She kept a photo of her mother on her nightstand, often holding it to her heart and wishing her mother had lived, believing life would have been much different, loving her mother despite never having met her.

Rose Aileene McGill grew up without a mother, living with a father who despised her. Eleanor Lenore acted as a surrogate grandmother, often caring for Rose when her father was incapable. Rose found little pleasure in anything, but she did like going to school at St. Leos. She was a sullen child, whose dark black hair often needed brushing and her clothes often needing mending. The older nuns, like Sister Marion, sat with Rose, telling her stories about her mother, her grandparents, and the Flora-Dora girls. Rose would sit on the concrete steps across from the church, the only remnants of the dress shop her aunts had owned, left behind by the fire.

She made two friends at school, Pattie Wells, the daughter of Jeremy, and Bernie Wells, and Valerie Koley, the daughter of a Ukrainian couple. Her father too was a miner and knew of James, but had no acquaintance with the man. The girls brought Rose out of her shell to the dismay of the nuns. They were a troublesome trio, playfully mischievous, disruptive, and belligerent. Pattie's parents were happy to meet young Rose having known Elizabeth, but they soon became annoyed having to be summoned to the school multiple times regarding the actions of their daughter and her friends.

As the trio reached puberty, Pattie and Valerie blossomed much sooner than Rose did. This new development got the girls into trouble. Pattie and Valerie where taking the lunch money from the schoolboys in the playground for peeks at there breasts. This went on for nearly a month before the nuns caught wind of it. The good sisters were appalled and shocked at such goings on at their little school. The newly named schoolmaster, Sister Marion, had little choice, but to expel the two girls. This saddened Rose, leaving her with no friends at school at all.

Summer breaks turned Rose into a prisoner, cooped up in her house day after day, confined to her solitude. At age seven or eight James began having his daughter do the cooking and cleaning of the house, telling her she needed to carry her weight. She dusted and did the dishes. She learned how to clean the coal dust from her father's clothes, no easy task for a small girl. She prepared her fathers meals, and everything had to be done before James arrived home from the mines no matter what time this might be. If she happened to doze he'd scream her awake, calling her a useless and lazy brat who would be better off dead. She was never allowed to eat with her father, getting the few measly scraps he would leave behind. She made up for this by stealing morsels as she cooked since he was not at home when she prepared his dinner.

The anniversary of Elizabeth's passing was a particularly hard day. Though James often returned home drunk, on these days he became an angry drunk. Rose hid in her little room, frightened at what her father might do to her. He never harmed, well never struck her, always remembering what his father had taught him about hitting women and children.

He pounded on Rose's door, ranting, blaming her for the death of Elizabeth. Rose curled herself up in the farthest corner of her room, guilt ridden over something she had no control over, missing a woman she never knew, but somehow loved with all her heart. She clung to her mother's picture, hoping that would protect her, not only from her father, but also from the horrible nightmares that tormented her.

James had begun playing cards on Friday nights, first at the speak-easy across the street, then bringing the game and all its players' home with him when the bar got too crowded. The fact that he had a child at home mattered nothing to him. He kicked in the front door, set his pickaxe beside the kitchen counter. He pulled the kitchen table into the living room and gave each player a tumbler full of whiskey before settling in to a nightlong drunkard's poker game.

In June, just after school let out for summer break, Rose began working at a small flower shop around the corner from their home. Mrs. Lilly Cunningham owned the shop. She had been friends with Elizabeth and her parents were friends with Rose's grandparents, Matthew and Nora. Her husband Kevin Cunningham worked in the mines along side James and played in the Friday night poker games, to the dislike of his wife.

It had been a hot, humid summer that year but, as if someone flicked a switch, August brought with it cooler and much more tolerable weather. The first Friday of the month marked the fifteen anniversary of Elizabeth's death, Roses birthday. There was no cake with candles for Rose, just the drunken grieving of a loveless father. This Friday he would come home with his card game in tow. Rose had made him dinner. He immediately tossed it out the back door into the overgrown weeds and tangled remains of the rose bushes Elizabeth had planted so many years before.

"Let the rats eat it," he hollered, slamming the rear door shut.

Involved in the game of cards was James of course, Kevin Cunningham, Bill Bob Jenkins, BB for short, Hammer

O'Reilly, nicknamed for the way he swung a pickaxe and a weasel of a man by the name of Edgar Koski. Popeye and Koski were friends and adversaries at the same time. Whether it was cards or drinking games, James and Edgar pitted themselves against each other in fierce competition.

What bound these two men, aside from their competitive spirits, was their hatred for Lucas Nash. Nash had gotten the better of Koski in a fight, but never of James. This made Popeye McGill a good ally for Koski to align himself. He wanting revenge for the beating he had taken from Nash some years before, Popeye knew this and was glad to oblige.

The card game began as it usually did, hollering over the first hand as if the dealer had stacked the deck. It turned ugly when James made a bet he could not cover. Koski had eyes for young Rose and dared Popeye to put up an hour with his daughter to cover the bet on the table. Kevin Cunningham objected to the notion, but could do nothing. James's mind did not consider the idea long before agreeing to the bet. Koski took the hand. James cocked a crooked finger, pointing to his daughter's bedroom. Koski knocked back his whiskey and wiped a dirty hand across his lips before leaving the table.

James refilled the glasses, staring with deep and desolate eyes into his own before drinking. "We can play four for a little bit, don'tcha thinks gents", stated James, shuffling the deck. James never looked up from his cards, nor did the men sitting beside him. If they had they would of have seen the soulless monster dealing a black hand.

Rose was hiding beneath her blanket clutching the photo of her mother when she heard the twisting of the doorknob. Koski entered Rose's room and sat on the bed. He folded back the blankets and pulled the picture from the little girl's hands, setting it on the table. Rose saw the distorted face of Koski in the moonlight spilling in through the window.

Rose wanted to scream, but feared her father would stuff his dirty sock in her mouth for doing so. She lay still as the man ran his grimy hand along the edge of the bed. Rose inched away, avoiding the touch of his fingers. When Koski's hands moved towards Rose, she shut her eyes. Putting herself in a distant place, she tried hard not to think or feel.

However, she could not distance her sense of smell. The stench of stale alcohol seeped from his pores and the moldy rot of the mines dripped off his skin. Rose gagged as the rank order coming from the filthy body of Koski sickened her.

Once he had finished, Koski let go of the girl and pulled up his pants. He warned Rose that she must never speak of what had just occurred. His father hadn't preached to him about harming women or children. Koski had no qualms with doing either. He left Rose two dollars on her nightstand. After the man left, Rose opened her window and vomited into the bushes. She had a pitcher of water and a glass on her dresser. She gargled with it and spit up again.

From that night, and every Friday night to follow, James made the bet. Sometimes, more than once, and on the worst of nights each of the men took their turn with Rose. Not James, he would get darker and bitterer with each passing Friday. His conscience in the voice of Elizabeth twisted his mind and his actions burned the dregs of his soul.

Rose, who had before pitied and feared her father, now loathed him. By the end of each Friday card game Rose wore the black soot of the miners and every Saturday morning she did her best to scrub it away, but she was stained, colored black by the touch each man that took their pleasures with her. No matter how long or hard she scoured she could never get clean.

Each of them left a few dollars on the nightstand as some absurd means of clearing their conscience. Rose took the money and hid it beneath a loose floorboard under her bed. She began to think of it as a means to an end. She counted the money every Saturday morning after cleaning up the mess from the night before, dreaming of escaping to somewhere beyond the dirty hands of the miners and far away from her father. She learned to stop the men before they would orgasm inside her, not wanting to get pregnant. Rose kept pitchers of clean water in her room, wiping away as much of each man's grime as she could and asked for more money if they tried to do anything out of the ordinary.

The abuse continued for years. Rose grew into a beautiful young woman, looking exactly like her mother and her grandmother before her. However, her dark blue eyes did not bare the same spark of life. Her face wore no smile, her cheeks no subtle blush. She had grown complacent to the dreams that grew more and more intense, believing nothing could be more terrifying than the life she now endured.

At seventeen, just days before graduation, the usual Friday night card game began without Kevin Cunningham. The players in the game changed all the time, but Kevin never missed a Friday night. He paid Rose the most for her services, and for her silence. A new player followed James into the living room, taking the seat across the table from Popeye and Koski, the seat usual reserved for Kevin Cunningham. The man was Lucas Nash.

Nash was at the pub waving around a wad of bills he had received for the sale of his house. He boasted about finally being able to leave this dirty town and had a ticket on the morning train headed west. Popeye McGill and Koski overheard Nash, seeing the roll he had stuffed in his hip pocket and cooked up a plan to separate the fat man from his money. Before they could invite him into the game, Nash approached their table, bragging on about his newfound prosperity. James offered him a seat at the table, asking him to join in the game. Nash won the next four hands before the group decided to move the game to Popeye's place.

Nash had already gotten comfortable when he took notice of Rose standing in the kitchen. He climbed out of his chair and stepped up to her introducing himself as "Laguska Natanuski," adding, "Or as your father knows me, Lucas Nash." His thick Slovak accent had deepened with age and from the dust of the coalmines.

He glared at Rose, looking her up and down while the other men set up the table for the night's game, "You are quite beautiful, like your mother and your aunts, except for that one, Mary. Ah, she was quite a tiger I recall; different, but still beautiful."

"You knew my family?" Rose asked surprised by what this odd, obese, troll of a man had said.

"Yes, I knew them, well it was not like we were ever, how do you say? Formally introduced or anything. We came to this country many years ago on the same ship," he answered, "Your father did not know that, but some how I think you do." He pointed to the scar across his face and nodded.

A chill ran through Rose. Her disturbing familiarity with this grotesque man, made her stomach churn, although she did not know why. Popeye yelled for Nash to come to the table, putting an end to a most sinister introduction of Lucas Nash to Rose McGill. She bid the men goodnight and went to her room. After approximately an hour, she realized she had not filled her pitchers, distracted by the strange new player in the game.

She slipped quietly from her room and into the kitchen with a pitcher in each hand. While she filled the first vessel, she overheard the conversation at the table turning angry. Accusations and denials flew back and forth. Nash believed James and his friend Koski to be cheating, which they fiercely denied. Nash lifted his large body from his chair, brandishing a dark barreled revolver and shot Popeye between the eyes, dead. Koski took a bullet to the throat. Blood gurgled from his mouth as he rocked back in his chair and crashed to the floor. A third bullet ripped through Hammer O'Reilly as he dove for cover.

Suddenly a loud thud stilled the room and Nash went face first into the card table. Glasses of whiskey spilled to the floor as playing cards and poker chips flew out in all directions. Rose had picked up her fathers pickaxe from where he had left it, leaning against the kitchen counter just inside the back door. She stepped in and drove it into the back of Nash's skull. He too was dead, as was Koski, but much more slowly than her father or Lucas Nash. Bill Bob Jenkins, spared from the violence, went to the aid of Hammer who was bleeding from the bullet wound in his shoulder.

Rose stood over Nash's fallen body, gazing down at what she had done. She looked at her father, still seated in his chair, a long dark stream of blood rolling down his face and dripping onto his dirty shirt, his eyes opened wider than she had ever seen. Koski's body twitched as his blood formed a puddle around him. Hammer and BB stared at Rose in shock, waiting for her to do or say something.

The smoke from the gun and two-bit cigars hung across the room. Minutes passed like hours, the silence broken by the sound of sirens whining ever closer. Hammer and BB, hearing the police cars approaching, bolted for the back door. The two men did not get very far. The police caught them on Main Street a few steps from the house.

Rose looked around as the first officers entered the house. "Now I've got to clean this mess up!" she stated stoically, avoiding the blood that flowed closer to her bare feet.

The police officer snapped handcuffs on Rose and moved her onto the stairs, removing her from the path of the red river that flooded the room. Outside a crowd gathered. The news of the murders skipped from one bar to the next that dotted the small borough of Ashley. More officers arrived, cordoning off the McGill house, stopping onlookers and reporters alike from entering the crime scene.

Rose sat silently staring out through the open door at the shocked faces of her neighbors, wishing only for the officers to shut the door, not being able to tolerate the glares of damnation. The scent of a strange wind blew through the open door, passing a twisted comb through Rose's raven hair. She straightened up; realizing freedom had come to her at last in a way she could never have foreseen.

The final cops to appear in the McGill living room were two plain clothed detectives who came in through the back entrance. The first was a tall dark haired man with a five o'clock shadow and deep piercing brown eyes. The other had thick blonde curls and fare skin. Both had on dress shirts with the sleeves rolled up to the elbows and cheap looking ties. The lighter haired detective had a baby face, what Amanda Collins would call cute. The darker officer had a rougher more serious look to him. They scanned the room before the blonde-haired dick approached Rose.

"Are you all right?" he asked.

Rose took a few seconds before answering, "Yes, I'm fine."

Rose was better than fine, she was free. Free of a father who turned his own daughter into a whore. Free of a life not worth living. She felt empowered, knowing she could do or be whatever she chose. This sudden strength filled her to overflowing and she liked it.

The detective continued, "I am officer Bob Sheridan, my partner is detective Billy Wilson. We are here to help you. Can you tell us what happened?"

Rose smirked.

Detective Wilson, who was still panning the room, jerked his head towards Rose. "You find something funny?" he asked, rather annoyed with her demeanor.

"Bill Bob was the name of one of the players in the poker game, is all," she answered, her blue eyes peering through her bangs.

The officers failed to see the humor in it. "Is that Bill Bob Jenkins? Is he the one who did this?" asked Officer Sheridan with some surprise.

"He didn't do nothin, just sat there like he wasn't even in the room," replied Rose as a lost expression engulfed her.

"You sure you're OK," detective Sheridan repeated.

"Yes, I already told ya, I'm fine," Rose snipped. "Surin ya need to be listenin if you're gonna hear something."

Rose rarely spoke with an Irish brogue, surprising herself with the sound of the words rolling off her tongue. She saw her reflection in the eyes of detective Sheridan, unsure of her own image. She threw her head back, flipping the strands of hair off her face and then turned to look at Officer Wilson who was staring at the tool protruding from Nash's head.

She proceeded to tell the officers what transpired, recapping the night's events in as much detail as she could recall, excluding the water pitchers, and hoping they would not discover the line of them in her room. Officer Sheridan, after hearing Rose's account, removed the handcuffs. A group of men in white medical coats bagged up the bodies and took them away, her fathers being last. Officers Wilson and Sheridan watched Rose as the men from the coroner's office carted out her father. They thought it odd that she showed no emotion, no tears, just a cold stare. Rose's reaction seemed out of place, like a puzzle piece that did not quite fit the picture.

The detectives took Rose to the police station where BB Jenkins and Hammer O'Reilly were telling their story. Upon seeing Rose appear in the squad room, both shut up, looking anxiously at Rose. The blonde baby faced detective asked Rose to sit, pulling up a chair beside his desk. Rose glared at the two men who had raped her more times than she could remember. A rye smile formed on her face and she winked at the two men. The smile and wink told BB and Hammer that she did not intend to reveal what they had done. Both men struggled not to show relief, going back to their recounting of the nights tragic and bloody event.

Once the detectives felt satisfied that Rose had told the truth, they released her from custody. Detective Sheridan drove Rose home. Her side of the double-block house remained a crime scene, taped off and padlocked. The door to the vacant apartment had a broken lock and the police officer easily forced it open. Rose thanked him for his help and he warned her not to disturb anything on the other side. He explained to Rose, she would be allowed in when the police completed their investigation. She told the young detective that she understood, thanked him again for his help, and bid him goodnight.

Rose watched through the front window as officer Sheridan drove off. Once sure detective Sheridan was out of sight and there existed no threat that he might return, Rose went to the second floor bedroom that faced the front of the house. She climbed out through the window, went across the front porch roof, and jimmied open the window that opened into what had once been her bedroom. The latch on the window had been broken since she was a child some thirteen years ago.

She went part way down the stairs then slid carefully over the rail onto a cabinet beside the staircase and hopped into the kitchen, avoiding the blood pool in the living room. Rose went to her room and removed all the water pitchers, storing them under the kitchen sink. Returning to her room, Rose Aileene pried open the loose floorboard beneath her bed, taking the stack of bills she banked there and replaced the plank. She wrapped a rubber band around the money and returned to the opposite side apartment to spend a long chilly night on the dusty sofa that had been left there by the last tenants.

Chapter 15

Black Rose

Between the horrific bloody episode and the haunting dreams, Rose barely slept that night. She lay on the couch, projecting patterns in the cracks of the plastered ceiling while wondering what life held for her next. It seemed she had just fallen asleep, when someone began tapping at the front door. Rose sat up on the edge of the couch, shivering in the chill of the morning. She wiped her eyes, watching the dust swirl and sway in the sunlight filling the room through the windows to the east. As she watched, menacing forms took shape in the grainy haze, frightening figures tortured and screaming for help. Another more insistent rap at the door broke the spell that held Rose still, affixed on visions she could not understand.

"Who would be knocking at the door this early," she asked herself while bending forward and throwing back her long black tangled hair. "Possibly the police," she thought, "wanting to continue their investigation. On the other hand, maybe, it is BB and Hammer released from jail, come to beg for my continued silence and forgiveness for the things they had done; possibly someone from the colliery or old Chester Lenore and his wife."

All these things ran through Rose's mind in the brief moments before answering the door. To her surprise, it was none of these, but her schoolyard friends Patty Wells and Valerie Koley. They had heard the reports of the murders on the radio and seen the morning headlines in the Wilkes-Barre Leader. Concerned for their friend and compelled by a twisted sense of curiosity, the girls found their way to Rose's door ahead of the pack of reporters and thrill seekers that poured down upon the McGill house that day.

Rose was very happy to see her friends. They too were glad to see her, and in much better condition than they imagined considering the news reports. Patty, who stood slightly taller than Rose did, wrapped her arms around her friends shoulders, while Valerie, who stood a mere five feet three inches tall, hugged both girls about the waist. Feeling the chill in Rose, Patty removed her jacket and draped it around her.

"Damn cold out for June," Patty said, holding onto her friend. "What in the hell happened here Rose?"

"Let's get some breakfast and I'll give ya all the gory details," Rose responded.

Rose found an old comb and a bar of soap in the upstairs bathroom and cleaned herself up as much as she could. She peeled a few dollars from her stash that she had hidden in a box behind the old claw foot tub. The girls hopped the morning trolley to the Hart Lunch where Rose bought the girls' breakfast. She proceeded to tell her friends with graphic detail what had occurred the night before.

Shocked and disgusted, Valerie nearly lost her breakfast, heaving as she ran to the restroom. The girls, seeing their friend sickened by the scene Rose's words painted, laughed aloud to the sharp-eyed disapproval of some of the other patrons of the restaurant. Patty was much less abashed at Rose's experience, asking more questions, requiring her to expand on the gruesome particulars.

By the time the girls returned to the McGill house many police officers and reporters were on the scene, including the two detectives. Rose pointed the men out to her friends from the trolley as it slowed to let them off. The handsome young detectives impressed both Patty and Valerie. They made sexually inappropriate comments that some old women overheard. Appalled by the lewd and indecent behavior of the girls, the women exited the trolley immediately. The two girls laughed boisterously, but not Rose, knowing the one bit of information she had not revealed to her friends.

Rose asked her friends to go home, not wanting them to get involved in a mess that did not concern them. The girls wanted to stay and to support their friend, but obeyed her request. They assured her they would come back when things settled down. Rose thanked them for being there for her before slipping down from the trolley and into the street.

Accosted by half a dozen news reporters, all with notepads and worn down pencils looking for the scoop, Rose froze. The two detectives interceded, taking Rose by the arms and guiding her through the salivating pack into the vacant side of the house, shutting the door behind them. Officer Wilson began grilling Rose again, focusing on why she did not seem to care that her father and his friend Edgar Koski had been shot dead right in front of her. Rose did not answer. Sheridan sat down on the couch beside Rose and put his arm around her.

"We know you're frightened, but we can't help you unless you talk to us," he told Rose in a soothing tone, playing the good cop to his partners bad.

Rose hesitated a while before answering. Seeing Officer Wilson pacing and getting more anxious and frustrated with every passing second, "I disliked my father and his friend," she blurted suddenly.

"Why did you dislike them Rose?" Officer Sheridan asked.

She told the officers, "My father has hated me since I was born, since me mother died giving birth. He blamed it on me. All my life he blamed it on me as if I could a done something to stop it. Koski was just a pig. I didn't like em just because I didn't like em and for no other reason than that."

The detectives asked more questions of Rose with the same results. Maybe they suspected something, but they were not getting it from Rose. She held tight and consistent with her story, never letting on about the Friday night sex toy she had become. Whether it was shame or something else that kept her secret, even Rose was not sure, but she never revealed it; not to the detectives or anyone else. The police had their answers for the card game that turned bloody. No mystery existed there, so the officers closed the book on the investigation; still wondering if there wasn't more to be told.

Rose cleaned up the mess in the old apartment, discarding the blood stained couch, kitchen table, and chairs, the soaked area rug and her father's throne. The things she chose to keep she moved to the vacant side of the double-block house. This was her home and only hers from now on.

Rose knew she needed things. The paint on the walls of the formerly vacant apartment was cracked and peeling. The left over furniture had tares and smelled of must along with some foul scent she could not identify. Making a list, she visited the stores along Main Street. The drug store for personal items, the hardware store for paints and brushes, and her grandfather's old sundry shop for anything she could not get at the other two stores.

The shop, now named Kolb's Varieties, had not changed much over the years. Possibly a few more lights not working and maybe more dust on the high shelves, but it was not so different from when Matthew and Nora ran the place so many years before. As Rose brought the few items, mostly cleaning products, to the counter she noticed a framed photo just off to the right near the cash register. Dora Kolb was working the counter. She looked at Rose as Rose leaned in to get a better look at the couple in the picture.

"Glory be! Ya look just like her!" Dora hollered. "It's like I'm seein a ghost."

"She is my grandmother", Rose said calmly, adding, "These are my grandparents, I think?"

Mr. Kolb, hearing his wives shouts, came shuffling up the aisle from the rear storeroom and stood beside Dora. Seeing Rose, his reaction mirrored that of his wife. He removed his spectacles, wiped them in his apron, and looked again.

"What are ya goin on about Dora?" He asked.

"This girl looks exactly like the woman in the picture," his wife replied. "She says the folks are her grandparents."

Rose asked the old couple why they had a photo of her grandparents hanging in their store. Mr. Kolb explained that it was hanging there when they bought the place. He said, "They looked so much in love that," putting his arms around Dora, who finished his thought, "It touched us deary. You could feel it. It's as if their love was captured in the picture and each time we look at it, Billy and I, well, we feel it too."

Rose ran her fingertips softly across the dust-covered glass. She gazed into the faces of Matthew and Nora, hoping to feel what the Kolb's felt. "From the stories she had heard about her grandparents, for this couple to feel their love in a photograph might just be true," thought Rose. For a brief fleeting moment, she thought she did sense something, but just as quickly as she realized the feeling; it disappeared.

"If you want the picture deary, it's yours to have," Dora said, secretly hoping the girl would not accept her gift. Dora's husband echoed the gesture.

"No," Rose decided, adding, "Maybe someday I'll return for it, but if ya would, can ya just leave it where it's at. It seems right to have it here."

Rose returned to the house with her arms full of bags. Old Chester and Eleanor Lenore where sitting on the front steps awaiting her return. They each took a bag, allowing Rose to free a hand to push open the front door. Once they had deposited the bags across the kitchen counter, Eleanor gave Rose a bear hug, whimpering over the death of James. Rose returned a faint unemotional squeeze and stepped away to store the items she had purchased. As she began to do so, Chester reached into his shirt pocket and pulled out an envelope, handing it to Rose.

"Your Dad had a life insurance policy through the mining company and when Elizabeth, well, when your mom died, he made Eleanor and me benefactors. We never thought it was right how he treated you and we feel you should have it."

She opened the envelope to find four thousand dollars in cash. Her elation over receiving such a large some of money quickly turned bitter cold. Her father did not want her to have it. She considered handing the money back to Chester, but instead reconsidered. "If this was something my father didn't want me to have," she thought, "then I'm keeping it!"

Chester added, "Now, some of this money will need to go to burying your father. Eleanor and I can make those arrangements if ya like."

Rose agreed to allow the old couple to take care of the funeral. Partially, because she knew nothing of doing such things, but also, because they had cared for the man much more than she did. The day of her graduation, as her classmates took the stage in the small recreation hall beneath St. Leo's Church, Rose laid her father to rest.

The service was short with very few mourners in attendance. The Lenore's were there, the sister of St. Leo's brought Sister Agnes, who was recovering from a stroke and appeared old and feeble. The Wells family, Valerie Koley, a few miners who Rose recognized from some Fridays past came to the cemetery. Amanda Collins-Dwight arrived with her third husband, Francis and stood beside Rose during the service.

Listening to the priest's final words, Rose resisted the urge to spit on the casket. The church bells of St. Leo's chimed and a misty rain began to fall as the box sunk into its hole. Amanda placed her arm around Rose's shoulder. It had been more than ten years since they had seen each other and Rose barely knew her, but she was aware that Amanda had been her mother's best friend, and appreciate the comforting touch. The last of the handful of mourners to pay their respects to Rose were the miners. They shook her hand and nodded, shuffling past, but never making eye contact, mainly because of their shame, but also because of Amanda.

Amanda had transformed from a pretty, playful schoolgirl into a beautiful woman. Her tall sleek body had filled out admirably. Amanda's long wavy blonde hair flowed over her shoulders, framing a flawless face. The miners felt unworthy to set eyes upon her. And Amanda, as she always did, played upon their frailty. She removed the thin piece of black lace that was pinned to her hair, covering her face to just above her ruby red lips and tossed her hair to one side. The simple men gulped, nearly swallowing their tongues as Amanda looked down then slowly up in their direction from the corner of her eye.

Rose studied every move Amanda made, watching how she turned the already weak-minded diggers into clumsy fools. She also paid attention to Amanda's husband Francis, who spent more time checking his watch than watching his wife. Amanda knew well how to manipulate the opposite sex, exploiting their basic urges to get what she wanted. In the case of her husband it was his ego, needing to have the most beautiful woman on his arm whether he knew what to do with her or not. Rose would not forget what she learned from her mother's friend that day.

After the funeral service, Rose returned home. Much work still needed to be done to make the place livable and comfortable. The extra money she received from the insurance policy would go a long way to solving that. There were still items on one side of the house that Rose wanted shifted to the other, things too heavy for her to move by herself. She contacted the company that had removed and disposed of the blood stained furniture. They agreed to do the lifting and shifting for an acceptable fee. Within a week's time the place was painted, polished, and refurbished.

Rose too, need a clean up. She washed and brushed the knots from her hair, cutting out the worst of the tangles. She spent a day shopping for new cloths, tossing most of what she had in the trash. Soon she looked and felt like a new woman and a new woman she would be, to an extent.

Rose kept her fathers big brass bed, but replaced the mattress and box spring with one she ordered from the Sears catalog. She also moved her little double bed to the spare room off the kitchen in the new apartment, replacing the mattress and box the same way. She kept the large dresser and chest of drawers and a full-length wood framed mirror that hung at the end of the upstairs hall. She found both her mother and grandmothers wedding gowns shoved in the back of a closet. Rose was amazed at the fine detail, especially of her grandmother's dress, which still had a few brown dried up rose petals clinging to it.

As she cleaned out the last of her parent's things, she found a stack of unopened letters in a case beneath her father's bed, along with some old photos of people she did not know. In addition to the other items, she found an old wooden box. She opened the envelopes first. Each was a notice from Michelle and Joshua Addison informing her father of the passing of her mother Elizabeth's Aunts and Uncle David. The postmarks spanned a ten-year period, with an account of Mary's passing being the latest. She opened the lid to the old wooden box last. There she found a water globe containing a black rose. She took a cloth and wiped away the dust, mesmerized by its haunting beauty. A chill ran down her spine and her hands trembled. She set the oddity down on the nightstand, knocking down a pile of papers.

Once her senses returned, she began cleaning up the notes that had spilled to the floor. At first, she paid no attention to what was written on them, but for some strange reason she stopped and began to read. The scribbling of her father professed a dread that came to him in the night darkening his dreams, terrifying a man who for all accounts feared nothing. Reading further, she recollected the nightmares that plagued her, the ones for which her father showed no sympathy. She now would have none for him and tossed the papers in the trash.

In a short month, Rose painted, polished, and shined, transforming the dingy McGill house into a quaint, contemporary home worth living in. The last piece of furniture Rose placed in her living room was a tall glass curio. She set her mother's picture on the top shelf beside the mysterious water globe. She used other whatnots to fill the empty shelves, with a small plain water pitcher occupying the last level.

Rose threw out anything that reminded her of her father; except for his pickaxe, which the police returned to her once they had closed the case. She put this beside the bed in the spare bedroom. While cleaning out the cabinets, Rose found a half-empty crystal decanter tucked in behind a line of empty or near empty liquor bottles. She sat back in her new wing backed chair, working off the top of the bottle, taking a nose full and thinking. She knew the taste from the tongues shoved in her mouth by the men who raped her. She certainly recognized its smell, the odor that oozed from her father's pores with his sweat and the underlying stench of every man who climbed into her bed on Friday nights.

Looking over her shoulder, she spied the calendar on the kitchen wall. It was Friday. She poured the whiskey into a tall glass, swirled it about and drank, choking on the first mouthful. A warm feeling circulated through her, running down her legs into her toes. Each swig afterward went down much more smoothly.

After finishing the tumbler of Irish whiskey, which was not her fathers, but her grandfathers, she fell into a deep sleep. She began to dream, seeing much more clearly the images of the black rose, blood slowly seeping from the pistil onto the velvety black petals. The blood dripped in single droplets from perfectly shaped edges and splashing into the white of eyes in rage. A shadowy image of a man swinging fists violently roused Rose from her slumber. She rubbed her eyes and stood up, nearly falling, wobbly from the alcohol. She went to the kitchen sink, splashed water on her face, and took a deep breath, trying to make some sense of her dream.

A knock on the door startled her back to reality. "Who would be calling on her this late at night?" She questioned.

Pulling back the curtain, Rose saw Kevin Cunningham standing on her front porch. She opened the inside door and stared at him through the screen door. Cunningham looked frightened, apologizing to Rose for disturbing her so late in the evening. He asked if he could come in to speak with her for just a moment. Rose thought about it, saying nothing and then opened the door just enough for Mr. Cunningham to get in. He cautiously closed the door behind him, his eyes locked on Rose as she poured a shot of whiskey and knocked it back.

"What is it that you want? "Barked Rose with her back turned to the cowardly man. She knew what he wanted. He wasn't there to apologize, as if he could. Or pay his condolences, which he should have done a month ago. No, it was Friday night and old habits die hard. Kevin Cunningham sat on the sofa as Rose went to the kitchen for another glass. She poured a whiskey for him and another for herself, not saying a word. Rose threw her jet-black hair back, looking down and slowly up into the eyes of Cunningham who nearly spilled his drink.

She finished her drink and took the man into the spare bedroom off the kitchen.

"Give me your wallet," Rose ordered.

Cunningham handed it over to her. She emptied it; taking every dollar he had and placed it on the nightstand.

"That is all the money I have", protested Cunningham, adding, "You know my wife, she will have my ass."

Rose smiled a rye unsympathetic smile. She was in control now and Kevin Cunningham's words cemented her position. The wrath of the wives raised the price of the pleasure desired by the pathetic men of Ashley.

"Would you prefer I tell your wife why you came to my house?" asked Rose, "Or maybe I should just call my detective friends and reveal the truth about your Friday night poker games?"

Kevin Cunningham said nothing. Rose pushed him back on the bed and pulled his pants to his ankles. Dropping to her knees, she dug her nails along Cunningham's inner thighs, leaving behind four long thin red scratches on each leg. She grabbed hold of him fiercely. He stiffened with her touch. Rose proceeded to do willingly what Edgar Koski and so many dirty bastards had done to her for so many Friday nights in the past. Cunningham discharged quickly. Rose wiped her lips with his shirt. Afterwards she told him she would be available on Friday nights for anyone willing to pay her price and pushed the man out the door.

"Look for the light to be on," she yelled to Cunningham who staggered on weakened legs across the crumbling red brick street to the pub.

Fridays at Rosie's became a regular stop for the miners, spending their hard-earned money for pleasures only Rose could provide. Her reputation spread rapidly, soon having too many callers for one night alone, expanding her business hours to include Saturday nights too. Rose bathed herself in the black dust of the miners, earning her the nickname 'Black Rose'. A name she would relish as she counted her money each weekend.

She continued to work during the day with Lilly Cunningham at the florist shop. The men of Ashley, for as simple as they seemed, kept the Black Rose a secret, shared only amongst themselves. Lilly Cunningham remained unaware of what her husband and his colleagues spent their paychecks on each weekend, but Lilly Cunningham was getting angry. Often Rose would overhear her boss complaining to the other women of the neighborhood about her husband most suddenly not providing for the family. These women shared the same complaint.

It was a Tuesday afternoon when a young woman came into the florist shop looking for an arrangement to bring to a friend in the hospital. Lilly greeted her pleasantly, chatting over what types of flowers she liked while showing her vases. When the woman spied Rose, straightening some display pieces behind the counter, her eyes opened wide and she whispered something into Mrs. Cunningham's ear. At first Lilly protested, objecting to the preposterous possibility that this woman might be speaking the truth. Soon her expression changed from disbelief to anger.

The woman left the store without purchasing the flowers as Lilly turned her attentions to Rose. She stared Rose in the eyes. Rose had no clue that her secret was out, asking her boss what the woman said to make her so angry. Mrs. Cunningham said nothing and then slapped Rose across the face with all her strength. Rose saw the pain in the woman's eyes, but offered no apology. She turned her a little, wicked, rye smile while rubbing the reddening side of her face.

A mischievous, deceitful look appeared in Rose's eyes. She unpinned her hair, shaking her head, letting her dark locks fall loosely about her shoulders. The dust of the day drifted between the two women. Lilly stepped back, realizing she did not know the person who now stood before her.

"I wouldn't of believed it, but now I see it's true," Lilly said bitterly. "You need to leave my shop and keep away from my husband!"

Rose let out a sadistic chuckle, "It's you that needs to keep your mister away from me. Why don't you ask him, see if he'll tell ya the truth. As for that woman. I don't know who her man is, but I'm sure he is as guilty as the rest."

Mrs. Cunningham chased Rose out of the shop, calling her "whore" and "slut"; telling her that she had brought shame to the name of a good family. Rose thought this funny. Knowing she was all that was left of her family and felt more bitterness and resentment for being left alone than shame. Now a different tale radiated through the streets of Ashley regarding young Rose McGill, this one had teeth. The wives made sure Rose was outcast. From the churches, from stores along the street, including Kolb's Varieties, even restaurants would not allow her a seat.

Patty and Valerie heard the words as well and went to see Rose, wanting to know if what people were saying was true. Patty thrilled at knowing the stories were accurate. Her parents had been giving Patty a very hard time about the parade of boys she had been taking up with and she wanted to escape their constant interference. Rose offered her the old apartment, knowing Patty did not care about the murders that had occurred there.

Rose uncorked a bottle of rye whiskey given to her by the bartender across the street for services rendered. Patty and Valerie had never drunk alcohol of any kind. Aware of this, Rose started them off with small amounts cut with water. Soon the girls were drinking straight from the bottle, laughing and talking about sex.

Valerie, despite her indecent exposure in the playground of St. Leo's, had done little more than fondling with a boy. She feared not knowing what to do and feared the wrath of her father if he ever found out. Patty laughed, counting off the boys she had been with and detailing rather graphically, what she had done with each.

After a brief silence, Rose offered to show Valerie how to touch a man. Valerie was drunk and confused, but agreed. Rose took her friend's hand and led her to the spare bedroom. She kissed Valerie on the right side of her neck and then the left. She unbuttoned Valerie's blouse and began softly massaging her breasts, running her fingers across her nipples until they were firm. Patty brought a chair in from the kitchen and sat back in the corner watching.

Rose finished disrobing Valerie and then disrobed herself. Standing in the sunlight of the window, she eased her right hand between Valerie's legs, while squeezing her left breast and biting lightly on her neck. Valerie said no with a moan and turned to face Rose. They fell back on the bed together and Rose slid her head down between her friend's legs, forcing her thighs apart. Patty began touching herself as Rose licked her way down Valerie until her tongue stung her excitedly. Valerie's back arched and she writhed in pleasure until one final moan and then collapsed on the bed exhausted.

Afterward, Rose told Valerie in a most businesslike manner, "If you make a man feel like that, you are doin it right."

Patty grabbed the bottle of whiskey and bounced onto the bed. There between her friends she shouted, "We are going to have such a good time" and took a big drink from the bottle, which she choked on and spit in a spray across the room. Patty's actions ignited a roar of laughter from her friends. With a gleeful smile that bordered on the diabolical, Rose pulled the bottle from Patty and drank.

Chapter 16

May I Introduce To You

The story of Black Rose spread through the quiet streets of Ashley like the Susquehanna River on a bad day, leaving behind a muddy film in its wake. The neighborhood women had the idea that they could put a stop to Rose's business practices by defaming her to the decent folk of the community. Their actions had an opposite effect. Rose had more knocks on her door than she had ever had before. Now it wasn't just the miners coming to call. It was businessmen, railroaders, dentists, and mail carriers; even a few women appeared at her door seeking the services of Black Rose. Men and women with more money, able to pay a higher price; Rose reveled in the profits of a bad reputation.

With the help of Rose, Patty moved in to the left side of the double-block house in just a few days time. Jeremy and Bernie Wells were infuriated at their daughter. Not just for leaving home, but also for moving into the McGill house. They had heard the stories, first disbelieving, having known Rose since she was a child. Then they became fearful for Rose, wondering what could have turned her to do such unmentionable things. Now with their own daughter following down the same path, they became angry, blaming Black Rose for the cause of their daughter's rebellious indecency.

Rose explained to Patty about what to expect from the men that came to her for pleasure. She told Patty, "Never to trust them, get the money up front, and never ever let them hurt you."

Patty questioned Rose on the last part.

Rose explained, "Usually the men are drunk. This is their version of courage; otherwise, they wouldn't step out on their women. Sometimes they are doin it because they're mad about something. Maybe their wife pissed em off, or their boss or some other shit. That don't give em the right to be takin it out on us."

"I keep my axe handy and in plain sight," Rose added. "Those that know respect it from the start, those that ask cus' they don't know, learn quickly enough. Helps to have made the news for killin a man, keeps people fearful."

"Maybe you should kill somebody," Rose added with a laugh.

To hear Rose say this frightened Patty a little, but she was familiar enough with her friend to believe she was kidding. Still, once it was out there and seeing the changes in Rose over the years, maybe some part of her wasn't. Not many weekends passed before Patty learned first hand what Rose was talking about, witnessing an incident Patty never forgot.

Friday night began in the usual way, with the girls primping and prepping for the line of johns ready to pay for their company. Rose flipped on the porch light, signaling to the street, they were open for business. The girls sat back and waited, but not very long. Within a few minutes time they each had a customer. The parade of patrons averaged three an hour from nine p.m. to one a.m.

Just after one a.m., Patty walked her last customer to the door, giving him a spank on the ass as she shoved him out the door. Suddenly, she heard Rose screaming, shouting threats, and profanities at the top of her lungs. Patty ran through the adjoining door to find Rose and a john in the living room, both where naked. She had the man pinned against the wall, the point of her father's pickaxe inches from his face.

Patty intervened, keeping Rose from killing the man. Rose wedged the point of her axe between the man's legs and dragged him screaming onto the porch. Patty emptied his wallet and then tossed it and his cloths into the yard. Rose yelled at the man searching for his underwear in the dark, threatening to cut off his balls and deliver them personally to his wife if she ever saw him again.

The police, after receiving a complaint from the neighbors, arrived on the scene. They knew well enough about Rose. One officer rapped on the door with his nightstick while the other peered in through the front window. Rose spotted the cop in the window and undid her robe, allowing the officer a good look before covering herself up and opening the door. Promising to be a good little girl, she slipped each a cow and a calf and sent them on their way.

Rose never explained to her friend what the man did to anger her. What she knew was that Rose wanted to kill him, or at the very least maim him so that he never raised his hand to a woman again. She would have done it too, if it were not for Patty. If this happened Rose would have gone to prison for murder and Patty for prostitution.

The anniversary of Elizabeth's death came and went uncelebrated, as did Rose's birthday. As far as Rose was concerned, it was the best birthday she had ever had. That Friday night Rose took twice the number of men to her bed, while Patty built a clientele of her own. By the time Rose shut off the porch light, both girls were exhausted, blackened with soot and smelling of the sweat of their customers. Rose poured them both a drink and they curled together on the sofa, trying hard not to think about what they just did.

Saturday repeated Friday, but without so many miners. A more professional string of johns bought the time of Rose and Patty. Each weekend repeated itself, working men on Friday, and professionals on Saturday. Sunday was a day of rest, when the girls counted their profits while sharing stories about their callers.

Rose warned Patty not to like the men she took to bed. "Takin em to bed doesn't mean takin em to heart," she told her friend.

Patty was having sex because she enjoyed it. It felt great to her every time she did it. She would have done all these men free; the payments were just a bonus. Patty may have only worked weekends, but she gave it away during the week. Rose prostituted herself because she had learned to, taught by the years of abuse she endured and the men who paid for her silence. She learned what felt good, which meant everything, and how to make those things feel great.

Their friend Valerie was a frequent guest at the McGill house, but never on the weekend. She did not mind hearing the stories, mostly told by Patty, but she never joined them. She viewed sex as something shared by two people in love not a toy to be played with.

Patty and Valerie sat on the couch in Rose's living room. Rose sat perched in her high back chair, sipping a glass of whiskey on the rocks when Valerie voiced her opinion of sex to her friends. Patty laughed and grabbed hold of Valerie's breasts, playfully squeezing and fondling. Rose did not laugh or smile, thinking about Valerie's impression of sex and love. She recollected the photo of her grandparents hanging in Kolb's Varieties. Dora Kolb said love emanated from the picture.

"Maybe," thought Rose. "You have to know love to feel love?"

The only love Rose ever knew was the feeling she had when she held her mother's photograph. She had heard all the stories about Elizabeth Grace and longed to have known her, believing her mother loved her if no one else did. She moved over to sit beside Valerie, kissing her softly on the lips, something she had not done to anyone, ever. She slid her hand around her neck, kissing her harder; deeper trying to taste the love Valerie spoke of, attempting to steal it from her mouth. Patty continued to play with Valerie, caressing her hips and thighs then moving her hands to Rose. Patty moved her lips to Rose, nuzzling her soft milky white neck as Rose continued to kiss Valerie.

Rose stopped abruptly, shrugging off the two girls' affections. She stood up and walked across the room. Sipping from her glass of whiskey, Rose stared out through the kitchen window to the west. A peach sun hung in a purple sky just above the autumn hillside. The sunlight warmed her skin and washed her face in color. Patty and Valerie watched their friend, wondering why she stopped what she had started.

Rose felt empty. Valerie's words had her thinking of things she had never thought. She walked across the kitchen to the back door, watching the sunset. Her eyes focused upon the overgrown entanglement of brush that filled the backyard. There she noticed one simple red rose caught in a web of twisted branches, surrounded by sharp whitish thorns and tipped in the hue of the sky.

As she gazed at the misplaced flower, it seemed to stare back at her, begging to be free from the vines that twisted about it; strangling it. Rose threw open the kitchen door and stepped into the yard in her bare feet. The weeds wrapped about her knees and ankles, threatening to trip her with ever step. Patty and Valerie watched curiously from the doorway, wondering what had gotten into Rose's head. Patty yelled after her, but she paid no attention, completely focused on the flower.

Her mother had planted the rose bush in the farthest corner of the yard to climb along what once was a whitewashed piece of lattice propped against the fence. Rose trudged through the thickets, vines grasping at her ankles as she went. The rose bush meshed with nightshade, its poisonous red berries dangling amidst the dying leaves of the shrub, with many large black wood ants crawling along its stems.

She reached between the bent twisted branches, thorns scratching her hands and wrist, to the stem that held the rose. She bent the branch until it split, releasing the flower from its prison cell.

Rose stepped lightly through the weeds, striding smoothly, her toes barely touching the ground. She held the rose gently between her delicate fingers, just beneath her nose. The glow of the sunset bathed the yard in color. The black silhouette of Rose Aileene pressed against the blushing sky. Patty pushed open the door, letting in the twilight colors, allowing them to fill the kitchen and run across the floor into the living room.

Patty and Valerie saw a different person return from the garden. Rose stood straighter, her black hair gleamed, and her once brooding, joyless dark blue eyes now sparkled like the first stars of the night. Rose put the flower in a small, patterned glass and placed it on the top shelf of the curio beside her mother's photo, moving the water globe down a level.

Valerie, noticing her friend was cut, spoke up, "Rose, you're bleeding." She took a cloth from the cabinet near the kitchen sink, dampening it and gently dabbing the wounds clean. Rose scratched the back of her hand and pricked the tips of her fingers on the thorns guarding the rose. Small deep red droplets formed and fell in singular drips, first landing on the edge of the glass shelf, then onto the floor. Valerie took her friends' hand and wrapped it in the cloth. A dazed look blanketed Rose and she became weak in the knees. Patty caught hold of her and sat her down in her chair.

"What happened to you, girl?" Patty question as Valerie poured Rose a glass of water. "One minute you were one person and now you're someone else," continued Patty. "What gives?"

Rose had changed in ways she had not yet realized. She had begun to feel something other than anger and resentment. Could something so cliché as stopping to smell the rose have made such a difference in the life of a person who had been so lost for so many years? Possibly, it was the fates, changing the game, or just taking it in a new direction. Rose dismissed the implication, but only time would tell.

"I'm fine," she replied, "Think I just had too much to drink on an empty stomach. It is dinnertime; let's see if we can get a pizza from Frankie's then some sleep. It's going to be a busy weekend."

The girls agreed that pizza sounded good, but they were not sure if Frankie's would serve them, particularly Black Rose. The three girls crossed Main Street and made their way up the hill to the pizzeria, expecting to be harassed but for once, they were not. Rose wore a hat and tucked her long hair into the neck of the jacket she had on, hoping not to be recognized. A disguise she learned to use whenever she needed to leave the house.

When they entered, Rose immediately recognized the man seated at the counter as someone who had been in her bed. He sat with his back to the door, smoking a cigarette and sucking the last of a soda threw a straw. He barely noticed the girls enter. The trio took a booth in the corner just inside the entrance near the window. The new Frankie, who had taken over the restaurant when old Frankie passed on, came to the table, writing down the order without looking up.

After a short while, the man at the counter slapped down a dollar and stood up. He told young Frank he'd see him around and turned to leave. The man stalled for a minute, spying Rose hiding in the corner. He smiled in the direction of Rose and said, "I'll see you tomorrow night," and continued out the door.

As the owner set the pie down on the girls table, two men entered, taking seats at the counter. Rose ducked her head, wishing not to be spotted again. Patty recognized one of the men as Wesley Edwards, a man she enjoyed being with before and after moving in to the McGill house. None of the girls recognized the other young fellow.

Wesley was a large man with a round scruffy face and a pleasant attitude. Nothing ever seemed too serious with Wesley. A joke or a laugh was his calling card and he always wore a cheerful smile. Patty enjoyed his lightheartedness and carefree attitude, which was in sharp contrast to her friend Rose.

Wesley ordered drinks for himself and his companion then peeked over his shoulder, immediately catching sight of Patty. He tugged at his friend's sleeve, encouraging him to come along with him to meet the girls at the table in the corner. The young man followed his friend, hanging back nervously behind Wesley. Valerie and Patty switched seats so that Wesley could sit near Patty as the other man slid a chair up to the end of the table.

Wesley introduced his friend. "Girls, may I introduce to you Dominic the Dago," kidded Wesley.

Dominic became annoyed by his friend and gave Wes a playful push before introducing himself, "Bon journo, mi chiamo." Dominic paused realizing he was speaking in Italian. He then began again. "My name is Dominic Rinaldi."

Patty and Valerie thrilled with the sound of Dominic, not only his Italian accent, but also the deep smooth tone of his voice as he spoke. Rose was less impressed and uncomfortable with the situation. Patty and Wes acted like teenagers on a date, something Rose knew nothing about. She muttered to Valerie, wanting to go home, while chewing on a cut of rubbery pizza dough.

Rose gave Valerie the money to pay the tab, excused herself, and headed for the exit. Dominic at the coaxing of Wesley hopped from his chair and pursued Rose. Stopping her before she could exit, he held the door shut, startling Rose who felt much less secure without her axe near by.

"Rosa," he began, stooping slightly to see her face hidden beneath the brim of her hat, "My friend and me, well, I mean I, would like to know if you would join us for dinner?"

Rose looked back towards the table at Patty and Valerie who watched in suspense to see what their friend would do. Rose stood up tall as she had in the garden that evening and pulled off the hat she wore to conceal her jet-black hair. Her dark blue eyes measured the man. His thick dark locks and smooth tanned skin, the strength in his broad shoulders, his gentle, deep brown eyes captivated her.

Wesley spoke up, "There is a dinner three weeks from today at the Hotel Sterling down along the river, that we been invited to and want to take you and Patty as our guests."

"What about me? I wanna go too," Valerie whimpered.

"I believe I know someone to take Miss Valerie. It is kindda formal, and there'll be a band and dancing," added Wes, doing his best to help his friend, hoping to persuade Rose to accept Dominic's invitation.

Rose paused to consider the proposition. Patty had already accepted, breaking the rule of getting friendly with a customer. Dominic had never been in Rose's bed or Patty's for that matter. Rose thought, "He must know my reputation". She could not be sure though without asking him outright, but wished not to embarrassment the man having just met him.

"Do you know who I am?" She asked loud enough for all to hear.

Dominic turned, looking to Wesley for help. He was confused by the question Rose put to him. Dominic's English was not great, but, having already been introduced, he wondered why Rose would ask him again. Wes looked away, unable to face his friend and the question no one wished to answer.

"I am Black Rose," she stated with a modicum of pride. "Have you heard that name?" she asked. Looking into his eyes, she could see that he had not.

Dominic answered "No" and questioned why people called her Black Rose. Rose explained to Dominic that the miners had given her the nickname and why they had done so, fully expecting Dominic to walk away, or worse. In the back of Rose's mind she wanted to go to the dinner, thinking, "How grand it would be to dance in the ballroom of the Hotel Sterling with someone as handsome as Dominic." Yes, she realized, she thought he was handsome, a compliment she had never awarded to any man, accept for the photos she had seen of her grandfather and her late great Uncle David.

Dominic the Dago surprised her and everyone in her party. "You are the most beautiful woman I have ever seen. What you do, I cannot judge. As for me, I would consider it an honor to have you on my arm."

Rose removed her hat and jacket, exposing the length of her black flowing hair that fell to the small of her back. She tossed it to one side, looking down then slowly up. Her eyes sparkled, the touch of a blush appeared upon her cheeks as the young man waited anxiously for Rose's response.

She warned Dominic that, "Many men and more women might take offense at the sight of me at this event."

Dominic straightened up and pushed out his chest.

"They will say nothing to you if you are with me. I will not allow it." Dominic professed sternly. Rose believed him and agreed to be his date for dinner.

Friday was as busy as Rose expected, but she turned the porch lamp off early. For this, Patty was thankful. Neither of the women had much desire to carry on that night. The girls curled up on the couch sipping whiskey and talking small talk. Patty leaned forward and kissed Rose softly on the lips. Then she kissed her neck and began working her way down. As Patty undid her blouse, Rose stopped her.

"Let us just lay here tonight Patty," said Rose. "Besides, too many men been with me this evening."

Rose and Patty fell asleep on the couch wrapped in each other's arms until a brick thrown from a passing car smashed through the window just above their heads. Another stone missed its mark and bounced off the wood siding with a thud. The girls fell to the floor and crawled into the kitchen to hide. Once they felt sure the vandals were not returning, they put on their shoes, grabbed the dustpan and broom, and cleaned up the shards of broken glass. Rose went to the basement and found some loose boards, a hammer, and a bag full of nails. Rose and Patty did the best they could to secure the window. Then Rose took Patty to her bed where they slept out the night.

Saturday night Rose did the same thing, turning off the porch light early. Patty worried with every passing car that night, fearful that more rocks might be slung and windows shattered. Sunday morning the girls counted their money over coffee and scrambled eggs. Though they did not make as much as they usually did, they earned more than enough money to buy new dresses for the dinner-dance. The next question was where to go for these dresses. Valerie came by that afternoon and the three girls decided to go north on the Laurel Line to Scranton. After a few drinks, their plans changed.

"New York City, that's where we need to go to get a dress," shouted Patty as she pranced about the living room, listening to her new radio. Valerie's eyes lit up with thoughts of the big city but she realized she could not afford such a lavish excursion. Rose excused herself and went to the bathroom, pulling out her stash of money from behind the tub. She counted out a thousand dollars and stuffed it into her blouse. She removed another five-hundred and cupped it in her hand before returning to the living room. Rose sat down beside

Valerie and held her hand, slipping her the roll of cash when Patty wasn't looking.

"Clear your schedules girls," Rose hollered, "New York City, look out, Black Rose is coming!"

Rose and Valerie jumped to their feet to join Patty just as the Hoosier Hot Shots hit the radio waves playing 'Darktown Strutter'. Rose had truly begun to feel happy, an emotion she had rarely known in her short life. Her joy disappeared when Rose noticed the flower she had rescued from the garden had withered on the shelf. Seeing the sadness on her friend's face, Valerie put her arms around Rose. "Everything that lives dies, Rose," Val whispered to her friend. "You enjoy it while you can." Rose hugged her friend. Hearing her words she returning to dancing and having fun for what may have been the first time in her life.

Chapter 17

A Night at the Sterling

The girls met Tuesday morning at the McGill house to catch the local trolley to the Wilkes-Barre station. They would have gone on Monday, but there was the matter of a broken window in need of repair before they could go anywhere. Wesley Edwards worked doing home repairs as a side job. When Patty called him, he was more than happy to help the girls out in exchange for services rendered. Of course, Patty enthusiastically agreed to his terms. Wes suggested they bar the windows, fearing this was not a one-time thing. He heard the talk in the town and worried for the girl's safety, particularly Patty.

A fog lay heavy over the Wyoming Valley when Valerie arrived at the McGill house Tuesday morning. She brought along her mother's blonde wig to help disguise Rose with the hope they might make it on to the Laurel Line without incident. Valerie helped her friend position the wig so that none of her black hair was exposed.

Valerie, being a thoughtful friend, also brought a fresh rose to replace the faded flower on the shelf. Rose, warmed by the touching gesture, gave Valerie a soft lingering kiss on the lips. The girls slipped out through the back door, slogging through the gnarled greenery in the backyard and exited through the rear gate. They snuck up between the neighboring houses to board the Main Street trolley, doing their best not to draw attention to themselves. The fog bank was a bonus.

As the fog began to dissipate, they boarded the Laurel Line bound for Scranton to catch the morning train to Hoboken. Valerie had been on a train once as a small child, though she barely remembered it. Her family came from Canada to Pennsylvania so her father could work the coalfields. Rose and Patty had never been on a train; they had never been anywhere further than Wilkes-Barre. Patty and Valerie thrilled with the adventure of it all. Rose was more subdued, but inside she too was excited to be heading for New York.

The Laurel Line arrived in Scranton with enough time for the girls to have breakfast before boarding the train to Hoboken. They overheard some of the other customers complaining about a mishap along the Hoboken line, creating delays of about an hour. The girls did not see this as an issue, allowing them more time to relax before the long train ride. They visited shops along Lackawanna and Adams Avenue, returning to the station just as the conductor made the last boarding call.

Once aboard the Phoebe Snow, Rose removed her jacket and wig. Her long black locks flowed in rippling waves across her shoulders, caressing her hips in a thick, glistening blanket of ebon. From the corner of her eye, she noticed a dapper looking man in a pinstripe suit, an ivory handled umbrella perfectly positioned and hanging from his wrist, watching her as she tossed about her raven mane.

Rose chose to tease the man playfully, slowly batting her sparkling blue eyes and then running her extended fingers slowly across her smooth white neck to her cleavage. The man followed Rose's hand with his eyes, his lips curling up beneath his salt and pepper mustache. She twisted her wicked rye smile to the man, startling him. He turned away quickly, dislodging his umbrella and dropping it to the floor, his face red with embarrassment.

The girls giggled like schoolchildren before moving to the dining car to have lunch. The valley dressed itself in autumn leaves from the outskirts of Scranton through the Delaware Water Gap, across the Paulinskill Viaduct and into Hainesburg, New Jersey. Rose, Patty, and Valerie watched in wonder, the swaying sea of red, gold, and burnt umber that passed outside the windows of the Phoebe Snow. Patty brought along a camera, snapping photos of everything from Rose's costume, to the fog billowing through the streets, and now the painted scenery.

As they rode further, the trees began to lose their luster, turning brown and less descript. Patty put away her camera, choosing not to waste her film. The train made short stops along the way, unloading and loading passengers at every stop, making its way to Hoboken. Once there, the girls would catch the ferry across the Hudson River where New York awaited.

In the big city, Rose took charge, seeming to know right where to go although she had never been there before. They hopped the trolley, riding it to 34th street and the garment district. All along Rose, Patty and Valerie were amazed at this wondrous city. They marveled at its buildings stretching up to touch the sky and the hordes of people on every sidewalk. Again, Patty's camera came out, snapping shots of everything, filling the roll of film. It was the big band era and the sound of swing cascaded through the city streets from every club they passed. The New York Yankees had just won their third straight baseball championship, sweeping the Chicago Cubs, causing a celebratory atmosphere on every corner far and wide.

On 34th Street, the three girls bounced in and out of shop after shop, seeking the perfect dress. So many of the stores were much too expensive, and they would have to return to the city to pick the gowns up. The girls stopped at a small confectionary tucked in among the hucksters and clothiers that aligned the avenue. They sat at a small table nibbling chocolate covered strawberries, professing how exciting and amazing the city is, but complaining about the crowds and the pompous high-nose people they had come across. A young girl at the counter overheard their conversation and recommended a shop just down the street, across from the butchers. Rose thanked her for the tip and the delicious candies as the girls continued on their quest.

When Rose and her companions reached the little dress shop across from the butchers, Rose stopped, gazing into the large glass storefront window. A group of shadowy images appeared to her, ghosts of the past gathered in the gloaming. A chill ran through her as an exhale of air rushed from the shop when Patty pushed open the door. Inside a young woman was removing a gown from a mannequin and talking to herself, or the display piece, the girls could not be sure. Hearing the chimes ring, announcing the entrance of new customers, another head popped out between two spinning racks of outfits. The clang of the doorbell echoed through the shop long after the door had closed.

"Ello ladies," the young woman began. "My name is Emily and this is my establishment. Well, mine and me sister, Maura Kate's. That be her hidin in the sale togs. What may we dress you in?"

Emily's thick cockney accent brought a smile to the girl's faces, having never heard such a strange and delightful way of speech. Rose, still goose bumped from her moment of déjà vu, hid in behind her friends, waiting for it to pass. Too much of this place and this shop was all too familiar to her, though she knew she had never set foot inside it before that moment. Patty introduced the trio to Emily and explained what they were shopping for, along with their predicament.

Emily spread the girls out, weaving in between them to get a better look at their shapes. She stopping at each, assessing and professing what she thought might look best, while Maura raced about taking measures of each girl. Emily took the longest look at Valerie, lifting her arms and placing her hands upon her hips. Maura wrapped her tape measure around Valerie, scratching a note on her pad and showing it to her sister. With Patty, it was the width of her shoulders and a pinch about the waist, but when she reached Rose, she stopped.

"You are a beauty now aren't ya love," stated Emily. "Not meanin any disrespect to your friends here. You are all quite handsome, but you are a smasher! Well, let us see what we can get dun fer ya. I got some things made up that with a wee bit of adjustment might suit ya lassies just fine. There are some stools up near the changin rooms. Get yourselves one and I'll bring ya what I have."

The girls sat down as Emily, shadowed by her sister, went to the dress rack. She returned shortly baring three gowns. She hung each from a post in front of the girl she meant them for, matching their body shapes and skin tones. Emily left again, trailed by her sister and returned this time with shoes to match the gowns. She asked Valerie to put the shoes on and stand up, placing the gown against her back and then her front. Emily did the same with Patty and then Rose, seeking their approval as she went from one girl to the next.

Valerie approved immediately and went to the dressing room to try on her gown. She was a hippy girl with larger than average bosom, but a smooth belly. Her height combined with her shapeliness gave her the appearance of being pudgy, but she was not. Getting a gown to show off her true figure presented a challenge to Emily. Patty wanted her dress to be much lower cut. She was a well-endowed girl and liked showing this feature off whenever possible. Emily replaced Patty's first selection with one more to her liking. Rose objected to Emily's choice for her and decided it might be easier if she explained to Emily her vision instead of having the girl running back and forth.

"Emily I would like something in black velvet, and form fitting," stated Rose. Always the seductress, she ran her hands down her bodyline, tucking in her pelvis as her palms slid over her hips. She rolled her shoulders back and wet her lips with the tip of her tongue.

"It should be backless as low as it can go and sliced down the front shamelessly," Rose laughed. So did Patty, but to their surprise Emily went to a closet behind the counter. Upon opening the cabinet, a scent of cedar filled the dressing area. Emily removed from the closet a gown wrapped in linen. She placed it on the post before Rose and gently detached the pins that retained the protective cloth.

Rose's image of the perfect dress described this gown in detail, with a few slight variations. A smooth shimmering black velvet garb with flecks of sparkling red thread woven through it hung before Rose. The plunging neckline ended at the bloom of a flower, delicately sculpted in red velvet and scarlet strips of satin, forming seven perfect pleats that trailed to ankle length. The back was as Rose described, bear to the base of the tailbone and slightly beyond. Emily lifted the gown from its hanger and handed it to Rose who went to the dressing room to try it on. Emily returned to the closet, coming back with a fine white lace shawl, the pattern of a rose etched in the fiber.

Valerie had exited her dressing room and stood before the floor length mirrors to admire her dress. Her gown was green to match her eyes. It flowed down off the shoulders, cutting generously between her breasts, but not as deep as the dresses Rose or Patty were trying on. It crisscrossed beneath the bust line, flowing outward in a pleated A—line to just above the knee. The material was silk, draped in chiffon. The unique design coupled with the high-heel shoes gave Valerie a longer, sleeker appearance. Patty got just what she wanted, a vibrant blue satin gown that exposed a most indecent amount of bosom, accompanied by a glittering quarter sleeve jacket to keep her from being arrested for indecent exposure.

However, Rose's gown astonished everyone. The dress clung to her curves like a second skin, as if the designer made it specifically for her body. The red metallic thread woven through the material caught the light at every turn. Emily slid the lace shall across Rose's shoulders as she stood before the mirror. Maura brought to Rose a pair of long white gloves and helped her put them on.

"Perfection," Emily said in a whisper. "That dress has been in the cedar shed for near forty years, when me dear old Dad bought the place. He said the former owners had left it behind. Guess they know'd you'd be cumin, hey lassie."

Emily rang up the three gowns, her prices were extremely reasonable. She seemed actually happy to get rid of Rose's dress. It cost Emily nothing to make, so the sale of it was pure profit. Rose and Patty had brought along more than enough money, purchasing the three dresses, shoes, gloves, and throwing in some new evening coats for good measure. Along the way, they stopped at a jewelry shop, purchasing earrings and necklaces to accent their new dresses.

The girls enjoyed a nice dinner before catching the trolley to the ferry launch. They caught the last train out of Hoboken heading to Pennsylvania, toting bags and boxes in every hand. The trio crashed repeatedly into other passengers, producing many angry glares as they moved along the aisle to their seats.

The girls did not notice or didn't care how disruptive they were being. Their loud laughter and generally obnoxious behavior annoyed many of the passengers in the car, who complained to the conductor as he came about checking tickets. The conductor approached the young women, scolding them like children. Patty and Valerie giggled, but apologized to the white haired old man. They turned to some of their fellow travelers, apologizing to them also.

Rose did not intend to apologize for having fun since it was something she rarely experienced. She felt happy and was not about to ask people, strangers to forgive her for letting it show. She did tone it down a bit; feeling tired from the long day, but never asked forgiveness of those she bothered.

The train arrived in Scranton late that evening. The girls, toting all their packages scurried to make the nine p m trolley to Wilkes-Barre, which was luckily delayed. Two women and four men where already aboard when the trio took their seats, situating their parcels so that others could sit. An older couple boarded, followed by three more men. The final group took the last seats in the back of the car. The man seated in the center had with him a strong box secured to his wrist by a handcuff. Once the last group settled in the car started forward, easing out of the station into the darkness.

The electric train reached the south portal of the Crown Avenue tunnel in no time at all, but slowed gradually as it reached the incline toward Moosic Mountain. The three men to the rear of the car were talking. Rose noticed the strong box when the group boarded, but thought little of it until she caught a glimpse of the guns holstered beneath their coats. From this point, she paid more attention to them than her friends, eaves dropping on their conversation.

"It was right about here," she heard the first man say. The other guard disagreed, claiming, "It was back down near Nay Aug, from what I heard."

Rose changed her seat, moving to the back of the car. The three men noticed Rose and took a pause in the conversation.

Once she settled back in her new position on the car the men began to speak again. They argued back and forth, but Rose could only hear bits of what they were discussing, their voices muffled by the noise of the trolley car clicking along the track. Frustrated by being unable to hear them fully, Rose boldly turned and asked them directly what it was they were debating.

None of the men responded at first, but Rose knew how to make a man talk. She batted her eyes and licked her lips, enticing the men just enough to weaken their resistance. Finally, the man seated in the middle began to speak. He told Rose the story of the 1923 hold up of the southbound Laurel Line. Rose listen intently as he recounted what he knew, while the other men interrupted with bits of the story they knew. Patty and Valerie overheard the men talking to Rose and moved to the back to join their friend so they could listen to the story too.

The man holding the strong box began, "It was midsummer, late July or early August, I can't recollect exactly. The paymaster for the coal company, Archie Henshall, carried three cases like the one I have, containing near $70, 000 dollars in cash; the mining company's payroll he was deliverin to Macanaqua. Three guards accompanied him as they did twice a month, putting the cases between their feet as they sat down in these very seats. Everything seemed normal from all accounts. A man reading a newspaper, a couple with a child, some other men, and a young woman, probably around your age, occupied the trolley heading to Wilkes-Barre.

It was just as the train came out of the tunnel when a passenger stood up and kicked open the door to the motorman's compartment and shot poor P J Durkin. Four other men stood up at this point, yellin, 'Hands in the Air, this is a robbery!' to the passengers and headed for the payroll master. All hell broke loose at that point with bullets flying all around. One struck the man reading his morning paper; Murphy I believe his name was, killed him dead. Another passenger took a bullet and the young woman panicked, leaping from the train into to the trees. Henshall tried to resist and took one in the leg. The conductor attempted to help the guards, but the robbers put a gun to his head and made him beg for his life, as the guards were overpowered.

The trolley rolled to a stop and the hoods jumped from the train with the payroll, making their way up an embankment to where a getaway car waited for um. The Police found the car abandon some time later, in a wooded area in Old Forge; was near a year before they caught up wit um. The first they captured in Homestead, Pennsylvania trying another payroll heist. Turns out, the guy they caught up to in Homestead and some of the other robbers worked for the coal company. They was fired a few weeks prior to the hold up."

The man paused for a while, talking to the man to his left. Rose waited, expecting more. When the man did not continue, Rose asked what happened to the robbers.

The man explained, "All but one was captured and electrified, 'Big Jack' Stammy was killed in a shoot out with the police after a failed bank robbery in Ohio. Some say it was his partner John Torti, who shot Stammy in the back before putting the gun in his own mouth. Damn fool blew a hole in his cheek before the cops got um."

The men rode the train to Wilkes-Barre along with Rose and her friends. There they bid them goodnight and boarded another train headed for Macanaqua. Patty flagged down a cab and the three girls piled in with their packages. The driver dropped Valerie off at her house first, before taking Rose and Patty home. Valerie left her new outfit with her friends. She knew her father would throw it into the yard if he knew who bought it. She would pick her outfit up the week of the party. At the McGill house, the cabby helped the girls to the door, bringing the bags in and setting them on the couch. Rose gave him a generous tip. While looking into his eyes, she asked the man his name.

"Jeffery it is Miss, Jeffrey Halliday," answered the man without hesitation.

Rose leaned in and gave the man a gentle kiss on the cheek. Jeffrey turned his head, blushing from his head to his heels. Rose thanked him and wished him a good evening. As she closed the door behind her, the man stopped and turned to Rose keeping her from shutting it, "If you ever need anything Miss, anything at all, you call the office and ask for Black Jack. I'll be there for ya, I promise."

Rose looked confused, "I thought your name was Jeffrey," asked Rose, "Who is Black Jack?"

"My cab is number twenty-one, so they call me Black Jack," answered the cabbie. "You remember that, number twenty-one, and Black Jack will be there before you can put down the phone."

Rose smiled, "Thank you Jeffrey, I will be sure to call. Goodnight."

Patty had opened the adjoining door to her side of the house and, after a quick bolt to the bathroom, was dancing about with her new gown in her arms. Rose wished her goodnight, took her packages from the couch, and went upstairs to her room. That night the dark dreams would not let Rose sleep. Each time she dosed they reappeared. She saw the skull of Lucas Nash opened up before her. Blood pooled about her feet, the petals of the black rose floating upon it. After four hours of tormented sleeplessness, she went over to Patty's bed and slept with her for what remained of the night.

The weekends continued as usual, with a steady flow of men and some women looking for pleasure at the McGill house. Patty and Rose did their best to accommodate every customer, taking in a substantial amount of cash in the process. During the week, Patty began spending more time with Wesley Edwards, going out to dinner or to the cinema, or just sitting on the sofa relaxing.

It was during one of the latter evenings when Rose over heard a conversation between the couple. Wes wanted Patty to stop being a prostitute. He told Patty that it bothered him that all these men where having their way with his girl. Patty liked being called "His girl" and told Wes she had been thinking about it and would continue to consider it. She then took him by the hand and led him to her bedroom where they spent the night.

Rose found herself considering it too, but for much different reasons than Patty. Whatever it was that drove her to do it, began to wane. However, she had just spent a large sum from her savings and would need to replenish her stash before seriously pondering putting out the porch light for good.

Rose was rationalizing. Money did not draw her to this life, nor did the need for sexual gratification, which is what had Patty hesitant. The Friday night poker games created an addiction, a habit that held on to Rose. However, the grip that held her loosened, despite all its efforts, with every happy moment she experienced.

A part of her liked being Black Rose. Her reputation as a murderous whore felt empowering. Another part of Rose longed to be free of her name and free of this town, which despised her so. This seemed impossible. More things than Rose understood were playing with her, including the bloody nightmares that always included the black rose. Those Rose believed to be inescapable no matter what happiness life bore. The fates were wicked puppet masters. As long as they pulled the strings, Rose would dance as they wished.

The days before the dinner-dance turned unseasonably warm with plenty of sunshine. Rose decided in a very spur of the moment thought, to take advantage of the nice weather and clean the weeds from the backyard. She chopped, cut, and slashed until every entanglement lay in heaps upon the ground. She raked the cuttings into piles and shoveled each pile into an old rusted wheel barrel, taking them out through the back gate to a wooded area and dumping them. She repeating this until the yard was cleared. Patty, seeing her friend working so hard, called Valerie and the trio joined to put the final touches on the yard.

Once they had finished sprucing up the yard, the girls began to talk, chatting about Thursday night and the upcoming evening at the Hotel Sterling. Patty began complaining about her hair and pointed out to Rose that she could use some professional help with her style too. Thursday morning Patty guided Rose and Valerie to a house set back in the woods off Old Ashley Road. The soft, muddy path looked to be unused for some time.

A grey striped cat and then another appeared from the bushes that surrounded the brown-shingled shanty that seemed to be leaning to one side. Patty stepped onto the porch; its boards creaked loudly with each step. She gave a firm series of raps, drawing more cats, leaping onto the porch between the weather worn aging spindles. The girls waited for a minute, Valerie wanted very much to leave.

Just as Patty knocked again the door swung open. A woman with short dark hair combed straight up, stepped out, staring angrily at the three girls. Her expression changed when she recognized that it was her niece Patty standing on her porch. "Patty!" she yelled hugging her and invited the girls into her house. Once inside cats of all colors came from every direction. Patty introduced the woman to Rose and Valerie as "Robin Jabbara, hairstylist extraordinaire."

Patty explained to her aunt what the girls needed and why. Robin, tossed aside a few cats, cleaned off a few chairs for the girls to sit down, and agreed to help them out. Robin pushed away a pile of miscellaneous junk from a counter, into an overflowing trashcan, and pulled forward an old radio. She tuned in a station playing popular music, and then sat Patty down in an old barber's chair that had seen better days.

The woman limbered up her scissors and began to clip, while singing loudly and far off key to whatever song played on the radio starting with the 'Tennessee Waltz'. She rarely knew the words, but sang loud and strong, with the cats in the background crying in tune with every missed note. Her spirit was contagious, spreading from cat to cat and, soon enough, to the girls who began singing too. It turned in to a very odd, but enjoyable afternoon.

Robin trimmed and styled each of the girls in no time at all. Once she finished their hair, she helped the girls with their makeup, dusting them gentle with a fine powder, and giving them a bottle of fragrant oil to add to the bath water, but she warned them not to run the water too hot and no matter what, keep their hair and face from getting wet.

"Don't wanna disturb all that good work I did, do ya girls?" she asked them as they headed for home. The girls agreed, thanking Robin for all she had done for them while promising to bring her photos of the night's event. When she took a quick look back to wave goodbye, Rose saw a cluster of cats running across the porch and balancing on the rail that wrapped around the side of the house.

Thursday night Wes and Dominic arrived to pick up Patty and Rose for the dance in a red 1937 Plymouth four door sedan. Wes borrowed the car for the evening from his older brother, promising to take good care of it. Wes washed and polished the vehicle, making it shine right down to the spoke wheel covers. His hope was to display to Patty that he could provide for her so that she would leave her life of prostitution. Patty was quite impressed, sliding across the soft white leather bench seat to snuggle up next to Wes as he drove. Rose liked the car and felt comfortable sitting alongside Dominic, but could not help but worry about the evening.

Valerie arrived at the hotel with her date, Gary, insisting that they wait outside so that the group might enter together. She and her young man stood near the entrance on River Street until Wes, Dominic and the girls showed up. It turned out to be a short wait. Valerie spotted the car rounding the corner from River Street onto Market Street, shouting out and waving to her friends as they passed.

Wes found a place to park just off Public Square. Once parked, he ran around the car to open Patty's door, something no one had ever done for Patty before. Dominic helped Rose out, taking her hand and the foursome walked the few short blocks to the hotel.

The avenues of Wilkes-Barre shined with the lights of Christmas adorning every building. Wreaths hung from every lamppost. A soft white snow floated through the dusk of the day, giving a shimmer and shine to the sidewalks leading to the Hotel Sterling. Large urns, overflowing with red and white poinsettias, stood beside each entrance and filled the lobby of the hotel. A huge, heavily decorated tree, wrapped in lights and white garland finished out a most beautiful scene.

The girls wore their new overcoats, having yet to reveal to the young men their gowns. A concierge greeted them in the lobby and recommended that the women check their coats. Rose looked at her friends, donning one of her usual smiles she said, "Here goes nothing, girls!" Dominic slowly eased the coat from her shoulders. Wes, seeing what Dominic had done, helped Patty off with her jacket as did Valerie's date, but neither managed to do it as smoothly as Dominic.

Wes and Gary's eyes lit up, their jaws dropped and their pants tightened, seeing the girls in their gowns. Dominic reacted much more maturely; his dark brown eyes sparkled with approval, the touch of a dimple formed in his cheeks as he smiled. Dominic took Rose's hand to his lips, never lowering his eyes from hers. He slid his arm smoothly around her waist, whispering in Rose's ear that she was the most beautiful woman he had ever known.

Valerie and Gary entered the ballroom first, turning many heads as they did so. Wesley and Patty came next, turning more eyes and provoking some whispering from the already seated guests. Dominic took Rose Aileene by the hand and stepped into the room, allowing Rose to enter behind him. Her long raven hair pulled to one side, poured over her left shoulder and flowed to her hip, exposing her uncovered back. Her gold earrings glistened in the light, as did the fine gold necklace that clung to the small of her neck. Dominic walked her slowly across the room. Rose stood straight; her lace shawl draped down from her elbows. She kept her eyes fixed on her friends, who, like the rest of the room, gazed in amazement.

Patty, noticing a touch of drool dripping from the edge of Wesley's mouth, jabbed him in the ribs with her elbow. Rose was breathtaking and because of this, no one recognized her as the cheap whore from Ashley. There was nothing cheap about Rose this night, nor Patty or Valerie. The threesome danced and laughed, mingling with some of the other younger guests at the party, but meeting some of the more prestigious patrons too.

Pennsylvania's newly elected governor Arthur H. James and his wife were the guests of honor. Governor James lived in Plymouth just across the Susquehanna River from Wilkes-Barre and ran his campaign with the promise of revitalizing the Wyoming Valley. This made him very popular locally. The governor and his wife went about shaking hands, greeting guests, and wishing each table a happy holiday season. Wilkes-Barre's mayor Loveland and former mayor Hart where in attendance and were accompanied by their families, enjoying a most festive evening despite their widely known dislike for one another. Coal barons and railroad executives rounded out the who's who of the Wyoming Valley attending the Night at the Hotel Sterling.

The girls and their dates spent much of the night dancing, forgetting about the fears they had about coming out in public with Rose. Almost no one noticed who she was, almost no one. Toward the end of the evening as conversations turned to leaving, a touch from behind on her bare shoulder startled Rose.

"May I have this dance?" a voice said to her, whispering in her ear.

Rose looked over her shoulder to see the detective Billy Wilson staring down at her.

Rose said nothing at all, taking the detectives hand as he led her to the dance floor. Dominic kicked back his chair ready to protest, but Patty grabbed his arm and pulled him back. Wesley replaced his chair at the table and pushed him back down in his seat. Patty explained to Dominic who the man was, keeping Dominic from starting a fight with a police officer.

"Don't worry," she told Dominic, "Rose can handle it."

"Well Rose McGill you look all grown up began the detective," spinning her around the dance floor. "Kill anyone lately?"

Rose, angered by his words tried to pull away, but the officer held her in place.

"You know that wasn't my fault, and no I haven't, but you're pushin your luck", Rose responded.

"Are you threatening an officer of the law," Officer Wilson replied, looking quite smug. "No, I'm threatening an asshole," Rose answered back, staring daggers at the man.

"What makes you so tough, kitten? Asked Detective Wilson.

A strange, funny feeling ran through Rose, believing she had heard that name used before. A sensation similar to the one she had felt in New York at the dress shop on 34th street overcame her. The officer noticed the distant look in Rose's eyes, immediately asking if she was all right. Rose did not respond, gazing into the distance, lost in a fog.

Detective Wilson brushed his hand across the blush of Rose's cheek. His touch returned her to the here and now. She looked at him with sad eyes and then slapped his hand away as the daggers returned.

"I'm a little young for you officer, wouldn't you say," Rose snapped.

"Just wasn't sure where you went to," stated the officer.

Rose pulled away from the detective. She thanked him for the dance, wished him a Merry Christmas, and then returned to her table. Detective Wilson watched Rose walking away, admiring her shapely ass. He admired her confident, her allure. He realized he had been ogling too long when an older couple bumped into him standing alone on the dance floor.

Patty and Valerie surrounded Rose when she returned to the table, asking her what was up with detective dreamy. Rose wanted a drink, caring next to nothing about the officer in question. She told the girls, "He was just trying to stir me up. Aggravating shit thinks he can do what ever he pleases, because he has a badge. Not with me he can't!"

Dominic, who had stepped away from the table, returned. Rose greeted him with a long sensual kiss. Wesley too returned to the table, getting the same greeting from Patty. Valerie's date did not get as lucky.

At the end of the evening, Wes took Dominic home first. Rose kissed Dominic goodnight as they stood in front of his apartment. It was the first kiss she had ever had that truly meant something. A kiss full of feeling and emotion that made her heart beat just a little bit faster. He held her in his arms. A cold wind swirled snowflakes about them and Rose felt differently. Dominic took Rose's hand, raising it to his lips. He bid her goodnight before helping her back into the car.

Chapter 18

Everything Changes

Wesley brought the girls home, saying goodnight to Rose as she unlocked the door to her side of the house, then sharing a long goodnight kiss with Patty on the front porch. Despite Patty,'s desire for him to spend the night Wes had to return his brother's car and declined. Inside the house, Rose took her grandfather's decanter and two shot glass from the curio and filled the glasses with whiskey. She threw back the first drink and poured herself another, setting the other filled glass on the coffee table for Patty.

Patty and Wes spoke in whispers on the porch before their final goodnight kiss, when Patty came inside. She plopped down on Rose's sofa wearing a gleeful grin. Rose perched herself in her favorite chair, her back straight, her head high, the decanter of whiskey at her side. She drank the second shot and poured a third. Patty sat up and saw the shot waiting for her on the coffee table. She swallowed it and Rose poured her another.

Rose could see in Patty's eyes there was something she wanted to say, but was hesitating, not sure how to start. Rose took it upon herself to begin the conversation.

"My bastard of a father use to sit in his big chair calling it his throne," she said.

"Well, you look like a queen. All you need is a tiara," replied Patty.

"What is it you're wishin to say Patty," asked Rose, seeing the look of someone struggling with something.

Patty was fraught with indecision. The months she had spent in the McGill house were fun and exciting, but it was time to leave. Patty knocked back the second whiskey before saying what she had to say, "Wesley and I have been talking, and well, I think I'm going stop working on my back."

Patty paused as Rose refilled her shot glass. "Not right away of course. I thought I would continue through the holidays into January. Maybe start the New Year differently. Wes thinks I should go home. Try and make amends with my folks, if they'll have me."

Rose finished her whiskey, stood up, and replaced the decanter on its shelf in the curio. She knew how Patty was feeling, she was feeling it herself, but it would not be so easy for her. Rose had no family to go back to, no boyfriend prodding her to leave her sinful life behind, only a budding desire for a change. She stared into the eyes of her mother in the photo atop the curio, wishing as she had when she was a child, wondering how different her life might have been.

Rose turned to Patty stating, "There is nothing that holds you to this place Patty. You are my friend, whether you are here or not. Wesley is a good man who only wants what is best for you. However, can you get by with only one man? Will he be enough to satisfy you?"

Patty thought about what Rose had said, then responded, "I love him, I know that much. The rest I'll figure out after the holidays." Patty stood up and gave Rose a kiss, first on the lips then on her neck. She ran a soft touch across her shoulder and down her arm. "You are a smasher Black Rose McGill," Patty whispered in Rose's ear with a nibble and invited Rose to spend the night in her bed.

Rose rejected the invitation and kissed her friend goodnight. After a few hours of nightmarish dreams, Rose went to Patty's room, slipping delicately beneath the sheets. Rose pressed her body against Patty, wrapping her arms around her. Patty kissed Rose's hand, then turned her hips and eased her friend on top of her. Following a long kiss, they made love until they fell asleep.

That weekend and every weekend straight into January, Rose and Patty were hard at work. The holidays brought a different class of people to the McGill house; a sad, lonely lot, looking for comfort in lives that had so little. Rose, struggling with her own demons, had not the tools to comfort sorrowful gents who wept at her bedside. She would give them what she knew how to give and send them on their way.

In January, Patty did as she proposed she would and returned home seeking her parent's forgiveness. Wesley accompanied her to provide moral support, knowing this would not be easy for Patty or her parents. Bernie and Jeremy Wells took their daughter in their arms, crying for the return of their child. They attempted to blame Rose for their daughter's actions, but Patty would not hear of it; taking responsibility for all she had done.

Dominic stopped in to see Rose on weekdays, taking her to dinner and a movie, but never sleeping with her. Not that he didn't want to, but he wanted to be more than just another john. He wanted a relationship with Rose, something Rose wanted too, but did not know how to have. Rose liked this about Dominic, caring more for him than any man she had ever known.

Dominic surprised Rose on Christmas Eve, showing up at her door most unexpectedly, with a tree and several boxes of ornaments to decorate it. In all the years Rose lived in this house, it had never known a tree at Christmas. The two rearranged the furniture and then Dominic wedge the trunk of the tree with stones from the garden into a bucket filled with warm water. Rose laughed, watching him struggle to stand the tree upright.

Once Dominic succeeded, Rose placed the first decoration on a limb, front, and center; a delicate white snowflake that sparkled as it hung. Dominic hung the next and before long four boxes of ornaments and entirely too much silver tinsel dressed a most delightfully overdone Christmas tree. Rose and Dominic sat by the tree for hours, talking and laughing, sipping wine, and watching the snowfall, until Rose fell asleep in his arms.

The winter passed slowly, with snow squalls lingering well into April that year. Rose had trimmed her nights of prostitution back to Fridays after Patty went home to her parents. She would have stopped all together, but old habits die hard. Saturday morning, she would count her earnings, dreaming as she did when she was fifteen of leaving this place to find a quiet life. Somewhere Black Rose did not exist and hoping that this new life included Dominic.

"How foolish," another part of her would say, "You are the Black Rose. No matter where you go it will be you and you will be it."

Rose slammed her fist on the table, frustrated by what she could not change; wanting to cry out, but she thought it a futile gesture. She took her money in one hand and a bottle of whiskey in the other to the upstairs bath. She stowed away the cash in her usual hiding spot and took a slug of whiskey from the bottle. Rose ran a hot bath, disrobing in front of the full-length mirror in the hallway as the water flowed.

She admired her naked body in the mirror, something she had not done since she first began showing signs of womanhood. Rose finally realized how much she had changed, that she had grown up, looking very much like her mother. She thought of Dominic as she ran her hands around her breasts then down the front of her. Turning to the side, she delighted in the smooth way her jet-black hair caressed her hips, happy with all that the mirror displayed.

"You are a smasher," she said to herself with a smile.

That Sunday Dominic, Wesley, Patty, and Valerie came to call on Rose. It was the first real warm day of the season and the group was going for a ride in the country. Wes had gotten his own car, a black 1937 Chrysler Imperial with plenty of room for five people. The group drove out to Harvey's Lake to have a picnic lakeside and enjoy a relaxing Sunday afternoon.

Rose and Dominic walked hand-in-hand along a wooded path beside the lake. The light green leaves flipped softly in the breeze as Dominic told Rose stories of his home in Italy.

"How beautiful the blue waters of the Mediterranean shimmered and the rolling hillsides, so green they would be this time of the year," he would say. "And Rome with its grand buildings and oh the wonderful food!"

Rose had few stories; her life was Ashley, which provided very few tales to tell. She could only dream of such places, but enjoyed the passion in Dominic's words as he described his homeland. At one point Rose lost her footing, slipping along the muddy pathway. Dominic caught her, gripping her tightly about the waist and leading her to a dry spot amongst the trees.

Following a soft lingering kiss, Dominic told Rose he was moving away. His Uncle Camillo and Aunt Theresa had written him in need of help on their vineyard in California. He explained to her how important his family was to him and that if they needed his help he must go; but he never invited Rose to go along with him. Rose waited for the invitation, but it never came.

They returned to the group where Patty waved her left hand under Rose's nose, showing off her engagement ring. Patty pranced excitedly about, hugging her friends and planting a kiss on Dominic, to Wesley's objection. Rose pretended to feel happy for her friend, but the news of Dominic leaving pained her deeply, not being asked to accompany him hurt her even more.

By the time the cherry blossoms bloomed along the Susquehanna, Dominic was gone. Patty and Wes set a date for the wedding in October. Patty wanted to marry with the colors of autumn surrounding her, remember the trees along the way to New York City the year before. Valerie too had become engaged, but not to Gary. She dated quite a few different young men before agreeing to wed a wealthy businessman by the name of Connell from Scranton.

Rose filled her free time tending to her garden. She repaired and painted the old piece of lattice, putting it back against the fence for the rosebush to climb upon. She added more rosebushes around the base of the house, primarily red, but some peach, yellow and white too. Around the front stoop, Rose planted annuals, mostly impatiens and marigolds. She would have loved to put up window boxes, but the bars on the windows made that impossible.

Although Patty, Valerie, and Wes stopped by every so often, their visits became less frequent as the summer moved along. They had a wedding to arrange, and though Patty wanted Rose as her maid of honor, she and Rose knew this was impossible. Valerie faced the same predicament and felt terrible not being able to include her good friend in her wedding plans.

Rose took it all in stride, knowing well her reputation and kept working every Friday night, satisfying the boys from the bars along Main Street. She started lighting the porch lamp later and turning it off sooner as the grip of her habit loosened with time. With every preoccupation, Rose became more detached from the demons that held her. Turns out, everything can change, even a rose.

Memories of times better spent began to have more meaning to Black Rose. She rearranged her curio, putting a fresh flower beside her mother's photo regularly. The water globe now occupied the last shelf, replacing the water pitcher, moving that to the cabinet beneath the sink. In between Rose placed souvenirs from New York City, her evening at the Hotel Sterling, photos of her friends and an assortment of ticket stubs from the Phoebe Snow, the Laurel Line and every movie Dominic had ever taken her to see. On the centermost shelve she placed the snowflake ornament, never wanting to forget the best Christmas she ever had.

That summer was a scorcher with temperatures topping out over a hundred degrees on some days. Rose did her best to deal with the heat, working in the yard in the early morning followed by a cooling bath and a generously spiked glass of lemonade. Rose's life seemed easy, her needs were few, however, the torturous dark dreams played on. Some nights she managed to sleep through, other nights she awoke in a hot sweat, gasping for air.

It was the morning after one such night, while Rose was working in her garden when a messenger came to the back gate with an envelope. The boy insisted she sign two forms before he would hand it over to her. She did so, thanked the young man, and took the envelope to the porch step to have a seat in the shade and relax. She took a sip of lemonade. Wiping the sweat from her brow, she cut back the flap of the envelope with her gardening sheers.

The notice came from an attorney by the name of C. Francis Binell, Esquire from the law offices of Binell, Binell & Smelling. Rose thought the name of the firm rather comical and chuckled, just a bit. The letter simply informed Rose of a meeting scheduled for her twentieth birthday, and that she was to bring two forms of identification. The notice confused her. Rose knew she had not scheduled any meeting for her birthday with these lawyers or anyone else for that matter.

She decided to call the offices of Binell, Binell & Smelling to find out who had set up this meeting and what it entailed. After more than a dozen rings, a woman answered the phone with a very raspy, gravely sounding voice, announcing the name of the firm and asking how she might help to direct the call. Rose introduced herself and stated her question as clearly as she could to the sound of the woman on the other end of the phone popping her chewing gum.

"Hold on please", was the response Rose received, then a long silence ensued.

Nearly five minutes had passed before the gravely voiced woman returned. "Miss McGill, we are usually not allowed to give any information over the phone, but in your case we have made an exception due to the unusual circumstances. Your mother scheduled this meeting for you some twenty years ago." After a brief silence, "That is all I am able to say at this time. Good day Miss McGill."

The receiver clicked. The woman hung up before Rose could say anything. The multitude of questions she had needed answers. Instead, the women left Rose spinning in the wind, anxious and unsure, blindsided by this meeting scheduled from the grave.

"Why had her mother arranged a meeting for her on this date so long after her death? And why was her father not included in the invitation?" these questions and more Rose asked, perplexed by the mystery of it all.

One thing she did know, her birthday was on Monday, and for the first time in her life, she wished to celebrate it. Getting Patty and Valerie on the phone, they made plans to go shopping followed by dinner at the Hotel Sterling. Rose wanting to recognize and enjoy her birthday, surprised and delighted Patty and Valerie, although they worried where they might be able to go. They agreed to meet on Monday afternoon at two o'clock in the square. This was perfect for Rose since she needed to see the lawyer downtown that morning.

The Friday prior to her birthday felt a bit cooler with less humidity. Rose prepared for her parade of Friday night business, shaving away her body hair, smoothing her skin with lotion, and relaxing herself with liquor. She switched on the porch light around 9:30 p. m. and laid back on the couch in a black satin robe and matching high heels, sipping a tumbler of ice tea mixed with Irish whiskey.

It took only ten minutes before the first knock on the door. A young red-haired kid, barely old enough to shave waved twenty dollars at Rose through the front door window. She pulled him in and scolded him for being so obvious. In less than twenty minutes, he was heading out the door, smiling as if he had hit the jackpot. This was his birthday; he celebrated by losing his virginity to Black Rose.

There were not many knocks on the door that night. Rather a slow business evening for Rose, but she had slow nights before. "Probably the heat," she thought stretched out across the couch flipping through a magazine. A quiet night suited her just fine.

Just around midnight, as she peered out into the darkness, having made the decision to turn out the porch light and call it a night, a long black Cadillac, trimmed in chrome and shining in the moonlight pulled to the curb. A man slid out from behind the wheel and stepped out onto the sidewalk smoking a cigarette. After a last drag, he dropped the butt and squashed it beneath his shoe.

Before shutting the car door he reached back to get something from the front seat, hiding it beneath the light sport coat he wore. As the man stepped from the shadows Rose's heart leapt, thinking it was Dominic the Dago. But when the man reached the light of the porch lamp, she knew it was not. He did however, look much like him, older, but dark, with brown wavy hair.

His footsteps fell heavy on the porch as he knocked three firm knocks on Rose's door. Rose peeked through the curtain cautiously to see a hundred dollar bill cupped in the man's hand. She had rarely seen a hundred dollar bill and never at her door to pay for the pleasures that she provided. She thought twice about it, but opened the door and invited the man in.

"Bon Journo," the man said once inside. "Sei tu quello che chiamano, Rosa Nera?"

Rose looked at him confused. The only Italian she ever heard spoken was the few sentences Dominic greeted her with the first time they met. She understood bon journo, but nothing beyond that made any sense to her.

Seeing that she did not understand the man translated, "Pardon me, are you the one they call Black Rose?"

"Yes," Rose stated firmly, "I am Black Rose."

"Molto buano," replied the dashing Italian in a smooth soft voice.

The man smiled, explaining to Rose that many had told him that she was the best lady of her kind in town, and the most beautiful. "You are the most beautiful woman I have ever seen," he expressed to Rose, taking her hand to his lips and kissing it gently. This and many other things about the man reminded her so much of Dominic.

He placed the hundred-dollar bill in Rose's hand, closing her fingers around it before reaching beneath his jacket. He removed from his inside pocket a rose, its petals black as midnight. Handing it to her the man explained to Rose that upon hearing her name he went to a florist in search of such a flower. To his dismay, the florist had none, but was able to tint the petals a dark black to make it appear so. He hoped it was to Rose's liking.

Rose, delighted with the gesture, giving the man an approving nod and inviting smile. She took his hand and guided him to the back bedroom, clinging to her gift in the other hand. Once there, things changed dramatically. The man slid his arms around Rose from behind, wrapping them tightly, like a boa constrictor curling about its prey. He bit her soft tanned neck, carving his teeth marks into her flesh. Rose screamed as the man, with a kick, slammed her bedroom door shut.

He spun her about and slapped her across the right side of her face, knocking out of her shoes and onto the bed. Rose lay on her back, hurt and dazed as the man undid his belt and bound it around his right hand. Pouncing on Rose, he struck her twice more with the belted hand. He reached down, unzipping his pants and pulled out his penis. Holding Rose by the throat, he forced himself inside her and began to hump, while Rose struggled to breathe.

Her arms flailed, sending everything they hit flying about the room and crashing to the floor. A sudden knock at the front door distracted the man. He looked over his shoulder, loosing his grip slightly. It was just enough for Rose's hand to find her father's pickaxe, which was in its usual place, leaning against the nightstand. As the man turned his attention back to Rose, she swung a glancing blow, cutting him just above the left eye.

The man's eyes filled with rage as he strained to regain his grip. Rose wound her axe again, exploding her assailant's ear, splattering it into pieces across the sheets. The man fell to one side. Rose kicked her way out from beneath him. The man spit a spray of profanities at her as Rose raised the axe with both hands clutching the handle. He looked up at Rose, the blood from his wounds dripping into his enraged eyes. Rose struck her final blow, burying the miners axe deep into his skull.

Rose stepped back, her hands and face covered and dripping with the blood spatter of her assailant. She looked down upon him, remembering what she had heard her father say so many years before. "Only a coward hits women and children," she spoke aloud. Rose noticed a small stream of blood making its way across the floor, the petals of the painted rose riding upon it. Stepping out of the room, she angrily swung the door shut.

Chapter 19

Happy Birthday Dear Rose

Rose McGill leaned over the kitchen sink, staring at the blood dripping from the tips of her fingers, asking herself why this man had turned so suddenly and without provocation. She poured a shot of whiskey, staining the bottle and glass with her bloody fingertips. She threw back the shot as a chill ran up her spine. Tying a knot in the belt of her black satin robe, she picked up the phone and called the police.

After making the call, Rose took her bottle and glass to the living room and sat on the couch to await their arrival. Her mind filled with images of family, friends, and strangers, spinning counterclockwise in her head. She leaned her head back, her face throbbing in pain, believing she heard the dance of raindrops falling on the porch steps. Rose listened to the rhythm, recalling tales told to her about her family, wondering how things must have been.

"Are you all right Miss," a young Ashley cop asked, seeing the discolorations forming on Rose's face and neck. Taking Rose by the shoulders, he shook her back to consciousness.

Recognizing the man as someone who had spent time in her bed on more than one occasion, she relaxed slightly and said she was OK. A second officer asked her what had happened. Rose, finding it painful to speak, directed the officers to the back bedroom with a wave of her hand. They returned shortly looking pale. The cops excused themselves and stepped out onto the front porch for air.

Once recovered, they returned to Rose asking questions regarding the dead man in her bedroom. Before she could answer more police cars pulled up followed by an ambulance from the coroner's office. Neighbors and bar patrons from up and down Main Street flocked to the McGill house, just as they had not so many years before. Rose buried her head in her hands, unable to comprehend what possessed this man, causing him to turn on her as he did.

The final two cops to enter Rose's living room where the two detectives, Sheridan and Wilson. Rose looked away, hoping they would not recognize her, focusing on a spider crawling down the textured wall to her right. The young officer from Ashley, with notebook in hand approached the detectives who stopped him before he could speak. They instructed him to secure the crime scene and that they would take it from there.

Detectives Sheridan and Wilson went to the back bedroom, returning a short time later. Rose waited on the steps, staring out at the strange, distorted faces that filled the street. The red and white flashes of the police car lights pulsated through every window and reflected off the eyes of the onlookers. It all seemed like a repeat of the same bad dream to Rose. The same nightmare she had endured night after night came to life and was now a reality.

Sheridan approached Rose first with notebook in hand. Rose prepared for the endless stream of redundant questions and belligerent attitudes coming her way. Her mind kept screaming, "This is not my fault," and straining to formulate a reason for the sudden turn of events so that she might explain not only to herself, but also to the officers what happened and why.

"Rose Aileene McGill," said Officer Wilson before his partner could speak. "Seems we have been down this road before haven't we?"

Rose tossed the hair back from her face. Her head ached and her left eye and cheek throbbed in pain from the punishment she had endured. The deep punctures from the man's bite became irritated by the touch of her robe. Rose tried to keep it away from the wound, wincing each time she moved.

"Are you alright?" asked Officer Sheridan, seeing the deep purple and blue bruises spreading about her eyes and around her neck. He handed her a tissue as a drip of blood seeped from a gash on her lip. She looked up at the detective, one small tear hung from the corner of her eye. He could see the pain and confusion on her face, truly feeling sympathy for her, despite her history.

"We've kept track a' you, my partner and me, since the last time you stuck an axe in someone's head Rose. Or should I say, Black Rose," said Officer Wilson, sarcastically; taking a seat in Rose's high back chair. "You have made quite a name for yourself in just a few short years. Well, do you have anything to say for yourself before we take you downtown?" he commented looking across the room at Rose.

Rose became angry. Looking straight at Detective Sheridan she barked, "I'm not alright. This was not my fault. The man tried to strangle me for no reason. Should I have let him, is that what you would have preferred I do? Then you'd be here to cart my ass to the morgue."

Officer Sheridan helped Rose to her feet, told her to go put some clothes on, and sent a uniformed officer along with her. Once she was upstairs, the two detectives began to talk. There was little question about what had occurred in the back bedroom, but they would need the details only Rose could give. Remembering how tight-lipped Rose had been the last time, they believed this would be a challenge or a rough road at best.

Once Rose returned to the living room, Officer Sheridan cuffed her. Detective Wilson continued to survey the house, looking at every nick knack, memento, and picture. He went out the rear door to the back porch where an officer stood guard. Wilson lit a cigarette, admiring what he could see of Rose's garden through the darkness before returning to the living room.

"You have done a very nice job with this place. As I recall it was a bit of a dump when your father lived here. Before Nash put a bullet in his head," stated detective Wilson, looking for a reaction from Rose. He got none.

Another plain clothed officer called to the detective from the bedroom. Wilson went to see what he wanted while Sheridan stayed with Rose. The murder of James McGill and Edgar Koski by Lucas Nash was the first case Sheridan and Wilson had been assigned to when they became detectives. They remembered every detail, right down to the cold expression Rose wore when the medics from the coroner's office rolled the bodies off to the morgue.

"Rose," Officer Sheridan asked, staring out at the crowd, "whose Cadillac is that?"

Rose told him, "The guy in the bedroom arrived in it, so I suppose it's his."

Billy Wilson returned holding a man's wallet. Sheridan turned and anxiously glared at his partner, who upon opening the wallet wore the same fearful expression. Wilson moved next to Sheridan who showed him what he already suspected. The two men muttered back and forth in hushed tones. Rose strained to hear, but only picked up bits and pieces of what the detectives were saying.

Finally, Wilson instructed Sheridan to get Rose down to the station. He handed a uniformed officer the keys to their car, asking him to move it to the rear of the house. Sheridan wrapped his arm around Rose, leading her through the kitchen and out through the back door. He paused for a moment, looking back at his partner, seeing him speaking to another uniformed police officer outside the bedroom door.

Sheridan then hustled Rose through the garden, out the back gate and into his car, shutting the door firmly behind her. Once behind the wheel, he adjusted the mirror so he could keep an eye on his passenger and pulled away quickly. The detective drove through the alley that passed behind the row of houses, parallel to Main Street until it ended. He then swung the car right followed by a quick left onto Main Street. Rose was confused and nervous, her face still throbbing from the pain. She asked repeatedly what was going on and whom the dead man was that had the detectives so worried.

Officer Sheridan did not answer driving silently through the dark empty streets. When they reached the police station, he moved Rose quickly into an interrogation room, locking the door behind them. Sheridan sat Rose down in a seat before a large grey table, and then took a chair across from her. Rose attempted to question the detective again, but he asked her to be quiet while he reviewed his notes.

The drab grey room smelled of stale coffee and cigarette smoke, with an underlying odor of bleach. After a long period of silence, detective Sheridan stood up, asked Rose if she wanted or needed anything, and excused himself. When he left, he locked the door behind him. Another long period of silence ensued as Rose sat waiting, wondering what might happen to her next. Thinking this time she was going to jail, if not for murder then prostitution.

After what seemed like an eternity to Rose, detective Sheridan returned accompanied by his partner Billy Wilson, a uniformed officer, and another man that Rose had never met. She knew by his demeanor that he was the one in charge. The uniformed officer stood guarding the door as the trio of men took seats across from Rose. They compared notes before turning their attentions to their prisoner.

The unknown man broke the silence, "I am chief detective Joseph McNamara. Would you please state your full name for me?"

Rose did as he asked, "Rose Aileene McGill," she stated firmly, still wiping the dried blood from her lip.

"Can you tell us what happened, Miss McGill?" continued the officer.

Rose told the officers everything that occurred as truthful as possible, stressing that she did nothing to provoke this man to turn on her as he did. Rose made it clear that if she had not done what she did he would have killed her. Chief McNamara looked at the two detectives on either side of him and then back at Rose. He examined the bruises on her face and neck, scratched a few notes on the paper in front of him, and then rocked back in his chair.

"Looking through your file I see you have done this before," he said glaring at Rose. Rose did not respond.

"Haven't you done this before Black Rose? Drove a pickaxe through a man's skull, killing him. Haven't you?" he yelled, lunging forward and pounding the palms of his hands on the table.

The officer seemed to want to frighten Rose, but he did not know Rose. Pushing her only served to solidify her resistance. Rose sat up straight, pushed back her shoulders, and stared the man down. She was not about to be intimidated by this man or any man.

"I have done nothing wrong. Not today or then either," Rose replied, "and you know it!" Rose settled back in her chair. After a short pause, "Now I would like to call my lawyers," Rose stated, crossing her legs and folding her arms. She leaned back comfortably in her chair knowing she was in control.

The detectives left the room, leaving behind the uniformed officer guarding the door. Detective Sheridan returned shortly and escorted Rose to a phone. She called the only lawyers she knew, Binell, Binell & Smelling. She reached the answering service and explained to the woman on the phone that she had been arrested and needed Attorney C. Francis Binell, Esquire to contact her at the Wilkes-Barre police station as soon as possible.

Detective Sheridan returned Rose to her chair in the interrogation room and then took the seat across the table from her. He sent the uniformed office for coffee for the two of them, then stood up and circled the room. Rose kept a watchful eye on the young detective, recalling what her friends Patty and Valerie had said about him that June afternoon following the night Lucas Nash shot her father and the pig Edgar Koski.

"What is it you're thinking Detective Sheridan?" asked Rose. The young detective sat back down and was about to tell her when the other cop returned baring coffee.

"There is a call for Miss McGill," said the officer, "It's her lawyer."

Once again, the detective escorted Rose from the interrogation room, sitting her down at his desk in the squad room and handing her the receiver. She explained to Attorney Binell that she was in custody, but that it was self-defense. The attorney apologized, stating to Rose that, "He was not a criminal lawyer. His firm dealt with estates law, wills and such, but he would call a friend who he thought would be of assistance."

Rose thanked Attorney Binell, asking him to please hurry, and hung up the phone. She returned to the interrogation room on the arm of detective Sheridan. Rose drank her coffee, which was now room temperature, and requested another. Detective Sheridan continued mulling over papers in silence. When Rose stood to stretch her legs Detective Sheridan told her to sit back down and then went back to his files.

Eventually, a young lawyer arrived in the interrogation room accompanied by detective Wilson. He reached out and shook Rose's hand, introducing himself as "Daniel Arden, Attorney at Law." The officer brought him a chair, allowing him sit beside his client. Attorney Arden dropped an overstuffed black leather satchel on the tabletop, tipping Detective Sheridan's cold coffee off the table and onto the floor.

Rose measured the young lawyer, thinking he looked barely out of high school much less law school. His bowtie twisted to one side resembled a plane propeller. The boy lawyer's cloths were completely mismatched; a brown suit coat, blue wrinkled and lint covered slacks and black scuffed shoes. Rose saw him as silly and doubted his competence.

"My apologies detective," began the young lawyer, fumbling with his case. "May I ask, has Miss McGill been charged with any wrongdoing at this time?"

The detectives glimpsed at each other, then answered a harmonized, "NO."

"I see," replied the young attorney. He stopped fussing with his paperwork and stared at the detectives asking, "Then why is she here?"

Detectives Wilson and Sheridan hesitated with the answer, looking at each other and then at Rose with concern. The young and seemingly incompetent lawyer showed his metal, taking Rose's hand as he repeated the question. "It is a simple question officers. If there are no charges, then why are you holding my client?"

Both the detectives began to explain at the same time. Officer Wilson stopped his partner and began, "The man Rose killed is of some importance Mr. Arden. His name is Vinjenso DeNapoli, better known as Vincent DeNapoli, son of Angelo DeNapoli."

A look of fear gripped the young lawyer and he began shoving his papers haphazardly into his bag. Rose had no idea who the man was even after the officer spoke his name. She had heard references to the DeNapoli family, but paid little attention to things she believed did not concern her. It was abundantly clear the attorney knew the name and it frightened him in a way Rose had never seen a man frightened.

The attorney stood up, pulling his satchel to his side. His voice trembled as he spoke. "Miss McGill, I cannot help you. I fear no one can. These fine gentlemen will explain. Good evening to you all."

Just as quickly as the lawyer had appeared, he disappeared. Rose glared angrily at the detectives, expecting an immediate answer, which was not forthcoming. The detectives glanced back and forth at each other and then at Rose. They realigned their files and closed them without an utterance.

"You need to tell me what is going on," Rose shouted, "and why my lawyer flew out of here like is life was threatened? Who is Vincent DeNapoli and why is everyone shittin their pants over him?"

Detective Wilson stood up and walked to Rose's side of the table. He sat on the edge and began to fill Rose in, "Vincent DeNapoli is the son of Angelo DeNapoli." "I got that part," interrupted Rose. "Angelo is a reputed crime lord who, when he finds out his son is dead, will want his killer dead. Anyone that gets in his way, he'd want dead too. That is why your lawyer hotfooted outta' here."

"So you are saying I'm dead?" Rose asked calmly.

"This man is unstoppable and he has people working for him everywhere, including here in this building", added detective Sheridan. "He owns judges and lawyers. Maybe even the one that just ran out of here. And if that's the case, he knows already."

"You need to protect me! It's your job, damn it!" hollered Rose.

"Why Rose McGill, I thought you were fearless?" commented Officer Wilson smugly.

The officers moved Rose to a holding cell where she would spend the next two nights under police protection. Monday morning Detective's Wilson and Sheridan removed her from the cell and returned her to the interrogation room. The detectives said very little, but brought her a coffee, sitting with her until a knock on the door brought them to their feet.

They let in a small, round, balding man, who sat down beside Rose. He introduced himself as C. Francis Binell, Esquire, at which time the two detectives left the room, leaving behind the uniformed office to guard the door. The attorney pulled a large neatly stacked pile of papers from his briefcase along with a fine silver pen.

The attorney handed Rose the pen, requesting that Rose sign numerous pieces of paper, not bothering to explain what the forms were for or why she needed to sign them. As Rose filled in her signature the lawyer spoke, "Since you were unable to come to my office I decided to come to you," he said with a smile.

He helped Rose flip the pages, pointing to a spot Rose had missed still in need of her signature, "Very tight security around this place. I swear they're protecting the president," he said.

Glimpsing up at the man from the endless stack of papers, Rose saw a simple grandfatherly gentleness in the lawyer's eyes. Clearly, he had no idea why Rose spent the weekend in a guarded cell. This she considered a sign of hope, thinking, "I might get through this after all." She signed the last paper and the attorney straightened the pile of forms neatly placing them back in his briefcase.

Attorney Binell reached into another sleeve of his briefcase and removed a large manila envelope and then closed and snapped the case shut. He placed it on the tabletop and slid it precariously in front of Rose. Upon the cover where four words, written in cursive by someone with beautiful penmanship.

Rose read the words aloud, "Happy Birthday Dear Rose."

"Your mother Elizabeth Grace came to me some twenty years ago," explained the old lawyer. "I was much younger and handsomer then." Attorney Binell smiled then continued. "I promised her you would receive this on your birthday and that I would answer any questions you might have. You look very much like your mother. She was a fine woman, a kind woman, taken much too soon from this world."

Rose pealed open the envelope and tipped it to one side, spilling out many envelopes in various colors and sizes. In addition, there were numerous photos of family and strangers, all signed and dated, with the caption of 'Happy Birthday' on each. There was also a stack of notebooks bound together with a blue ribbon. Attorney Binell sat with Rose as she opened each envelope and read the letter within.

Some of the envelopes contained checks, the awards of insurance policies from her mother, grandparents, great aunties, and Uncle David. The sum of which, made Rose Aileene McGill a mildly wealthy young woman. She glimpsed at Attorney Binell who handed her two more envelopes. These envelopes also contained checks. One was for the sale of the business on Main Street, the other for her grandparent's home on St. Mary Street.

Attorney Binell explained to Rose that the large envelope, which held the checks from her aunts in Maryland, arrived later. He also informed her that there is more for her at his office since he could not carry everything. She would need to come to his office at a suitable time to retrieve them. Rose agreed as she continued to root through the items.

Glancing at the photos, she read aloud the notes from those persons she did not know. These mostly spoke of her grandparents and the bond they shared. The first came from an old priest by the name of McCormick, which was very generic, simply wishing her a long, blessed life and advising her to forgive the sins of others and find peace in her heart and mind by doing so.

Letters from twins by the name of Lynch were next, followed by a note from a couple named Clancy and one from a man named Jeffrey Haggerty. Genie and Daniel Haggerty, whose composition was quite lengthy, finished with the signatures of all their children accept for Heather, whose name Genie forged in a crest of angel's wings. Rose quickly realized these notes were a time capsule of sorts, revealing her roots as seen through the eyes of many.

A letter from her father slipped out from between the note from her mother and grandparents. A note she certainly did not expect. She blamed her father much like her father blamed her and she did not intend to forgive him no matter what his note said. Rose set it aside and read her grandparent's letter first.

"Dear child," it began. "Your grandfather and I consider it a great disappointment that we are not there to share in your life. We hope that it has been a splendid one, full of happiness, joy, and adventure.

Live has blessed your grandfather and me with a love so strong and pure. This we wished for your mother, and this we wish for you. Sometimes you must look past what your eyes see to find what is most important. Truth and beauty often disguise themselves. To recognize them you must first open your heart.

Here I fear I must also mention the darker side of things. The black rose is a fateful spirit, demonic and beautiful all at once. It is a gift and a curse. What path it may lead you down we cannot know. What we believe is that it needs to return to whence it came, but you may hold the real answer. We love and pray for you, your grandparents, Matthew and Nora Flannery."

Rose rested for a moment, trying to understand the references to the black rose, realizing that the visions that haunted her also haunted her grandmother. She fingered through the photos, locating one of Nora as a young woman, seeing herself looking back at her. She dug further, searching for a picture of her mother. Again, she saw herself.

Rose tore open the letter from her mother, which sounded similar to the one written by her grandmother, concluding with her mothers thoughts on the nightmares that tormented her. Elizabeth, additionally, wrote about why she chose the name Rose Aileene. It had been spoken to her in a whisper as she slept and feared that if she did not do as the voice asked something terrible would occur.

"Something terrible did occur," thought Rose. "My mother died, leaving me to deal with life on my own and a father who deserved no less than he got."

The old lawyer put his arm around Rose, trying to comfort her as best he could. Rose read the notes from her great aunties and uncle, matching each with photos of the person whose letter she was reading at the time. She found her great aunt Cora's to be most unusual, not the note, but the picture. In Cora's photo, she stood beside a gown on an old wire mannequin; the dress Rose wore to the Hotel Sterling. For some reason Rose was not surprised, knowing there was something too familiar about the little dress shop in New York. She smiled and thanked Cora in her heart for the beautiful dress she made, realizing that her great aunt stitched it just for her.

She saved her father's note for last, not caring what the man had to say. The letter, however, did raise an eyebrow. He began with a heartfelt apology, which he had written prior to his child's birth. James knew he had not the tools to be a good father and he prayed his wife would guide him through. He expressed his love for Elizabeth, concluding with a lesson for his child. One he hoped would have some worth and serve her well in her time of need.

It said simply, "In your darkest hour, trust in what and who you know. Be wary of strangers, they will only mean you harm."

The words Popeye McGill expressed to his daughter took some time for her to digest. Rose considered them as she returned everything to its envelope. She advised Attorney Binell to take all the policies and cash them out for her and that she would meet him at his office by the end of the day. Rose told the old lawyer to expect further instructions for him at that time, although presently she had no idea what those instructions would be. Attorney Binell promised to do as Rose requested and wished her a good day.

A plan began to take shape in Rose's mind. She would need the help of her two friends, Patty and Valerie, along with the cab driver, Jeffrey Halliday. Rose circled the room with the envelope pressed against her chest. Lost in her thoughts she had not noticed the uniformed officer who had been guarding her door left with Attorney Binell, leaving Rose alone and unprotected.

The door creaked open slowly, catching Rose's attention. Rose dropped the envelope and grabbed hold of the chair nearest to her. In doing so, she bumped the table, spilling her cup of coffee in a line across the floor. She moved to the farthest corner of the small room. A large man in a dark suit and fedora stepped into the room and rushed at Rose with a knife. Rose stepped quickly, keeping the heavy gray table between herself and the knife-wielding assassin.

The man cut Rose off, trapping her with her back against the wall. As he stepped towards her, he did not notice the coffee on the floor. He slipped in it as he lunged. Rose swung the chair with all she had, striking the man squarely across the face. The weight of the man slammed hard upon the dirty floor, dropping the knife at Rose's feet.

Without thinking, Rose picked up the knife as the man rolled over. Before he could protect himself, Rose stuck the blade into the man's chest. She let go of the handle when the man grabbed hold of her arm. Rose clawed at his eyes, trying to break his hold, but he was much too strong. Rose kicked at the man; still she could not get free. Suddenly, the door to the interrogation room opened and Detective Wilson raced in, pulling Rose out of the man's grasp.

Rose's assassin reached beneath his jacket, pulling out a chrome-plated snub-nose 38 and aimed it at Rose. Detective Wilson, seeing the gleam of the weapon, reached for his gun. The sound of the shots reverberated off the dingy walls followed by a profound and lingering silence.

A scent of sulfur filled the room and a thin grey smoke cloud hung like a web, mingling with the dust that sifted beneath the cool white light of the ceiling lamp. The blood spatters dripping from the walls formed perfect pools upon the floor. The tick of the clock counted off each second that slipped away unnoticed.

At the sound of the shot or shots, no one could be sure, hearing the echo of the bang, the few officers that occupied the squad room leaped from their chairs and rushed to the interrogation room. Detective Sheridan arrived first to find his partner holding the limp body of Rose in his arms and the assassin lying prone against the far wall. Other officers piled up behind Sheridan, looking over his shoulders, trying to see what there was to see.

Detective Sheridan, seeing his partner checking Rose for a pulse, asked if she was dead.

"I can't tell," Officer Wilson, said, "I don't feel her breathing, but I think there's a pulse."

Detective Wilson scooped Rose's lifeless body into his arms, pushing back the crowd of cops that filled the doorway and ran down the narrow corridor to the back exit accompanied by Detective Sheridan. Officer Sheridan slid past his partner to unlatch the door, finding it unlocked. He shoved it open wide, holding it until Wilson was out and then ran ahead to open the car door.

Officer Wilson slid Rose carefully onto the back seat and then sat down beside her. Detective Sheridan eased behind the wheel and switched on the lights and siren. The tires kicked stones into the air as he raced from the parking lot in the direction of the hospital. Once they were far beyond the sight of the police station, Officer Wilson leaned in and whispered into his partner's ear. The car took an abrupt change of direction.

Sheridan spotted a cab and swung in behind it, pulling the car to the curb. Wilson climbed into the front seat as Sheridan stepped out of the car and into the cab. What happened afterward, one could only guess. Detective Wilson drove off without looking back. Sheridan had the cabbie take him to the medical examiners office and then to the morgue, meeting up with Detective Wilson there.

The two detectives returned to the police station reporting Rose Aileene McGill, alias 'Black Rose' died of a single gun shot wound to the face. They carried with them paperwork from both the emergency room doctor who had treated Rose and the morgue to corroborate their statement. Chief Detective McNamara read over the statements, knowing that none of the other officers at the station during the time of the shoot could confirm or deny what Officers Wilson and Sheridan professed as fact.

Chapter 20

White Rose

It was a warm, sunny August morning when the casket of Rose Aileene McGill went into the ground; the graves of her mother and father on her right, that of her grandparents to her left. The short service at the burial sight had few attendees. Rose's best friends, Patty and Valerie shed tears throughout the ceremony and although their fiancés did their best to comfort them, they were inconsolable.

Patty's parents put aside their resentment for Rose, as did Kevin and Lilly Cunningham, choosing to remember the child rather than the woman. A group of men one could only guess to be Rose's regulars seemed to take the loss very hard. They clustered in the background, beyond a line of unkempt headstone looking quite despondent. C. Francis Binell stood along side the two detectives Sheridan and Wilson with their heads down, but eyes up watching suspiciously.

Amanda Collins-Benoit arrived last, accompanied by her fifth husband, a young Frenchman who looked to be in his mid-twenties. Detectives Sheridan and Wilson rubbernecked as Amanda strode smoothly past and stood between Patty and Valerie. At age forty, it could now be said that Amanda had become even more desirable with age. No one was more aware of it than she was and, as she usually did, Amanda toyed with the men in attendance, turning a flirtatious glance at the detectives as she passed.

Three nuns from St. Leo's Church knelt by the gravesite as the priest spoke his final reflections of Rose. He snapped shut his bible to the ring of the church bells in the distance, bidding the mourners a good day. Amanda rested her arms around Patty and Valerie as they turned and walked from the grave. The two girls, who had been looking down through tear-filled eyes during most of the service, raised their heads, noticing the number twenty-one cab easing slowly out of the cemetery. It exited through the main gates and turned right, rolling slowly down St. Mary Street hill.

Many residents of Ashley and the surrounding boroughs thought the loss of Black Rose a good thing. The neighbors, who had enough of sirens disturbing their sleep and strange drunken men roaming their otherwise quiet neighborhood, welcomed the end of her sinful life and the attached collateral. The men in the bars along Main Street felt much differently, toasting Rose the following Friday and every Friday until the memory faded.

The legend of Black Rose, the axe-wielding prostitute with the looks of a Hollywood starlit, became exaggerated over the years by the residences of the little borough of Ashley. Her victims numbered a dozen and the incident at the police station had her shooting her way out, only to be gunned down in a barrage of lead. Some found this story humorous while others believed it wholeheartedly.

Then there are those who believed quite a different story. This faction was of the opinion that Rose was not shot in the interrogation room at all. They held to the idea that the detective, Billy Wilson, outdrew the would-be assassin. These people believed her casket was empty or her body replaced by a Jane Doe stolen from the morgue. Those that supposed this tale to be truth also thought Rose lived hidden away from the reach of Angelo DeNapoli.

The young detectives did their best to dissuade any notion that Rose lived. They knew Angelo DeNapoli would continue to seek revenge for his son's death if he believed otherwise. They too would find themselves targets, along with anyone DeNapoli believed could lead him to Rose. Making sure he believed Rose died that day was essential to the safety of every person at the funeral. If not there was sure to be a bloodbath, and they would be among the dead.

Whatever the case, the house on Main Street along with the majority of its contents went in auction with the proceeds going to pay for Rose's burial and legal fees. This is according to Attorney C. Francis Binell who held power of attorney for the meager McGill estate. People questioned why some items were not at auction, such as the memorabilia and decanter that occupied the glass curio and the missing dresses from her bedroom closet. Further inquiries arose regarding the deadly pickaxe, which in reality the police kept and eventually destroyed.

Along Springfield Road on the northern edge of Belfast between Flannery's hill and Barrett's Post another story began. Genie and Daniel Haggerty purchased the land, which bore the stone put in place by Matthew Flannery. They built a fine public garden dedicated to the memory of their daughter Heather. The stone became a focal point for people along the road and put onto a pedestal when the Haggerty's contracted to erect the new park.

This September day, a deep blue sky spread out in all directions. From Dunmore Head to Dublin and across the Shetlands, no more perfect a day could be imagined. Springfield Road dressed in gold with a soft breeze spinning through the willows and birches and down Kil Pipers Hill.

A young woman in a large hat and sunglasses sat on a bench beside the monument, observing a young man with a bouquet of white roses accented by orchids dashing between cars along Springfield Road. She watched him as he skidded on some bits of glass by the granite curb. He stepped into the grass and walked up to the monument, pausing briefly to take a deep breath before kneeling down and setting the flowers at the base of the stone.

The young woman, peering up from beneath her big hat and over the top of her dark glasses, questioned the man as to why he placed flowers where he did. The young man did not answer at first, noticing a soggy pile of petals in the dirt beside his bouquet. The woman removed her glasses, stood up and stepped to the side of the stone. The man buried the dark, withering remains before straightening his legs. Just as he began to speak he noticed the woman's eyes; deep blue sparkling eyes that astounded him.

The woman smiled and looked away, fearing she had revealed too much of herself. Another young person rushed past, setting a single white rose on the stone, followed by another, and another. Some continued along the walkway that cut between the flowerbeds to enjoy the gardens on this beautiful day. Some others went back the way they came, towards the businesses that lined Springfield Road.

The woman questioned the man again. He realized he could not look her in the eyes and talk at the same time. She was more beautiful than any women he had ever seen. The man bent down, pulled a rose from his bouquet, and handed it to the woman asking her name.

"You agree to tell me about the roses and I will tell you my name," the woman replied.

The young man quickly agreed.

The mysterious blue-eyed woman told the man her name in a deep sultry voice that dissipated in the breeze, causing the man to drift into a daze. The woman took his arm and they walked through the sunlit garden. The man introduced himself as Matthew Douglas Lynch II and began telling the story of the celebration of the white rose, which began before the turn of the century.

"My father and grandfather told me the story of two young lovers who met at that very spot and fell perfectly in love," said the young Mr. Lynch. "Their love it has been said affected everyone from the hill to the post and then some. After they left for America, my grandfather met my grandmother there by the marker. My father admits to have fallen in love with me mother while walkin through the gardens. However, it isn't just me family; surin many loves have been born at the stone."

"But why the white roses?" asked the young woman.

"That is because the woman's wedding gown was woven with white roses and she wore a crown of white roses on her head. My grandfather says theirs was a pure love and the white rose symbolized that purity," explained Matthew Lynch.

The couple continued their walk along Springfield Road, enjoying the warmth of a late summer day. Young Matthew pointed out landmarks all along the road. They eased past the Haggerty house. The woman insisted on stopping to peek into the garden through a gap in the fence. They passed by a small vacant shop before crossing the street. The mysterious attractive woman listened, seeing the faint images of the people that had lived there before. She could see their faces smiling in the shadows, nodding approval that Black Rose had come home.

Back in the states, Angelo DeNapoli buried his son Vinjenso in a large lavish ceremony attended by hundreds of